IN THE MARGINS

Gail Holmes

ultimo
press

Published in 2024 by Ultimo Press,
an imprint of Hardie Grant Publishing

Ultimo Press
Gadigal Country
7, 45 Jones Street
Ultimo, NSW 2007
ultimopress.com.au

  ultimopress

 A catalogue record for this
book is available from the
National Library of Australia

In the Margins
ISBN 978 1 76115 311 2 (paperback)

Cover design Hazel Lam
Cover images Background by ptashca / iStock; retro books by Alisa Zahoruiko / iStock; book
stickers by Anna Mariukhno / iStock
Author photograph Courtesy of Kristian Gehradte
Text design Simon Paterson, Bookhouse
Typesetting Bookhouse, Sydney | 11.7/18.8 pt Fairfield LT Std
Copyeditor Ali Lavau
Proofreader Libby Turner

10 9 8 7 6 5 4 3 2 1

Printed in Australia by Opus Group Pty Ltd, an Accredited ISO AS/NZS 14001
Environmental Management System printer.

 The paper this book is printed on is certified against the
Forest Stewardship Council® Standards.
Griffin Press – a member of the Opus Group – holds
chain of custody certification SCS-COC-001185. FSC®
promotes environmentally responsible, socially beneficial
and economically viable management of the world's forests.

Ultimo Press acknowledges the Traditional Owners of the Country on which we work,
the Gadigal People of the Eora Nation and the Wurundjeri People of the Kulin Nation,
and recognises their continuing connection to the land, waters and culture. We pay our
respects to their Elders past and present.

For my mum, Millie.

And for Andy, my husband, and our children Chris, Morgan, Ben, Darcey and Lauren.

Part 1

'If I be waspish, best beware my sting.'

WILLIAM SHAKESPEARE, *THE TAMING OF THE SHREW*, ACT 2, SCENE 1

1

Staffordshire, England
September 1647

The stone cross perches high on the chapel roof. It is framed in the bedroom window, a solitary disturbance to the trees and fields that stretch west towards Craggy Hill. Usually it irks me, but this morning the cross is pale against the pallid dawn sky, almost insignificant. Almost.

Throwing back the bed covers, I take the two frigid strides to the basin and thrust my face into the cold water. Gasping, I reach for the drying linen then smooth my hand over the damp plait that hangs over my shoulder like a rope. Henry always says you could tie up a horse with my hair. I glance back at the empty bed, wondering why he didn't wake me when he left. I'd slept fitfully, dreaming of hands pulling me down as I struggled and fought against them. I'd woken to find the bed linen twisted around me, as though the struggle were real.

I dress quickly, pulling on woollen stockings and fastening the buckles on my stoutest leather shoes. As I stand up a wave of dizziness overwhelms me, and I grip the back of the chair until it passes. The buttons of my bodice strain as I breathe—I'll have to let the seams out soon.

I pass the boys' room, where they haven't yet stirred, and go downstairs. The fire blazes in the hearth of the cold kitchen at the back of the house. Peg, her wind-raw cheeks glowing red in the firelight, rolls out pastry for pies. Bread is already baking in the oven and a warm, oaty smell fills the room.

'Has Mr Wolfreston gone, Peg?'

'Tom Dyer fetched him to see to that pauper queue that were lining up outside the chapel this mornin'.'

'But it's too early.'

'Well, I saw two women huddled in the porch when I came by. One had a babe.'

I wrap my heavy blue shawl around my shoulders and fasten it with a brooch. 'I'd better take over some bread if it's ready,' I say, eyeing Peg carefully, expecting the usual confrontation. Peg doesn't hold with me giving fresh bread to the 'paupers and scavengers' that come begging to the church.

But today she only wipes her flour-dusted hands on her apron before taking a basket from the floor and setting it on the table.

'I made these already,' she says, lifting a cloth to reveal two warm round loaves. 'For Mr Wolfreston's breakfast, mind, not them scavengers.' She turns briskly back to the pastry, hiding the twitch of a smile.

I close the back door behind me. The red-brick frontage of Statfold House looks less austere than usual; the house is almost pretty with its frost-covered lawn before it. A short way down the lane, the chapel sits among the handsome rowan trees Henry's father planted just before he died. I hurry past the graveyard to the vestry entrance.

The odour of ash, tallow and damp wool enfolds me as I enter the small room where last night, after a day of picking pears, I had bent over the church accounts, calculating what was left for the poor. The embers had died in the fire and the wind had echoed low in the chimney when I finally closed the ledger. I wrote in the parish records: *This harvest is meagre. If this dearth persists and war returns, what hope is there?* Then I had walked in the howling darkness back to the house, where Henry slept in the chair by the fire with the *Mercurius* newssheet lying on his lap.

Inside the chapel now, Henry sits at a table with Tom Dyer, the warden, who has the cash tin. Stretching along the rear wall is a queue of men, none of whom I recognise. They look like war veterans—former soldiers who roam the country hunting for work, peddling goods and begging for dole. None wear the red tunic of Cromwell's New Modelled Army. Vestiges of their old uniforms hang from hunched shoulders. Lank hair falls about prominent cheekbones. Without their regiment colours it is impossible to tell whether they are loyal to Cromwell or are defeated Royalists who support the imprisoned King. One man wears an old officer's coat, and it looks so incongruous on his gaunt frame that I wonder if he has killed someone for it. He catches me staring and I turn quickly away to the woman standing in front of Henry.

'Jane, widow of John Harding, Statfold village: one shilling,' Henry says.

Tom Dyer hands a single coin to the woman, who keeps her head bowed as she accepts it. She'll be back here within a few weeks,

I know. Her husband had been the blacksmith and part-time grave-digger before he was killed in a skirmish near Lichfield, leaving Jane with their young daughter. She has already claimed three shillings for the return of his grave-digging tools to the parish.

I rip one of the loaves and offer her a large piece. She tucks it inside her shawl and mumbles her thanks without looking up.

Henry watches as I break up the rest of the bread and lay it on the cloth near him. 'Are you any better?' he murmurs, and I remember feeling sick in the night. I should tell him I am with child, but he will only worry and confine me to bed, as if that would make any difference.

I slip out of the chapel, past the red-berried trees and spy the widow hurrying down the lane towards the village; Jane Harding would not want anyone to see her ask for poor relief and I am about to turn away, to grant her privacy, when her shawl slips from her thin shoulders and I see that she is hunched and shaking.

'Wait!' I call.

She turns abruptly, tottering among the swirling leaves as if she might fall over.

I stride over. 'Forgive me, Mrs Harding, but do you not have relatives who can help you?'

The widow pulls her shawl around her, gathering herself. 'There's no one.' Her northern accent, once so warm, is brusque. 'I'm looking for work. Do you know of anyone hiring? I can sew, wash, clean, I'm good with horses, I can do the butchering, even the tallow for candles . . .' She trails off.

My stomach lurches and I cover my mouth. The collection of tallow for candles is a despised job involving wrestling with carcasses to extract the last of the fats and squeezing those fats till all the stinking tallow juice oozes out. But it must be done, for wax candles are too expensive for everyday use.

Fortunately, she doesn't seem to have noticed my disgust. She's staring across the field with desperation hanging around her like the burrs in her matted shawl. 'He was just a drunkard,' she mutters. She wants me to know that she is no self-deceiving fool; she is not mourning her dead husband but the loss of her old life.

'I'll talk to Mrs Edwards; the girl who does her linens has moved away.'

Her pale eyes seek mine. 'And what of my Grace? What chance has she now?'

As I watch her walk away, I remember my mother's blue eyes burning into mine on the day I refused Henry Wolfreston's first proposal. She had followed me into the summerhouse at Hazelmere and stood with her arms folded inside her shawl, despite the warmth of the summer evening. 'This is your chance of a better life,' she had told me.

Every mother wants a better life for her children. Grace is a quiet, thoughtful girl of seven. She often sits near the village pond making chains with the wildflowers that grow there. Sometimes she brings some little flower to me. It is hard to imagine such a child laundering and skivvying for a penny here and there. There must be something that can be done.

After the noon meal is finished, Henry sits at the table reading the *Mercurius*. He has hardly spoken since he came back from the chapel, so I send our two boys into the garden and sit down beside him.

'Is something troubling you, Henry?'

'Nothing important,' he says, but there is something in his expression that indicates otherwise. I watch him a moment wondering if he'll say more, but he merely turns a page.

'Henry, I've been thinking.'

'Oh?' he says from behind the newssheet.

'About teaching the Harding girl to read.'

He snorts. 'Why would you do that?'

Henry's scorn surprises me. I had expected some resistance, as the village boys can't even read, but it is not such a ridiculous idea.

'To give her some chance of a better life,' I say steadily.

He looks at me with his eyebrows raised, as if I am trying to trick him into something. 'You sound like a Leveller, Frances.'

'Well, Mrs Harding is rightly worried about her daughter's future; I'd like to help her.'

Henry lays down the *Mercurius* with a sigh. 'And how exactly will reading do that? It's not a skill she'll ever need.'

'If she can read, there may be other things she can do, other possibilities. She could read out the newssheets and notices to villagers. She could read labels so could perhaps help an apothecary, or work in a bookshop in Tamworth. The children's lives follow the same pattern as their parents. Always dependent on the harvest or lack of it. There's no other hope for them. But an education of some sort *can* make a difference.'

He stretches and pushes back his chair. 'I'm not sure teaching children to read is where we should be directing our efforts. Besides, you have this house to run, George and Middy to look after. And you know that Middy needs so much of your time.' He stands, kisses my forehead and picks up his hat from the side table where he left it. 'I've got to go and help Tom collect the parish tithes. The farmers are reluctant to part with them.'

'What?'

'There's some trouble because the harvest is so poor. We will get the magistrate involved, if need be, but hopefully it won't come to that.'

He pauses at the door. 'Don't worry about Jane Harding; she still has her looks and will probably marry again. And in the meantime, the parish will help her and her daughter.'

I watch his tall hat sail past the window. Many people will suffer this winter, but I cannot shake off this thought that I should help Jane Harding's girl. She is not my daughter, so why do I feel compelled? I glance at the *Mercurius*. Every newssheet and every book in my library, from Chaucer's story of Constance in 'The Man of Law's Tale' to Shakespeare's *The Taming of the Shrew*, seems to tell me where my duty lies. But I know that if I do nothing to help this girl, I will regret it.

I am still in my seat when Peg comes in to clear the table.

'Oh, dear Lord, why is he still here?' Peg says, glancing out the window as she picks up the wine jug. She taps the glass with her free hand.

Following Peg's gaze, I see a man playing at sword fighting with George and Middy, all of them holding sticks.

'Who is that, Peg?' I ask.

'One of those scruffy peddlers. Wanted to sell you something, ma'am. I told him to be on his way.' Her face glowers.

'It's all right, Peg, I'll go out and see to him.'

As I approach, he drops the stick, bows to George and ruffles Middy's hair. A heavy buff captain's coat lies discarded on the ground, and I realise he's the gaunt soldier who had stared at me in the chapel this morning. He's smiling, though there's something crafty about it.

'Ah, Mrs Wolfreston,' he says. 'I have something special for you.'

I lower my voice. 'I don't want to buy anything from you. And I don't want you near my children.'

His eyes rest on Middy, as if figuring something. 'They're good boys. Now, I beg for one moment of your time, Mrs Wolfreston.' He searches his satchel, his hair falling over his face. He takes out bootlaces, buckles and buttons. Squinting, he digs further and brings out red and blue ribbons, a folded piece of yellowing lace and an array of carved wooden whistles. He searches my face again, looking for clues, desperate to make his sale.

My arms are folded. I want rid of him. I don't trust him.

'You must like stories,' he says.

Some spark of interest in my eyes must betray me, for he quickly spreads several thin books of varying quality on the grass. I shake my head.

He takes something else from his bag and, kneeling like a courtier with a gift for a queen, he holds it out and says, 'I also have this.'

It is a small book, bound in calfskin with gilt stamped on both covers—*His Deuine Weekes & Workes*, by the poet Du Bartas. My French is very poor, but this is a translation, printed by Humfrey Lownes of London in 1605, and I have heard of it. The opening lines are about the first day of Creation. My eyes leap forward, hungry for more.

I close the book abruptly and give a guarded smile. 'This is a fine one,' I concede. Much too fine for a peddler to be hawking, I think but do not add.

His face glows like a stallholder who has negotiated a good price. 'I knew you would appreciate its worth. I heard in Tamworth you collect books.'

I hesitate, wondering who on earth has told this man about me. Only family, friends and visitors know about my books. Feeling some resentment, I hold out the volume, indicating that he should take it back.

'How did you come by it?' I ask sharply, for I am sure he has stolen it.

'I came by it fairly,' he says.

He must be able to tell from my fixed expression that I don't believe him. He turns his head so that the boys can't see his face. 'It was a gift from an officer, ma'am. I . . . I helped him out at Naseby.'

'Be on your way, sir.'

'It *is* mine,' he insists. 'I'm only selling it because I've got nothing.'

I stand unmoved.

His eyes harden. He packs his bag then nods towards the boys, who stand watching us with their stick-swords still in hand.

'Two good lads you've got there. Hope these wars are done before they're grown up.'

As he limps towards the lane, Middy trails behind him, calling, 'Sol-jah.'

George looks up at me, frowning. 'He's a nice man, Mamma.'

I stare after the soldier. Why have I treated him so harshly? He has done nothing to me; he is merely trying to make a living. And I've as good as called him a thief in front of my boys. I am ashamed of my capacity for small cruelties.

'Wait,' I call.

He turns. Even from this distance, I can see that he's angry.

'I will buy your book,' I tell him. 'Come and my cook will feed you.'

He gives a defeated nod.

While he follows me to the kitchen, Middy and George talk to him. He answers them pleasantly but does not look or smile at me again. I berate myself for thinking the worst of him, and yet I am uneasy for calling him back into our lives.

2

Before retiring that evening, I carry a candle sconce into the library and sit in the flickering shadows at the desk. I savour this last part of the day when the house is still. Each night I record the household events in the margins of my copy of Grey's Almanac. With all that besieges us, I worry that everything I know may be lost forever. Tonight I note that four kittens were born, that the plums on one tree were ruined by frost, and that Middy said 'sol-jah'. Middy is seven, the same age as Grace Harding, yet he can say only a handful of words. I record each new word and treasure it.

I open the Du Bartas at the title page. There is no time left today to read it. Anyway, I am weary from picking fruit and tramping over to see Mrs Edwards, but I can at least complete this last satisfying ritual. I run my fingers over the page, then take out the quill and ink and inscribe above the title:

Frances Wolfreston Hor Bouk
Bot of a soldar

None of Cromwell's Puritans would carry such a refined book by a French writer. Only a Royalist officer could have gifted such a book, so the soldier in the buff coat must be the same. Henry would not be pleased if he knew that a Royalist had been in his house. The soldier told Peg he was heading north, and I hope he is already a long way from here.

I gaze at the Du Bartas and the two penny godlies in their thin card covers that I bought in the churchyard at Tamworth last week, wondering where I might place them on my bookshelves. Since I married, I have collected more than two hundred books. Many are thin quartos and penny godlies that take little space, but I also have many fine books with leather covers and gilt decoration. The Du Bartas volume will look well among them.

From the corner of my eye, I see something creep by me. I turn warily but it is just Henry's shadow looming large on the wall as he approaches. He kisses my forehead and puts his hand on my shoulder.

'Henry, if I couldn't read, would you have married me?'

'What a question.'

'But if I couldn't read, I would not be able to help with your sermons or manage the accounts and the parish ledgers and records. I would not be very useful to you at all.'

He sits on the edge of the desk, looking at me. 'I didn't marry you just because you can read.'

I nod, although I am not convinced.

'Frances, if you want to teach this girl to read, then do so.'

'But you think it's not a good idea.'

He gives a little laugh. 'And will that stop you?'

He stands by the fireplace, drawing a line on top of the mantelpiece with his finger. In the flickering firelight, his face looks lined and troubled.

'What's wrong, Henry?'

'There is something I have been meaning to tell you. The bishop has sent word that the recusancy laws have been tightened.' He pauses, tapping his finger now. 'Parliament is intent on weeding out the recusants in every parish. So, we can be lenient no more. We must record the names of every man, woman and child who does not attend the Sunday service—and record the reason.'

I stare at my books on the desk. The quill shakes in my hand. I wipe it and place it down.

'Mrs Edwards is keen to oversee this, but you will have to note the names in the records weekly, Frances.'

'But . . .' My words catch in my throat. 'But what of those folks who cling to the old Catholic ways, like . . .' I hesitate and look at Henry. It seems like a betrayal to name folk to him, and yet he knows all his parishioners as well as I do. 'They don't cause any trouble, Henry. They pray quietly in their own homes.'

He looks at me as if I'm trying to make things unnecessarily difficult. 'We don't need to record that, provided they come to Sunday service.'

'I don't like this, Henry. It is too harsh, too intolerant.'

'It doesn't matter whether we like it. It is the law.' He brings his clenched fist down quietly onto the mantelpiece. 'It is worse in Ireland and Scotland than here.'

'That is scant comfort,' I retort.

'Why is this bothering you so much? The laws have existed for years; the Puritans are merely enforcing them.'

'You make it sound reasonable, Henry.'

Henry sighs and seems to deflate. 'No, it is not reasonable. It's severe. But it is how things are. We expected it.'

'What happens to them . . . the recusants?'

'A charge for each week missed, larger fines for repeat offenders. If they persist, then the sequestration of their land or, in the worst cases, prison.' He sighs again, seeming to expel a little hope. Then he says softly, 'Are you coming to bed, my love?'

'Shortly,' I say.

I listen for his footfalls on the stairs then I take out a sheet of vellum. I need to write to my mother and let her know. She, of all people, would understand my concerns, but I can't seem to find the words. What on earth can I say that will be of any use? Words must be chosen with such care these days. I stare at the single line I have written. The candle, one of our last beeswax stubs, has burned down till all that is left is the flaming wick standing in the molten wax. I watch it fall, then I sit there in the dark, my eyes adjusting to the faint glow from the dying embers of the library fire, thinking of my mother.

I last saw her in the second year of my marriage to Henry, when I had to spend several weeks confined to the house. An unexpected fever had set in when I was expecting our first child, and I lost the baby. I was sick, with aches all over my body. The doctor, who was a serious man, bled me with leeches for several days. He told Henry that I must stay in bed until the fever was completely gone and I had regained my strength.

The view of the chapel from our bedroom window upset me, so Henry made a bed downstairs in the library, where I could see a copper beech tree framed in the window instead. For weeks, I watched the bare branches of the copper beech sway in the wind. I felt as if a great part of me was missing, and that I was too weak to look for it.

I had been installed there a few weeks when I woke from a nap to see someone sitting in the chair near the window.

'Is that you, Mamma?' I said.

'It's me, angel.' As I heard her affectionate name for me, a ribbon of something fluttered through the missing part of me.

When I woke again, she was there. I hadn't seen her for nearly two years; her blonde hair had more streaks of grey and her blue eyes seemed paler, but her soft face was still handsome—more handsome than mine.

'How did you . . . why are you here?'

'Well, Henry wrote to your father and asked him to send me and he agreed.'

'He agreed? Was he worried about *me*?' I said, surprised.

Her blue eyes narrowed. 'Of course,' she said.

She rose and walked to the window, and stood looking out, clearly annoyed that I should talk so about him.

'Did you come by horse?' I asked.

'Yes.'

'How?' I almost laughed at the idea that she would attempt such a thing. My father hadn't let her ride alone since she fell from the saddle when she took the horse into town when I was nearly twelve.

'I can still ride a horse, Frannie,' she said. Then she chuckled. 'Although I can hardly sit down now.'

I fell asleep again, and each time I woke, my mother was there. Occasionally I saw her kneeling in prayer but mostly she stood by the window or sat in the chair close to the bed.

One day I said, 'Tell me a story, Mamma.'

'Silly,' she said, smiling.

My mother had a great love of theatre and had seen many plays performed in the days before the theatres were closed down by the Puritans. She could recite impressive swathes of verse and she taught her children to read from the playbooks of William Shakespeare, Ben Jonson and Christopher Marlowe. She walked around with a playbook in her hand acting out each part, while I and my brother followed or stood where she put us on her stage and gradually, we learned the parts. Our two little sisters watched from the grass, where they played with animals fashioned from wooden pegs by old Ambrose, the field hand.

In the scene recounting the death of Julius Caesar, she made us all take turns playing Brutus and then Caesar, so that we understood how it might feel to be betrayed by someone we trusted. 'Betrayal is silent and invisible,' she would breathe into our ears.

'Please, Mamma,' I said. I pointed to the bookshelf, where a copy of her favourite playbook stood. 'It's there. Read it to me.'

She shook her head, and I knew then that it was too painful for her.

With a fleeting smile, she quoted from it:

'Then God be blessed, it is the blessed sun,
But sun it is not when you say it is not,
And the moon changes even as your mind.
What you will have it named, even that it is,
And so it shall be so for Katherine.'

Her warm voice lifted the beautiful words and they drifted around the library, caressing the book covers, tucking into the pages, treading across the margins, settling in the spaces, and lulling me back to sleep.

Henry wrote to my father again after Lottie died, asking for my mother. My father expressed their deepest condolences but wrote that it was not prudent for him to allow my mother to travel alone with the war so recently ended. Henry offered to write again asking them both to come, but I knew that would be futile. Now, I gaze at the last embers praying my mother is safe and well.

3

On Sunday, I sit in my usual place in the chapel. The stained-glass window throws shards of red and yellow onto the wooden pew. Middy traces the edges of the coloured segments with his fingers, while George watches with a solemn expression as his father climbs the pulpit steps. Henry talks of God and duty to England. His voice rolls out in thunderous rumbles. He insists that everyone attend church regularly, that it is an obligation, that expectations are high and that the magistrates will serve fines for every single service missed. As Henry explains that Mrs Edwards will monitor attendance, the parish matriarch stands and gives a saintly smile that makes me wither inside.

I glance around, wondering who is missing. The regular churchgoers seem to be here. There are two I know to be absent: Robert Caldwell, who has not been to church since his accident, and Hannah Smythe, a widow who lives in an isolated cottage on a path off the back lane to Rivermead. I cannot remember ever seeing Hannah Smythe at church. There may be others like her that I am not aware of. It seems to me that Henry's sermon would be of most benefit to the people who are not in the congregation — this is a part of the church service that I have always thought deficient.

As if reading my mind, Henry requests that the villagers encourage and assist their fellow parishioners to come to church. 'This will make our parish stronger,' he bellows.

Mrs Edwards gazes at him, her face glowing with fervency. She is a formidable presence. I shudder at the thought of her 'assisting' Robert Caldwell to chapel. Poor Robert Caldwell, who lost his wife in childbirth and the use of his legs to a pair of runaway oxen on the Tamworth Road.

At the end of the service, I wait in front of the porch while Henry talks with a visitor to the parish. Mrs Edwards catches my arm and leans in towards me.

'I can't talk long, Mrs Wolfreston. My cousin Judith is visiting from King's Norton.' She nods at the sharp-nosed woman standing with Henry. 'I have three names for you to put in the records today.'

'Three?' I ask.

'Hannah Smythe, Robert Caldwell and Margaret Crowell.'

'Who is Margaret Crowell?' I have not heard the name before.

'She is a widow who lives over the hill from the Kavanaghs on common land.'

'Will you talk to the Kavanaghs?' I ask. 'Ask them to let her know before we do—'

'Before we do what?'

'Record the names.'

Mrs Edwards raises an eyebrow. 'Has the rector agreed to that?'

I glance at the boys who are waiting nearby.

'Mrs Wolfreston, this is a serious business.' She is frowning at me, her lips pursed. 'People already know that they are meant to be at church.' She glances over at her cousin and then says, 'We will not delay in recording their absence.' She taps her stick on the ground before me. 'Good day, Mrs Wolfreston.'

I watch as she takes her cousin's arm and propels her through the small crowd.

My mother's voice echoes in my ear: *''Tis mad idolatry to make the service greater than the god.'*

'George,' I call. 'Tell Papa I won't be long. I'm going to see Mrs Smythe.'

Hannah Smythe is wrapping dock leaves around her hands, weaving long strands around her fingers. When she is satisfied that her hands are covered, she tugs several strands of stinging nettles from a bush as easily as flowers. She continues along the path to her cottage, eyes sweeping the grasses and plants under the hedgerow for what she needs, singing 'Scarborough Fair' in a tuneless voice.

'Mrs Smythe,' I say as she reaches the stile that I'm resting on.

Hannah flinches in surprise.

'How long have you been sitting there, Mrs Wolfreston?' she says.

'Not long,' I say. 'I came over the fields.'

'I can see that.' She gestures to the mud on my Sunday boots.

I nod at the dock leaves wrapped around Hannah's hands. 'That's a good idea.'

Hannah looks at her green fingers then smiles. 'Well, it is, but I don't suppose you came this far off the beaten track to talk about how to pick nettles.'

She was as blunt the last time I came looking for her, with Middy in my arms. 'I expect you must be quite desperate to come here, Mrs Wolfreston,' she'd said.

'You weren't at church again today,' I say.

She pushes the nettles into the sack that hangs from her shoulder by a piece of rope then she leans over and yanks out some more. 'That's right,' she says without meeting my eyes.

She continues along the path and I follow behind.

'Mrs Smythe . . .'

She keeps walking.

'Please. I've come here to warn you.'

A bramble bush encroaches on the path, and she stops and begins to strip it of its remaining berries. As she reaches up to the higher branches, her sleeves slip, revealing several faded circles of scars on her wrists. I have seen them before, but my breath catches at the sight of the chiselled lines. There's something familiar about the shape and I wonder again how she got those marks.

'I wanted to let you know that things are changing. Mr Wolfreston spoke of it today in church. I wanted to make sure you got the message.'

Hannah turns to look at me with her brown, burrowing eyes.

'The law has tightened,' I explain. 'You'll be fined now if you don't come to church every week.'

'I can pay no fine.'

'Your non-attendance will be recorded. The sheriff's officers will check.'

'To what end? I own nothin'.'

'They could imprison you, Hannah.' I close my eyes, unable to hold her gaze. I imagine her chained, pulled roughly by sheriff's men to the village green for public shaming before being taken to the women's prison.

When I open my eyes, Hannah is holding out some misshapen berries. 'You look pale. You'd better be eating some of these.'

I take the berries and eat them slowly, watching as Hannah drops the remaining berries into her sack. She notices the blackberry juice staining my fingers and hands me some leaves. She watches with satisfaction as I use them to rub the stain from my hands.

'Just come to church, Hannah,' I implore her. 'You don't have to believe, just come.'

She looks at me sharply. 'There are people who would see you hanged for saying that.'

High above us, a flock of geese flies south. I wish I could fly with them and escape these cursed times, when every word must be measured. The flock passes swiftly. A few stragglers trail behind, battling to catch up. I watch till the last one disappears.

'I want to help you, Hannah,' I say. 'I owe it to you for helping me when I was labouring with Middy—'

'You don't owe me.' She adjusts the sack on her shoulder with what seems like a shrug. 'Good day to you, Mrs Wolfreston,' she says curtly. She pushes past the blackberry bush and is gone.

How on earth, I wonder, do you help someone who simply refuses to be helped?

4

I sit at Henry's desk in the library watching four little heads bowed over their work, feeling quietly satisfied. Much has happened in a few weeks.

I came upon Jane Harding in the churchyard and suggested I teach Grace to read. She seemed displeased and said, 'I'll need to think on it.'

However, two days later, when I opened the back door to fetch some eggs, Grace Harding was standing there with her bonnet on. 'Me mam sent me,' she said. Grace wore a clean linen under an old tunic. Her mother had scrubbed her, and her thick, fair hair was soft like wheat tips.

I brought her inside and she warmed herself near the fire, where Middy sat holding two ginger kittens while Peg silently ladled out the potage. She cocked an eyebrow as I set out another bowl for Grace.

'I told Jane Harding I would give Grace breakfast if she would send her up to learn to read,' I said briskly.

Grace ate the potage with a steady focus, as if she'd been instructed not to gulp.

After breakfast, the children followed me into the library. George quickly settled down to his schoolwork. He will be going to the church school in Lichfield next year and must work every morning. Grace watched me as I wrote out the alphabet on some parchment. I explained to her that these are letters that each have a sound, and that they make up the words we use to talk. Her eyes widened as I started sounding out the letters. She repeated them hesitantly, her voice fluttering like a bird's wing.

'That's it, Grace,' I said.

When George finished his work, I asked him to sit beside Grace and go through the letters with her again. By the end of the first morning, she was able to recite half of the alphabet and write the letter A. I noticed that George was patient with the girl, though he shouts when Middy takes books from the shelves or scribbles on the vellum. After Grace had gone home, I mentioned my observation to George.

'Because she's clever,' he said. 'Middy can't learn.'

'Middy can learn some things, George.'

'I know,' he said. 'He's good with animals.'

Last Monday, Grace sounded all the letters out and learned to recognise small words like 'at' and 'it'. When I praised her, dimples formed in her cheeks as she smiled. It was the first time I had seen the solemn child smile. I was about to tell her this when Peg tapped on the library door to say someone wanted to see me.

Mrs Kavanagh stood outside the back door, her fox-red hair windswept. She had a fat, brown hen tucked in her arms.

'I hear you're teaching the Harding girl to read. I wondered if you could teach my youngest two?' Behind her, two flame-haired boys held their caps in their hands. 'The harvest's done for the year, such as it was, so their father can spare them.'

I took the hen.

So, the library begins to feel like a schoolroom now. My heart warms as I listen to the children reciting their letters. Their open faces seem to absorb the lessons easily.

I glance over at Middy uneasily. He has taken books down from the shelves and built an unstable tower on the floor. I watch curiously as he rests the tip of his finger in the dimple of his chin before taking a book from the middle of the pile and laying it flat on a low empty shelf. He repeats this process, there seeming no logic to the sizes of the books, yet his face is creased with concentration.

'Mrs Wolfreston, what letters are in my name?' Grace asks.

I smile at her and take up the quill. As I write each letter of her name, I sound it out. She watches carefully, the tip of her tongue caught between her lips in concentration. She runs her finger under the letters and repeats: 'G-R-A-C-E.'

'Yes,' I say, and she gives a shy smile.

'Stop that, stupid,' George says.

I look up to see George shoving Middy.

'You're making a mess,' he shouts.

Middy falls backwards, and the tower of books topples across the flagstones.

'George!' I say sharply, helping Middy to sit up. 'That's no way to behave.'

George juts out his chin and his cheeks fire up. 'He's stupid, Mamma. You shouldn't let him near the books.'

Hot metal seems to sear into my temples. I want to chide him, but I am so angry I can't find the right words. I'll have to deal with him later, I decide, when the other children have gone.

Ignoring George, I say brightly, 'Let's put these books back where they belong, Middy.'

But Middy immediately takes a book from the heap on the floor and carries it to the low shelf.

I bite my lower lip and turn away. Outside, the leaves on the copper beech are on the cusp of turning. I picture Middy grown up, unable to carry out simple tasks without help, and I wonder who will care for my boy when I am gone.

'Mrs Wolfreston,' Grace whispers. Her soft hair is tucked behind her ears, and she is pointing at Middy. 'Look.'

Middy studies the low shelf. He picks up a book and moves it, and I realise what he is doing. He has sorted the books by colour and hue: card, tan, light brown, dark brown, three shades of blue and two of red.

I place my hand on Middy's shoulder. He smiles up at me, his blue eyes keen. I realise that I too am guilty of making assumptions about what Middy can and can't do. I have five students here, not four.

In the afternoon, Candace Broughton and I stroll up Craggy Hill. A short distance ahead of us walk Henry and Charles, Candace's brother. I am glad they are out of earshot because I can't wait to tell Candace about the little school that's forming in my library.

Candace is the daughter of Sir James Broughton, who owns much of the land around these parts. She is the most handsome woman in the district, a fact I can admit now without envy, though when I first saw her in the churchyard in Lichfield, fluttering her lace fan at Henry, I was reminded of the white fantail pigeons that strut in the garden in springtime. I resented the freedom of her loose, blonde curls as she laughed and the way she touched his arm with her smooth, pale hands. Henry, who has known the Broughtons since he was a boy, asked me why I avoided her. I complained that she had nothing useful to say. He told me that I was overestimating her beauty and underestimating her talents. He was right, but only on the latter point.

She walks beside me now, her emerald dress shimmering in the sun, making the grass and the trees look duller by comparison. She is talking excitedly about a poetry book she has written, but I am confused, for I am sure that Henry told me that Charles has recently had a book of verse published.

'It is the very same book,' she cries.

'You wrote it together?'

'No, I wrote it.'

I look at her, puzzled. 'But, Candace, why would you write it for him?'

She raises a hand to shield her eyes from the sun at my back as she returns my gaze.

'What other way is there to publish my work than under a man's name? Anyone who knows Charles would know that he has no interest in verse. His only interest is politics.'

'But it is a falsehood,' I say, thinking how unfair it is that women must make such a pretence and gain no credit for their work.

'You're one to talk,' she replies.

'What do you mean?'

'Charles told me that you take care of all the parish accounts and records.'

I have always considered myself virtuous in helping Henry so, but Candace makes me doubt myself. 'Henry is not the only man with no talent for accounts,' I say.

We walk on in silence until we reach the top of the hill. In the broad valley below, a cathedral is just visible in the distance. I imagine my mother standing on a hill on the other side of the valley, for a few miles from Hazelmere is a summit from which the cathedral can be glimpsed on a clear day.

'The more important point is that you are to be congratulated on writing an accomplished book of verse,' I say finally.

'Thank you,' she says, as if she had been waiting for me to realise this. 'And people will read it and enjoy it,' she adds.

Never knowing that a woman wrote it, I do not dare say.

She sits on a boulder regarding me. 'I suppose someone who writes their name on every single book that they own would find it hard to understand someone who writes their name on so little,' she says, with a tinge of sarcasm in her voice.

'Not on every book yet,' I say. 'And I write my name because I do not want to find myself in a situation where my property can be taken from me.'

'Do you not trust Henry?'

Henry and Charles are waiting for us a little way down the hill. Henry waves up at us.

'Whether I trust him or not, Candace, the law is the law. And not even rich women like you are free of it.'

She frowns.

'I'm sorry,' I say hastily. 'I didn't mean . . .'

She flutters her fingers as if it were already forgotten, but she strides down the hill away from me.

I hurry after her, regretting my rudeness. It is impossible to talk with her on the way back as Henry and Charles walk beside us. To make matters worse, Henry insists on congratulating Charles again on his book.

When we reach Statfold House, Candace seems disinclined to linger, but I ask her to inspect my recent book purchases. She follows me into the library reluctantly but smiles when she sees the Du Bartas poetry book. She reads several lines aloud and her whole face glows with pleasure.

'May I borrow this, Frances? My father's cousin William often quotes these lines to me,' she says, tapping the page. 'He is coming to visit us shortly, and I would like to discuss this with him.'

'Yes, of course,' I say, reminding myself to note it in the almanac.

She barely hears my answer as she stands by the window turning the pages, reading the lines with a poet's hunger. It seems cruel to interrupt her.

'I would like to meet your cousin when he comes.'

'And I am sure he would be impressed by your collection of books. I think his family are also collectors. I will ask him about it.' She says this without lifting her eyes from the page.

'Candace, I've been doing something new.'

'New? In Statfold?' she says, arching her fair eyebrows as she turns another page.

'Look,' I say, pointing to the table which has children's catechisms, prayer books and parchment scraps positioned in three neat piles.

'What are you up to?' she asks, glancing at the table.

'I've been teaching three of the village children to read. They already know the alphabet and two of them are reading a few small words.'

She shrugs. 'It is good of you, Frances, but I am surprised the parents see the use of it.'

I stare at her, surprised that she is so dismissive.

'What?' she says, finally closing the book.

'I thought you would be interested, Candace. You regularly talk of the importance of a good education. Wouldn't it be useful if they could read a public notice or a newssheet when they grow up? Or if they were able to write letters to their family and friends, as we can?'

I indicate a scrap of parchment which is filled with Grace Harding's scrawling letters and words. 'There are two boys and a little girl. She wrote this.'

Candace stares at the girl's rudimentary writing as if it were a puzzle.

I clear my throat and say, 'I was wondering about starting a parish school.'

She looks at me and then back at the parchment. 'A school in Statfold?'

'Yes. It would be open to all of the children in the village and the nearby hamlets—mainly in the winter, after the harvest is in. What do you think?'

Candace paces around the library for a few moments and then stands at the window, staring out at the copper beech tree. When she speaks it is with resolve. 'My father told me of a man, a Leveller called

Winstanley, who has written papers on this idea of having schools throughout England for all children to have an education.' She pauses. 'I am keen on this idea, but I wonder who would pay for these schools, especially now with all funds diverted to pay the army.'

'Well, for our parish, it would be the cost of a tutor and a place to teach. That is not much.' I add quickly, 'Henry mentioned that the church recognises the need for people to be able to read to understand the *Book of Common Prayer*, so we may be able to persuade the bishop to donate something.' I hesitate. 'We will also need the support of patrons.'

Candace is holding up the parchment. Her brow furrows as she follows the curves with her fingers. 'Grace . . . it says "grace" here.'

'She has written her name, Candace.'

She smiles. 'It is exciting, Frances. My father might be interested. May I show him this parchment?' She looks at me warily. 'But I'm not promising anything.'

I clap my hands. 'Think of it, Candace—Statfold Parish School.'

5

After dinner the following Sunday, I write up the Grey's Almanac. I mark my pupils' initials on the days they have come to the house this last week and I note the walk with Candace. Then I settle down to read *The Constant Maid* by James Shirley. It is a delightful leather-bound volume with a rich odour of walnut that seems to hint at the treasure within the pages. It is such a funny story about muddled love that it cheers me each time I read it. It makes me want to write myself.

I make a note in the margin next to a good line:

A very pleasant comedie.

I study my comment. It has not captured the sincerity of what I feel, and I am dissatisfied with it, but it is written now and cannot be changed. I press on the blotting paper and leave the pages open to dry the ink.

'Frances?'

Henry stands in the doorway. He has his cloak on and his face is flushed from the wind.

'I've just been talking to Tom. He says there's no recusancy list in the parish records, just a few lines drawn but no names added.'

I look at his questioning eyes and sigh heavily. 'I'm sorry, Henry. I forgot.'

He rubs his left cheek. 'You are meticulous, Frances. You did not forget.' He says 'forget' as if it were a lie.

With a heavy sense of dread, I push back the chair and reach for my shawl. 'I have the names. I'll go write it up now.'

As I hurry past him into the hall to get my cloak, he calls after me. 'Do you realise the trouble this could cause for me?'

When I reach the chapel vestry, Tom Dyer is still there. He lifts the parish books out of the vestry chest where they are stored under lock and key.

I open them on the table, while Tom pokes the fire back into life and adds a weighty log. He is about to add another.

'Leave that, Tom. This won't take me very long. It's only been a few weeks and there are not many names.'

'Very well, I'll gather up the prayer books.'

My fingers shake as I prepare a list to record names, weeks, attendance marks and reasons. Henry's words resound in my head. *You are meticulous, Frances.* I falter on the first name and reach for the blotter, cursing Henry under my breath for giving me this poisonous task.

Tom returns and stacks the books on the shelf beside the table. He looks over my shoulder at the list.

'If you don't mind me saying, Mrs Wolfreston, I think you need to record his given name. He's called Robert, but his true name is John Robert Caldwell.'

I stare at the incorrect name, wondering how to fix my mistake. Crossing a line through the first name will make the table look less reliable. Henry may think I am trying to hide something.

Tom opens the chest and brings over more books. He lays the parish records of births, marriages and deaths on the table. He opens a long book and turns to C. There are Caldwells listed there who have been in the parish for more than seventy years. He points to John Robert Caldwell, born in Statfold in 1607.

'This is him.' Tom looks quietly pleased at finding my mistake, and I feel foolish to have made such an obvious error.

'I'll be more thorough with the other names, Tom.'

Why do I feel the need to explain myself to him?

'Is it all right if I finish now? Mr Wolfreston said I might go as we're up at dawn for market day.'

'Of course.' I watch him pull his rough wool cloak over his jacket. There are lines around his eyes from lack of sleep. 'Tom?'

He looks back at me expectantly.

'Thank you,' I say, tapping the register gently.

'That's all right, Mrs Wolfreston. Don't be working too late yourself, ma'am.'

As Tom opens the outer door, frigid air streams around my skirt and I shiver. The candle on the desk flickers and jumps as the door closes with a bang.

On my list are the names of five who have missed one Sunday service; two of them have missed the last three services. I work my way through each one in turn. I find the first few names easily, running my fingers down the birth register. Most people live their whole lives in Statfold. I am relieved that Margaret Crowley, Peter Robinson and

Jeffray Overly heeded warnings and returned to church after missing only one week. Robert Caldwell's three-week absence can be easily explained, although the sheriff may not accept his disability as a valid reason for not attending church. Hannah Smythe's name is last.

Despite my warning, Hannah Smythe has still not attended chapel.

My fingers run down the birth register looking for her name. It is not there. Of course, I realise—Smythe is her married name. Chiding myself, I go back to the start of the birth register and check every entry for the name Hannah. My belly flutters. Is it the baby, I wonder, or impatience with my task?

Eventually, I conclude that Hannah wasn't born in Statfold.

Sighing, I open the chest again and take out other records. The marriage records date back to 1570. I work my way through them till I find Smith and then Smythe. There are two possible entries. One was made in 1590 so seems too old. The other, made in 1622, reads: *Mr John Smythe and Miss J. Coulter.* I stare at the record for a long time, trying to determine what this means. She is called Hannah, but perhaps her given name is not that but simply something else beginning with J. But why would the registrar not record the given name fully in the marriage record? Or is J. Coulter not Hannah at all but a previous wife of John Smythe?

With the registers splayed open across the table, I cradle my head in my hands. The recusancy record already has the first line crossed out in black. I do not want to make more mistakes.

The draught from the door gives a long, muted whistle. I glance at the dwindling fire; this is going to take longer than I'd thought. I turn the pages of the birth register and begin the search for Coulter.

6

We rise early the next morning for market day. I went to bed late after a fruitless search for Hannah's name. Then I couldn't sleep for worrying as I couldn't bring myself to write her name on the recusancy list. We drive two loaded carts to the harvest market in Tamworth. Henry and I ride in the first with George and Middy. They sit in the back on an old blanket, leaning against bushel sacks full of wheat and oats. Tom Dyer and Peg, in her best bonnet, follow in the second cart; Peg is talking animatedly to Tom Dyer, who looks to be enjoying her company. The road is busy with carts, farm folk and peddlers carrying their wares to market. I fidget with the ribbons on my hood; it would be faster to walk. It's a relief to finally see the turrets of Tamworth Castle above the trees.

Henry and Tom Dyer unload the goods and Peg takes the boys to the market square. I set off for the bookshop. I weave through the crowded street of overhanging buildings, passing several butcher stalls with pigs, rabbits and whole sides of beef hanging on hooks. The smell of the raw meat makes me suddenly queasy and I turn into a covered lane that leads to the next street. I rest for a moment on the corner, leaning against a wall with a hand to my belly.

A woman selling pies approaches me. 'They say it's a sign that the baby is taking well, when you feel sick like that.'

'Is it that obvious?'

'Only to them that knows the signs,' she says. She stands by me awhile, talking about her little ones at home, not bothering to call out to passers-by to buy her pies. 'Well, you've got a bit more colour now,' she says after a few minutes, examining my face.

I buy pies for the boys. She chooses the best two and wraps them with care.

The bookseller is a brick-fronted two-storey building with a small printing press upstairs and the shop below. At the front of shop, John Townsend, the rotund owner, sells newsbooks and tobacco. He has drawn quite a crowd this morning and the place reeks.

'I won't be long, Mrs Wolfreston,' he calls wheezily.

I hold my breath as I edge past the men smoking pipes and chewing tobacco. I pass shelves of theology books, political texts and scores of the new almanacs for 1648. On a short section of wall, three woodcut prints that I recognise from newssheets have been hung for decoration; the first is of Oliver Cromwell leading men into battle; the second shows the witch-finder general who died recently, standing with his staff; and the third depicts a trio of witches with huge warts and black cats. I study the prints closely. Usually it is the intricate workman-ship of woodcuts that fascinates me, but I find myself drawn to the positioning of the women beside these two powerful men like a cruel jest or ruse. Though I am no witch, it leaves me feeling diminished and I move on quickly.

At the rear of the shop, a long bookcase that stretches from floor to ceiling is filled with playbooks, verse and other literature.

On a round display table, a large book is propped up on a stand. I run my hand over the glossy leather cover, breathing in its rich, heavy odour. The gilt title reads: *Mr. William Shakespeare's Comedies, Histories & Tragedies.* I imagine how splendid the book would look on the drawing room table when guests came visiting.

'Only fifty pounds.' John Townsend stands beside me in his work apron. He is almost sixty yet still climbs the ladders to retrieve books for favoured customers.

I give a little grunt. 'I could never afford that.'

'No matter, I have something better for you.' He holds up two quartos bound in card: 1599 and 1636 editions of *Venus and Adonis.* He taps the older of the pair proudly. 'This one is a second edition.'

I gaze longingly at the quartos. *Venus and Adonis* is William Shakespeare's first published work. He wrote the poem when the London theatres were closed because of the 1592 plague. It tells the story of the goddess Venus, who becomes so intoxicated with the handsome young hunter Adonis that she pursues him. But Adonis spurns her love. My mother had the 1593 first edition when I was a child, so I am familiar with it, but I know that there are some changes in the later editions. I wonder if Mr Shakespeare cared that some of his words were changed. Perhaps he cared more that people enjoyed his work than whether a word was amended here or there. For some reason this makes me think of Candace and her poetry that no one will ever know she wrote.

While I am counting out my coins, I say, 'I have a favour to ask. I am teaching a few children to read but I have nothing for them to write on. I wondered if you have any scraps that you might give me?'

He climbs the stairs to the printing room; as he opens the door, the scents of turpentine and ink drift across the shop. When he returns, he is holding a large bundle of parchment offcuts from the printing press. 'Will this suffice?'

'You are a kind man, Mr Townsend.'

He laughs. 'Well, they might buy a book from me someday,' he says.

The market square is heaving with people. I hold my satchel and the pies to my chest and squeeze through the jostling crowds. Henry and Tom Dyer stand at a street corner, trying to keep both horses calm. Henry wants to leave but Peg and the boys have not yet returned. I climb onto the cart to search for them from a higher vantage point.

In a space in the middle of the crowd, a bull stands tied to a stake. Nearby, several snarling dogs are restrained by their owners. The bull bellows and paws, ready to charge, and the crowd reels backwards. A woman groans as she is thrust against the cart. Every instinct tells me to leave, but there's nowhere to go. I feel sick as I scan the crowd, praying that Peg has not brought the boys to this bull-baiting.

The bull heaves on the ropes and the stake seems to shiver, but it holds. A cur is released; it snaps and bites. The bull attacks but is pulled back by the ropes. It snorts, its black eyes shining, then lunges again. The rope yanks it back and it bellows. It reminds me of the awful noise our milk cow made when her calf died, and she tried for hours to revive it.

The bull rouses and tries once more. But this time it falls to its knees. The crowd cheers. A woman near me shouts, 'Kill it.'

Suddenly I see a young boy approaching the fallen bull. Only the back of his head is visible, but I know him at once.

'Middy, stop!' I call.

Henry gasps and begins to push through the crowd.

'Middy!' I shout. 'Stop!'

My son turns his head, looking for me, just as the dog, sensing his approach, turns from the bull and sets upon Middy.

My screams shred my throat. The pies fall as I reach out to Middy. I am floating as Middy turns, his long hair rippling. I see his dimpled chin. Screams from the crowd are drowning mine. The crowd shifts, there's a flash of steel, and then Middy disappears and I stumble in the footwell of the cart.

I clutch the cart seat, winded and gasping. 'Middy!' I call, my voice rasping.

And then a man wearing a buff coat appears, pushing through the crowd. He's holding Middy. There is blood on Middy's right leg. The soldier hands Middy up to me and I clasp my son so tight that he yells.

'Oh, what if I lost you, Middy?' I exclaim over and over, until I realise that Middy is crying.

'The bite's not too bad,' the man says.

I lift my head to thank him for returning my boy and realise he's the soldier who sold me the Du Bartas book.

I open my mouth, but no words come out.

Henry, who has returned to my side, shakes the soldier's hand and says something to him, but I cannot hear it. All I can hear is my boy saying, 'Bull.'

That evening, I lie next to Middy, watching him sleep, trying to sleep myself. Every time my eyes close the events in the market square play out again, and I lurch awake. I almost lost *another* child. To calm myself, I try reciting poetry, but it does no good. Eventually, I recall my mother's smooth voice saying, 'You worry too much, Frannie.' She had a way of soothing me when I was agitated or upset. 'Count slowly, angel,' she would say, 'and listen to each number.' And then, when my breath had settled, she would stroke my forehead and tell me stories until I fell asleep.

I reach out and stroke the damp fair hair from Middy's forehead. 'Mamma,' I murmur. 'Oh, how I miss you.'

I've never talked with anyone about the children I have lost. Henry doesn't like to dwell on such things. Even when my mother came to comfort me when I was sick, we didn't talk of the baby that never breathed. My mother had her own experiences of that, so she knew well the great emptiness that I felt, and I had long since learned that a woman must contain her feelings. So, Mamma distracted me by asking me of the people in the parish and the fruit in the orchard. I asked her to tell me about our family or the people in Hazelmere, but she said, 'There's nothing to tell,' or, 'I cannot remember that now.' Instead, she recounted the plot of a book or a play from memory. As she talked, her face relaxed. Her voice dipped and soared. But she did not laugh in anticipation of a funny piece of action, as she used to. Oh, she had such a good strong laugh when I was young.

Things changed after the accident. That day, my father went looking for her and brought her home. He carried her into the house and straight upstairs. Her body was limp and her head lolled over his arm as he took her into the bedroom. I hung back by the bedroom door watching as he laid her on the bed.

She gave a long moan, and I ran to her. I stared at her pallid skin, the circles under her eyes. 'Papa, we need the doctor,' I said.

'She just needs to sleep,' my father said dismissively. 'There's nothing broken.'

'But Papa—'

'Go, Frannie, and keep the others away. Your mother needs her rest.'

I lingered by the door watching as he lifted my mother's head and slipped a pillow underneath.

He turned to me, his eyes glistening like wet pebbles. 'Go. I will look after her.'

My mother rested in her room for days. Whenever I went to see her, my father was there, sitting by the bed with his head hanging.

One afternoon, I saw my father fall asleep in the chair by the fire in the dining room. I crept upstairs and into my mother's room. She lay in the bed, her face ashen, her eyes closed.

'Mamma,' I whispered close to her ear. 'It's me: Frannie.'

Her eyelids fluttered. Slowly her lips parted, but no words came.

I took her hand and squeezed it. 'Mamma, what do you need? A drink?'

She opened her eyes. 'Read to me, Frannie.'

'Yes, Mamma.' I looked about the room for a book and spied *Venus and Adonis* lying on the floor near the bedside table. I picked it up, turned to the bookmarked page and began to read.

'No,' Mamma murmured. 'From the beginning.'

Thinking she must be fevered, I said, 'This is the first page, Mamma.'

Her head turned on the pillow, letting me know that I was wrong.

At the start of the quarto was a note—a letter written by William Shakespeare to an earl, dedicating the book to him. I turned the pages till I reached the verse and began to read.

I read on and on, expecting Mamma to stop me at any moment, but she didn't. As I finally neared the end, I glanced at her. She was looking past me towards the window, her expression so wretched that I almost cried.

I thought of that book again when she tended to me on my sickbed in the library all those years later.

'You look upset, angel,' Mamma said as she placed her hand on my forehead, checking for fever.

'I was thinking about Venus and Adonis.'

She frowned.

'I don't like Venus,' I said. 'She pursued and hounded Adonis so. I feel sorry for him.'

Mamma turned away then, her eyes searching and settling somewhere on the bookshelves. She took a wavering breath in, as if trying to remember something. 'Venus hoped to experience love with Adonis in all its passion but was left bitterly disappointed by what human love did to her. Her heart was truly . . . broken.' Mamma tried to smile as she looked at me, but her chin wobbled a little in the light. 'It's Venus you should pity, angel,' she said.

I gaze at Middy now. If I hadn't taken so long in Townsend's buying those copies of *Venus and Adonis*, I would have returned to the square sooner. Perhaps I could have prevented Middy from going towards the bull. I shudder at the thought of what might have happened if that soldier hadn't been there.

7

Henry sits near me on the window seat as I bend over some overdue needlework. Since the bull-baiting, he has taken to sitting beside me after the noon meal, watching me. He used to watch me like this when we were first married, as if he expects that I might disappear. I glance up at him. It irks me that he's younger than I am. He looks boyish, even with his beard. I suddenly recall how affectionate we were just after we were first married, and I feel myself smile—he used to be tender.

'What are you thinking?' he asks.

'Nothing,' I say, my cheeks growing warm.

His eyes crinkle, a soft smile forming, as if he knows I was thinking about him.

As I press the needle through the fabric, he says, 'I spoke to Sam. I told him he could stay on and look after our horses and the cows over the winter.'

The needle pricks my finger and I wince in pain. 'Are you sure we can trust him, Henry?' I say. For the past few days, Sam, the soldier in the buff coat who saved Middy, has been sleeping in our stable and helping with odd jobs. 'We don't know anything about him.'

'He saved our son, and he's starving,' Henry reminds me. 'It's the least we can do.'

I remove the pins from the bodice seam and continue the running stitch. 'You're right,' I say with a sigh, but there's an unease in me.

As if reading my mind, Henry says, 'I saw him this morning, leading the boys around the stable yard on Lady. Middy was laughing.'

I smile. 'The boys do like him.'

'I'll show him how to drive that carriage. Then he can bring my mother over to visit or take you and the boys there,' Henry says.

'I'd rather ride Merlin; that carriage is far too cramped.' I notice his frown and add quickly, 'But it is kind of Charles to lend it, and your mother will be glad of it.'

He looks over at the rowan trees, rusting orange in the afternoon sun, and I know he is remembering his late father. After Henry and I married, his mother moved out of Statfold House to live with his sister in Melbourne, a pleasant town which lies some twenty-five miles north.

'What on earth . . .?' Henry says, peering along the lane.

Mrs Eugenie Edwards and Mrs Mary Dawson are passing the church and turning towards Statfold House. Mrs Edwards' outdated ruff protrudes above her cloak. She strides with her walking stick held high as if it were slowing her down. Mrs Dawson, slim and elegant, wears her hat with its prostrate peacock feather. Henry always says that feather is too afraid to stand up.

'It's likely about recording the recusants. I'll be in the chapel if you need me,' Henry says.

As he steals out of the garden door, I put down my sewing. I call to Peg then smooth down my hair and remove my apron. As I reach the hallway, there is a loud knock on the front door. I take a deep breath to calm myself before signalling to Peg to open it.

'What took you so long?' Mrs Edwards says to Peg.

'What a pleasure to see you, ladies,' I say, showing them into the drawing room. 'Do you want me to call for Mr Wolfreston?'

'No, it's you we've come to see,' Mrs Edwards says.

She balances her stick against the side table, where some books are piled, and sits in the adjacent chair. She gives the books a prod and her lips move as she reads the title of one then gives me a sharp look.

Mrs Dawson sits on the edge of a nearby chair. 'We heard about your boy being attacked at the bull-baiting. Is he all right?'

'He is well, thank you. His leg will have a scar, but it was a lucky escape, and we are very grateful for that.'

Mrs Dawson glances towards Mrs Edwards.

Mrs Edwards says, 'I expect you'll be wondering what brings us here on this pleasant afternoon?' She smiles but it falters like a kite that fails to catch the wind. 'Mrs Wolfreston, I suppose you are proud that word has spread all over Tamworth even up to Derby that you have a'—she pauses as if she has just eaten something bitter— '*library*, and that you are collecting playbooks.'

'Well, I find it disappointing that a woman can't do anything without it being talked about in town. I have collected all manner of books since I was married. I have as many books about conduct and theology as I have literature. And as you know, Mrs Edwards, the bishop himself is fond of playbooks.'

Mrs Edwards gives me a frosty look.

Mrs Dawson, clearly uncomfortable with this exchange, adds, 'Of course, reading the *Book of Common Prayer* is a worthy endeavour.'

'Yes, yes,' snaps Mrs Edwards, 'but there are more productive ways to spend your time than reading these.' She picks up two of the books from the side table and tuts. '*A Midsummer Night's Dream, The Famous Historie of Montelyon.*' She tilts her head, waiting for me to respond.

'My children are fond of those stories.'

She points at the table in the corner. 'Is this where you've been teaching the village children to read?' Her words prick like needles.

'No, the children are—'

She interrupts: 'Are you a licensed teacher?'

'No, of course not. I am only helping a few young children learn their letters.'

Mrs Edwards and Mrs Dawson exchange a meaningful look.

Mrs Edwards clears her throat. 'Mrs Wolfreston, we have not been consulted, but if we had we would have told you that this enterprise is doomed to failure. There is absolutely no need for the commoners to read. It will not put food on their tables. Besides'—she frowns at me as if I were an unruly child—'there is a way that things work here, and you are interfering with that.'

'But the church wants more people to read in order to improve their understanding. Surely teaching the children to do so is a good thing?'

Mrs Edwards grasps her stick and bangs it on the floor. 'Gentry children, yes, but not commoners.'

My eyes widen but I keep my voice level. We are barely gentry ourselves, the three of us, but I fear pointing this out would not help my cause. I say, 'Why is teaching commoners a problem?'

Mrs Edwards rolls her eyes. 'As you well know, some ladies in the parish do not read and would be put at a social inconvenience by this.'

'But . . .'

Mrs Dawson's face reddens. 'Have you any idea how it feels when you cannot read yet commoners' children are reading right there in front of you?' She flaps a hand in front of her face.

A log spills onto the hearth. I pick it up with the tongs and take my time prodding it back into the flames. When I look up, she seems a little calmer.

'That must be upsetting, Mrs Dawson. But I can teach you to read too, if you would like? Discreetly, of course.'

Her mouth falls open. 'How dare you intrude so, Mrs Wolfreston? You have no right to change the way of things in Statfold. Are you so wrapped in your own *vanity* you cannot even see that?'

I clasp my hands so tightly my fingers hurt.

'Mrs Wolfreston, will you stop teaching these commoners?' Mrs Edwards demands.

The fire crackles between us and the logs shift and grumble.

'No,' I say.

For a moment Mrs Edwards looks lost, as if she had not considered that I might refuse her. She stands up, looking down at me.

'Come now, Mary,' she says, without taking her eyes off me. 'We have both been humiliated enough by this shrew.'

She stalks from the room. Moments later I hear the front door slam. I stand at the window watching them stride towards the village. Mrs Edwards thrusts her stick before her like a weapon. Shaking, I make my way into the library. I stand in the middle of the room, surrounded by my books, as Mrs Edwards' rebuke spins through me. *Shrew.*

8

I woke in the library to find my mother standing by the fireplace, her hand touching the small tapestry of St Paul's Cathedral that hung above the mantel. When she realised that I was awake, she said, 'Do you remember when we walked around London, angel?'

We had visited London with my father when I was eleven. My mother persuaded my father that it would be educational for me to see a play. They took me to the Globe Theatre to see a comedy by William Shakespeare called *The Taming of The Shrew*. During the performance, I became concerned that my mother had chosen a story where a husband tries to curb the spirit of his strong wife Katherine by depriving her of food, but my mother sat beside me laughing. My father laughed too, and I wondered if I understood them at all. My father held my mother's hand and looked at her sweetly. But the following morning at breakfast, he was brusque, as if the intimacies at the theatre were forgotten.

After breakfast, my father had to leave to meet with someone, so Mamma and I strolled among the wild grasses and foxgloves in Lincoln's Inn Fields. She asked me what I thought of the play.

I trailed my hands over the silky grass tips, unsure how to respond. I didn't want to seem ungrateful for the treat, but I had found the play disturbing.

'Katherine disliked being told how to behave,' I said hesitantly.

'Yes,' my mother agreed, looking rueful. 'She argued and fought with everyone, as if she knew better.'

'She was clever,' I pointed out. 'Perhaps she did know better.'

'She is a shrew—get the ducking stool!' my mother joked. 'I'm afraid strong or clever women are not appreciated, Frannie. They are often called shrews.'

'Petruchio was mean to her.'

'Petruchio knew that he must be her equal to persuade her to change, that he must be as witty and clever as she.'

This couldn't be right, I thought. Was my mother defending Petruchio's cruelty as he tried to tame Katherine?

As if she knew what I was thinking, my mother explained, 'Katherine's chances for happiness were limited by her disposition. Petruchio showed her that if she changed, she could be happy.'

'But to starve her?'

'He also starved himself.'

She looked thoughtful as she gazed at a marshy pond, where a crane dipped its long neck into the water.

'I think she allowed him to believe that he "tamed" her because he had earned her respect and trust. She believed she could be happy with him. She realised there must be give and take to make a marriage work.'

I wanted to say that sometimes one person only gives and the other only takes. How did I know this so surely? I looked at her, but she looked steadily away.

The crane flapped its wings and took flight, something small hanging from its beak.

After a moment my mother said, 'Marriage is a compromise and'— she paused—'it is almost like a comedy . . . how we try to alter each other so.'

'So, the sun must be the moon, as Petruchio demands?'

She gave a sweet chirrup, like a bird. 'Sometimes. But at other times Katherine will decide when the sun is the sun. For she is not stupid; she knows what is real and what is a necessary fabrication. He has taught her the difference, has he not?'

'It is difficult to fathom,' I said.

She tucked her arm under my mine. We walked until we reached a hillock with a distant view of the river. Clusters of boats were moored at wharves, their wooden masts piercing the sky.

'Look, Frannie,' my mother said, her face alight.

Hanging above the river like a lost pearl, the moon was shining in the morning sunlight.

How close we were.

Now, I watched my mother standing in the library by the tapestry, her face shining with memory.

'Yes, Mamma,' I said. 'And I remember the moon.'

She smiled at me.

The next day, I woke to find her sitting by the window and gazing out, with my catechism unopened in her lap. Seeing her like this, I felt a deep sorrow. It reminded me of when I sneaked upstairs to see her. I found her sitting by her bedroom window, the shadows of the low sun on the lead making a grid on her face. I wanted to tell her how much I missed her but she didn't turn around. She kept staring out of the window at the sinking sun, and I crept away.

When we were little, my mother taught us to pray every morning and night in the way of the old religion. My father knew this, but he didn't seem to mind so long as we went to church on Sunday and told no one. He knew my mother was Catholic when he married her, and at that time there was more tolerance than now. But then my father told us we were not allowed to pray with her anymore. We did not mind this, and if my mother minded, she did not say. I knew she continued to pray in her room when she thought no one could see her.

She had a small book of verse, *Shakespeare's Sonnets*, that she kept hidden in her skirt pocket. Father never knew that when he took us to church on Sundays, my mother had that book with her. My mother's face tilted towards the vicar as he spoke, but her mind seemed to be elsewhere. Sometimes she caught me looking up at her, and then she would place her gloved hand next to mine on the pew, so that our little fingers touched. I knew then that she was running over a verse or a play in her head. It was our secret.

'Oh, you're awake, Frannie.' My mother stood up and laid the catechism on the table. She gestured to the window. 'The tree will bud soon,' she said.

I felt then the depth of my mother's unhappiness. But she hadn't always been like this.

So I said, 'Tell me about the day you fell off the horse, Mamma.'

She turned from the window and looked at me, her face in shadow. 'You must be mistaken. I have never fallen from a horse, Frannie.'

'You must remember,' I say. 'You fell from the horse when you went to town. Papa had to go and fetch you home.'

She turned back to the window, but I had caught the frown on her face. I watched her, puzzled; for some reason she seemed annoyed by the subject.

'You were sick after that,' I reminded her. 'You had to stay in bed, as I do now.'

Turning, she snapped, 'Frannie, we both know that I didn't fall off any horse.'

I stared at her. 'I'm sorry, Mamma. I—'

'No.' Her eyes flared. She looked close to tears, but she didn't cry. To this day, I have never seen my mother cry.

9

George and Middy have breakfast in the kitchen. Grace's bowl and spoon lie untouched on the table. I sit with the kitty in my lap, waiting for Grace, but she does not arrive for her lessons.

'She must be sick,' I say aloud. But I notice Peg avoiding my eyes. 'Has something happened in the village, Peg?'

She shrugs and busies herself making bread. You can't get anything out of Peg, if she decides against it.

The Kavanagh boys arrive soon after, red-faced and with muddy shoes; it has been raining since last night. I ask the elder boy, Joe, if he has seen Grace in the village, but he says he hasn't.

I settle the boys down to their work, but the morning is unsatisfactory, and they seem to accomplish little. They bicker and tease each other, and at one point I have to scold George and Joe.

I send the Kavanagh boys home early, and then sit beside George and Middy in the kitchen eating lunch.

'Did Joe say anything about Grace?' I ask George.

George looks at Peg, who has turned from the cookpot to stare at him. He looks back at me, an uncertain frown forming on his forehead.

'He said he saw her playing at the pond.'

I glance at Peg, but she has turned back to the cookpot.

After lunch, the rain has eased, and I set off to the village. George and Middy run ahead along the lane, looking for puddles to tread in.

'Which way are we going, Mamma?' George calls when they reach the crossroads.

I point towards the centre of the village. 'First, we're going to see Mrs Harding.'

'Is she still called missus when her husband is dead?' George asks.

'Yes, George.'

Jane Harding's white cob cottage lies in the middle of the village, just beyond the millpond. As we pass the adjacent large barn, where her late husband worked as the smithy, Jane spots me from the window of her cottage and opens her front door before I reach it.

'Come in, Mrs Wolfreston.'

'Stay where I can see you,' I say, gesturing for George and Middy to wait outside.

The house is a single room with a flagstone floor. There is a bed in the corner, a table with two chairs and another chair pulled close to the fire. The house smells of damp hay. Jane leaves the door ajar, and we stand just inside.

'Is Grace well?'

Jane's face is ashen. She twists a corner of her apron between her fingers. 'She is, but I dare not send her up to you.'

She gestures to a chair, but I give a quick shake of my head.

'Mrs Edwards came by yesterday afternoon,' she says. 'She was quite riled up, told me that I had no right to send Grace to learn to read without letting her know. Said she might have to let me go.'

I glance out of the window, and see the boys make their way towards the pond.

'Did Mrs Edwards say why Grace couldn't come?' I struggle to keep the bite of anger from my voice.

'Something about it being sinful to raise expectations, and how only schooling licensed by the parish is lawful. I told her it wasn't really a school, it was just you teaching Grace and the Kavanagh boys, but . . .' She looks around the meagre room and gives a wry laugh. 'She seems to think we might get above ourselves. Oh, don't get me wrong, I'm grateful for the work, but what's it to her if little Grace learns to read?'

I glance outside again to check on the boys. Grace is wandering through the long grass next to the millstream on the far side of the pond. She climbs onto a large rock and sits with her chin on her knees, watching the clear water flow over the paddles of the mill wheel and disappear into the murky green pond.

'What I'll do with her, I don't know.' Jane Harding's young face is taut and lined in the morning sun. 'Mrs Edwards won't let me bring her with me.'

I put my hand on her arm. 'Let the dust settle on this awhile.'

I step outside and she follows me. Several villagers pass, murmuring polite greetings. I notice Hannah Smythe approaching with a large bundle of sticks tied to her back. As soon as she spots me, she hurries off in another direction, keeping her head bowed. She must hate me for hounding her.

My boys have gone to stand by Grace. George whispers something to her and the solemn girl turns to wave at me. Tears sting my eyes, and I walk away before Jane Harding can notice.

George and Middy come running after me.

'Where are we going now, Mamma?'

'Home,' I call, without waiting for them to catch up.

'Mamma, stop!' George tugs my sleeve as he reaches me.

I stop, squeeze my eyes shut and then breathe out slowly through my nose.

'Mamma . . .' he says.

'What is it, George?'

He's staring up at me, his head tilted to one side and his hand still resting on my arm. I sniff and look around. Behind us, two geese are waddling to the pond. I realise that in my haste, I've come the wrong way. Patting George's hand, I point along the lane.

'Let's go this way past Mrs Smythe's, then we'll cut across the field.'

George exchanges a look with Middy. He knows the path across the field will be muddy. I am always telling them to avoid it.

By the time the lane reaches Hannah Smythe's house it's far too narrow for a cart and is crisscrossed with long brambles. Hannah is outside her cottage, trying to clear a path through fallen leaves with a shovel, the bundle of sticks still tied to her back.

She looks up at the sound of our approach, scowls when she sees that it's me. Her eyes drift to the boys—to Middy, who bends to move a long bramble branch away from her feet. She gives him a smile.

'These leaves are as slippery as ice when they're wet,' she remarks. 'What can I do for you, Mrs Wolfreston?'

'Bees,' says Middy.

'That's right, Middy,' I say, smiling as I now have a good reason for having walked this way. 'I wondered if you had any honey and beeswax I could buy, Mrs Smythe?'

She puts down the shovel and we follow her along the narrow path to her door. There's a cow tied up nearby.

I wait while she goes inside, and the boys run off to explore the henhouse and the vegetable beds and, beyond them, a small field.

Hannah returns with two small jars.

'This is all I have. It was a cold winter last year, so there's been fewer bees.'

I peer into the jar containing the beeswax. There isn't much. I could stretch it to two or three candles at most. The honey jar isn't quite full. I hand her a coin.

The boys trudge through the long grass along the edge of the muddy field.

'That's my lavender,' she says, watching them.

I nod. 'You haven't been coming to church,' I say softly.

She chews on her lip and says nothing.

'I can't force you to come, but I have to write you up in the records.'

'You told me that before,' she says.

My heart beats faster. She's not making this easy.

'The problem is that I can't find your name in the parish records.'

'Well, I married John Smythe in Statfold. It's nowt to do with me if the records are wrong.'

'There's no Hannah listed,' I say. 'John Smythe married a J. Coulter.'

Her eyes are wide when she finally looks at me.

'Is that your name?' I ask.

She gives me such a sharp look that I shudder. Then she turns and walks back to the house.

Following her, I say, 'It's just that I need to make sure I'm not writing the wrong name in the recusancy record.'

'Just write Hannah Smythe if you have to, though I don't know whose business it is.' Her voice is shrill.

'Well, I told you before . . .'

She picks up the shovel and turns to me, the colour high in her face. 'I never meant to cause this trouble. I just want to be left alone.'

The shovel scrapes through the mud on the path, tangling among the brambles. She wrestles it free. 'Old Mrs Wolfreston wouldn't be bothering me like this,' she mutters angrily.

The mention of my mother-in-law jolts me. She had a good reputation in the parish, and for years after I arrived people would compare Henry and me to his father and mother. The comparisons were often unfavourable.

'That's not fair, Hannah—I've been protecting you. I didn't record your name, hoping you would return to church after we last spoke.'

She says nothing.

'My husband could get into trouble because of this,' I say quietly.

'You don't need to do anything on my account.'

'Yes, I do. You helped me when no one else would.'

'I keep telling you, you don't owe me anything for that.'

I stare at her. 'But you saved my life, Hannah,' I protest. 'You saved Middy.'

She sniffs. 'I didn't do it for you. I did it for . . .' She looks away quickly towards the field, her lips forming a thin line. 'All right, I'll come to church on Sunday,' she says.

I smile. 'You will?'

'Now, let me get on,' she says, picking up the shovel.

The baby is heavy inside me as we climb the hill and follow the path between two fallow fields. The boys run ahead as we reach the top, but I stop to catch my breath. Turning back the way we had come, I can just make out the figure of Hannah Smythe. She hadn't told me her true name, I realise.

Beside me is a parish boundary marker. To the east is Rivermead, nestled beside the trees that also hide the river from view. Behind me is Statfold village.

'Mamma, look!' George points towards home.

Protruding above the trees is the chapel, with its stone cross perched on the roof ridge, and beyond that the first floor and the chimneys of Statfold House are visible. Through a gap in the trees, the stables border the yard and, behind them, the orchard slopes down towards the low woods that snake all the way around to Rivermead.

Sam is coming out of the woods at the bottom of the orchard, his buff coat glowing yellow in the afternoon sun. He walks a short way, then looks around as if someone has called him from the woods. He pauses, then turns and makes his way up to the orchard.

'Sam,' Middy says.

'Yes, Middy,' I say, quietly. I look again at the stone marker and mentally trace the line of the fields towards Statfold. Hannah Smythe's cottage lies right on the border of the two parishes. Perhaps the Rivermead parish records may reveal something about Hannah Smythe.

10

The next morning, Candace arrives as I am taking the Kavanagh boys through the lesson I had planned. She watches from a chair by the library fire, occasionally nodding to show her support. We had arranged for her to observe the lessons so that she can discuss my pupils' progress with her father. It is a such a disappointment to me that she cannot see Grace read.

'Good work, teacher,' she says, as we make our way to the drawing room after the boys have gone outside to play. 'But where is the little Harding girl?'

As I relate what has happened with Grace and Mrs Edwards, Candace sighs audibly. She walks over to the window and stares at the chapel.

'That damn woman,' she says. 'She doesn't like anyone.' Her green eyes are flecked with brown in the sun streaming through the glass. She raises her chin. 'But I don't think Mrs Kavanagh will pull the boys out, even if Mrs Edwards and Mrs Dawson press her to. She won't be bullied. And neither should we, Frances.' She taps a gloved finger on her chin. 'I think you should invite Mrs Edwards for dinner while

Charles and I are here. She respects my father, so will be flattered by our company.'

'That will not change her mind,' I say.

She tilts her head considering this. 'No,' she agrees. 'You must also apologise. Eat lots of humble pie!' Her hollow laugh echoes in the large room.

We sit on the window seat and the warmth of the sun eases me.

'This is worth doing, Frances,' Candace says, serious now.

Suddenly aware of the bulge in my belly, I take off my shawl and lay it over my lap.

'I know,' I say. 'I just fear that, whatever I do, she'll put a stop to it. She is such a devout Puritan she even hates that I collect books, particularly verses and playbooks.' I glance at Candace. 'Puritans take all the joy from life. They have closed the theatres, banned actors and now you can't even enjoy reading a play in your own home. It feels wrong to me that they should dictate how we live. Yet I am a rector's wife, and I am meant to behave as they do.'

Candace lowers her voice, as if she's worried someone may over-hear. 'It seems to me the Puritans forget there must also be compassion and care. People like Eugenie Edwards cannot see past their elbows. We must work around them. They were never taught the joy of verse, and the purpose of plays and books in educating us and freeing our souls. They have never had the benefit of fathers like ours, who taught them to read widely and think for themselves.'

I am surprised that Candace would compare my upbringing to hers. Henry must have told her that my father taught me to read. After all, my father had boasted to Henry that he had taught me everything I knew; that I managed the household accounts for him, that I would make an excellent wife, and that my father need pay him only a small dowry with such an asset. Although the Wolfreston family sought the marriage, this dowry is a perennial source of embarrassment for me.

'It was my mother who taught me to read,' I say shakily. 'My father taught me much later, and only theology and accounts. He is a . . . a strict man, Candace.'

Her brows knit together. She starts to apologise but I hold up my hand to stop her.

'You couldn't know. I have not even discussed my childhood with Henry.'

'What is she like, your mother?'

'My mother?'

Candace looks at me now and I can see she wants to understand. But what can I tell her? Candace's poems are full of light, of hope, of verse that lifts and sweeps the heart into an afternoon's dream. There is no hint of the darkness that lurks in corners or creeps under doors. Does she know of the long, slow pain that a silence can inflict? That it can gouge crevices where it seeps inside you and, though you might cover it with a smile or a pleasant word, it is always there underneath?

Candace is watching me steadily.

'You once asked me why I have not married,' she says. 'And I told you that I have not yet met the right person.' She clasps her hands tightly together. She takes a deep breath. 'But the truth is I don't ever want to marry.'

I sit up. 'Why?'

Her lower lip trembles. 'When Charles was away at school and my father was in London, I had to stay with an aunt for a period.

What I saw there, in that house, how my aunt was treated by my uncle . . . it appalled me.' She's breathing hard, staring at her clasped hands.

I put a hand on hers. 'Did he hurt you?'

'No, he did not come near me, and I wrote to my father asking him to come and take me home.'

She breathes in through her mouth. Her breath catches in her throat and for a moment I think she will cry. 'When I was leaving, I asked my aunt if I should tell my father about her husband. She stiffened with embarrassment. She looked through me as if I had insulted her. I felt such a fool. *If this is marriage,* I thought, *I want none of it.'*

I pat Candace's hand and she looks at me, her eyes moist.

'Perhaps her life would have been worse if you had told your father,' I suggest.

She looks out at the chapel. The rowan's bright orange leaves are drifting into piles.

'Perhaps,' she says flatly. 'Perhaps not.' She turns to me. 'Anyway, I wanted you to know that I'm not as naive as you may think.'

'I don't think you're naive. You are the wisest woman I know.'

She squeezes my hand. 'If you ever want to talk about anything, I am here.'

The baby flutters inside me and I give an awkward smile.

Candace stands and reaches for her shawl. 'Anyway, your mother must be very proud of you—collecting all those books after she taught you to read.'

After Candace leaves to go home, I take out several books that I have bought in the last few years since the war began: *The Arraignment of Lewd, Idle, Forward and Unconstant Woman*; *A Christall Glasse for*

Christian Women; and a new one: *The Good Womans Champion: A Defence for a Weaker Vessel.*

The first book reinforces Chaucer's lessons on womanhood, extolling obedience, reverence, quietness and steady work. But it makes me think of the oxen in the field, harnessed for work their whole lives, beaten by some, cared for by others, depending on the whims or character of their owners.

Look at Jane Harding: she was a lovely young woman, but she could barely look anyone in the eye when her husband was alive. She seemed to disappear. She could often be seen wandering the lanes with Grace in her arms. I brought her into the kitchen once. She supped some broth while the rain dripped from her hair. She wouldn't talk to me, just held her babe close and rocked in the warmth of the fire. Yet in the months since he has died, she seems to lift her head higher.

Then there's Mrs Kavanagh, who seems like she would barge over you if you stepped near her. Yet one day, when George fell and cut his head on the millstone, she swept him into her big arms and ran, heavy legs pumping under her tucked-up skirt. 'Your boy, Mrs Wolfreston,' she shouted as she came up the lane, sweat pouring from her brow. She didn't stop till she had barged into the kitchen. She was more swift and more capable than any man.

'We must work around them,' Candace had said of women like Mrs Edwards.

It occurs to me that Mrs Edwards probably considers women like Candace and me to be 'Forward and Unconstant' in our ideas and habits. Lord, she probably considers all women except herself to be thus. Unfortunately, she is not the only one who does.

How glad I am that there are other books which are a little more generous about women's virtues. My mother once said to me, 'Always take care what you write in the margins, Frannie, even in an almanac. Remember that everyone can see it and judge you for it.'

I open *The Good Womans Champion* and I write in the margin:

In praise of women, a good one

I leave the book open to let the ink dry and go into the garden to find my boys.

That night, I tuck the boys into bed and read a tale about the knight of Montelyon. When I close the book, Middy is already asleep. His fair hair is spread over the pillow like a halo.

'Sam is showing us how to trot on Lady,' George says.

'Well, I'm glad it's not Merlin,' I whisper. 'He is so grumpy that he would throw you.'

He doesn't smile. 'Middy is better than me. He can make her trot already. She listens to him. Sam says he has a gift.'

This is the first thing Middy has ever done that his brother cannot do. A smile is bouncing around inside me, but I keep it contained.

'Good for Middy, but don't worry, George,' I say, 'You will probably do it tomorrow. Anyway, we appreciate things more if they don't come as easily.'

He turns onto his side, ready to sleep, but he is frowning, so I stroke the spot between his eyebrows, smoothing away his cares, as I used to when he was younger.

'Sing, Mamma,' he murmurs with his eyes closed.

I sing 'Fare Ye Well, Lovely Nancy' and watch George till he is fast asleep. I brush a hair from Middy's forehead and continue singing softly.

When I go back downstairs, Henry pours me some ale and we sit by the fire.

'What were you and Candace talking about earlier?'

'About the merits of teaching girls to read.'

He looks surprised. 'Not this again,' he says. 'People don't want change. It threatens their way of life.'

'I think the poor do want change,' I say. 'That's why the Levellers are gaining support.'

'The poor don't have anything to lose but landowners like Mrs Edwards do.'

Henry leans his head against the chair and closes his eyes.

After a few moments I say, 'Henry?'

He murmurs irritably, 'What?'

'I need to talk with you about something else,' I say.

I want to tell him I'm with child. I want to tell him that I don't want to be confined to bed this time, that it does no good.

He sits up, blinking. 'Is it about the recusants?'

'No . . .' I shake my head, caught off guard by his question. 'No, it's . . . I just meant to tell you that Candace has offered to save one of their next litter of hound pups for Middy.'

His eyes light up. 'That'll do him good. It may bring him on a bit.' He sits forward, wide awake now. 'Are you all right Frances? Have you taken on too much with all this teaching?'

My heart pounds but I force a smile. 'I'm just tired. I think I'll go up to bed.'

As I climb the stairs, I remember his question about the recusants and remind myself that I must talk with Tom Dyer about the Statfold and Rivermead parish boundary and exactly where Hannah Smythe's cottage lies.

11

The plum trees in the orchard are gaunt and knobbled in a sea of muddied orange leaves. While I prune the smaller apple trees, Sam is removing the dead wood from them. I usually enjoy figuring out how to improve the shape of the tree for a better crop but today I have been distracted. I have ripped two small holes in my skirt and cut my finger.

Mrs Edwards has avoided me these last few weeks. She has left notes with Tom Dyer about church attendance rather than meet with me after Sunday service. I thought about writing to her, but an apology would be a falsehood. So, I left it to Henry and Candace to persuade her to come to dinner today.

Candace has counselled me that I should remain quiet, allow the men to be controversial in their views of education and then seek to develop some middle ground with Mrs Edwards. I stare at the bloodied white rag on my finger, hoping I do better at dinner than I have with the trees.

George and Middy are puffing white plumes into the crisp air as they wind through the trees, dragging the pruned branches to the clearing for burning. As I pass them, George calls, 'Where are you going, Mamma?'

I hold up my finger. 'To clean this and get changed for dinner.'

Middy points to the heap of branches.

'Sam's going to let us light the bonfire later,' George says for him.

Both boys' eyes are shining with excitement.

Peg has several pies and meats laid out on the table, and more food in the oven. She's muttering under her breath, counting the cooking times for each item, when she looks up and notices my hand.

'Lord have mercy, what have you done?'

While I bathe my finger, Peg tears a clean cloth for a bandage. She ties it tight around my finger. We both stare at the red stain growing on the fabric.

'It's all right,' I say. 'It'll have stopped bleeding by the time they get here. Is there anything I can help you with, Peg?'

Wisps of hair are plastered to her temples, and her cheeks are even redder than normal.

She breathes in through her nose. 'Not with that hand, ma'am,' she says. 'You go and get yourself ready.'

At five o'clock, Charles and Candace Broughton bring Mrs Edwards in their new carriage. Henry rushes forward to take her hand as she steps down from it.

'Welcome, Mrs Edwards, come in and warm yourself.'

She has dispensed with the ruff this evening and wears a lace shawl over her black dress. She is a handsome woman without that ruff.

Henry escorts her into the dining room and, as she passes, she says without even a hint of a smile, 'I trust you are well, Mrs Wolfreston.'

I am about to follow her when Candace grabs my arm. 'Can I have a word, Frances?'

I smile awkwardly at Charles, who is standing beside his sister and looks resplendent in a red waistcoat embossed with gold brocade.

Candace nods at Charles.

'I'll go on in,' Charles says, looking amused.

The silk of Candace's dark blue dress shimmers in the candle-light. She no doubt intends to impress Mrs Edwards with the sobriety of her gown, but the contrast with her blonde curls is startlingly elegant. Her beauty is difficult to supress.

'Something's wrong,' Candace hisses.

'What do you mean?'

'She hardly said a word in the carriage.'

How unusual for Mrs Edwards to be silent.

'She's just enjoying watching all of us pander to her,' I say, as we reach the door.

The setting sun casts a warm glow in the oak-panelled dining room.

'This is a quite a feast, Mrs Wolfreston,' Mrs Edwards observes.

The table is laid with a white tablecloth, and in addition to the usual vegetables and roasted meat, Peg has made pork and mutton pies. Pies are a great favourite of Mrs Edwards.

'Are your boys well?' Mrs Edwards asks. 'Are they dining with us?'

'They are eating in the kitchen,' I say, smiling around the table. 'George and Middy have been building a bonfire all day.'

She peers at me, eyeing the bandage on my hand disapprovingly. 'Middy. That's an unusual name. What is it short for?'

'Middleton,' I say, tucking my hand out of sight below the table.

'Middleton,' she repeats slowly.

I look at Henry and he gives a subtle shrug.

Mrs Edwards looks around for her walking stick and, finding it hanging from the back of her chair, gives a sigh.

Henry says, 'It was good of you to give the widow Harding a job. It has made a difference to her and her young daughter.'

'I try to help those less fortunate, Rector.'

The only sound is a crackle from the fire and the steady drum of Charles's fingers on the table.

'And how is George, Henry?' says Candace. 'He must be preparing to go to choir school?'

'He will start at Lichfield next year. He is looking forward to it.'

'It's an excellent school,' says Charles.

Mrs Edwards looks around the table. She takes some pie onto her plate and cuts it into small pieces.

Candace nods at Charles and he leans forward, the brocade of his waistcoat catching the candlelight.

'What do you think of this idea of common schools, Henry? It's has been put forward by the Levellers, but I hear many politicians, and even some Puritans are supporting it. Is the church for it?'

It is hardly subtle, and I almost wince as Henry says, 'I haven't heard too much of it, but it's a good idea. If it were based around the church's teaching, I think it would be a benefit to the parish to have a school. What do you think, Mrs Edwards? I've always valued your views on parish matters.'

Mrs Edwards is twisting her wedding band.

'Mrs Edwards,' I prompt her gently, 'Henry was just asking about your views on common schools.'

'Well, education is a matter for the church,' she says. 'It doesn't concern us ladies.' She takes a small piece of pie and chews it distractedly.

Candace and I exchange frustrated glances. I lean back in my chair, watching the sun sink behind the trees. The candles in the sconces fight to light the dimming room. Henry rises and lights more candles before putting more wood on the fire.

'I met an interesting woman over in the churchyard in Tamworth last week,' I say. 'She was visiting from Nottingham, and she asked if St Editha's had a children's lesson on Sunday.'

'What's a children's lesson?' Mrs Edwards asks.

'She told me that in her parish, straight after church service, someone teaches the children the meaning of the Bible readings in a simplified way. The children ask questions to help their understanding of the texts. She said the children enjoyed it greatly.'

Mrs Edwards says, 'It's not a bad idea. We should discuss that with Mrs Dawson when she returns from her visiting her sister.'

Candace shoots me a sympathetic glance.

'Mr Wolfreston, there is something I need to raise with you,' Mrs Edwards says. 'I've received a letter from my cousin, Judith Oxley. You may remember meeting her last month?' She barely waits for Henry's affirmation before continuing. 'Judith sends some news from her parish, but I am not sure it will please you.'

'I'm always interested in your news,' Henry says, taking a long draught of wine in anticipation.

She rests her hands either side of her plate, waiting till everyone is looking at her.

'Judith is married to a man of modest means. He is an overseer for the magistrate's office, and he's been involved in sequestration, I think they call it. It's a difficult task, so much land to administer, rent to collect and so on.' Mrs Edwards pauses and dabs her mouth with her handkerchief. 'Well,' she continues, 'the government has been taking *two-thirds* of land there from some recusants.'

'That is happening in many places south of here, Mrs Edwards,' Henry says.

'And a great money-making task it is for the government.' Charles gives a cynical laugh.

'I tell you that to set the scene, sirs,' Mrs Edwards says, her face colouring. She looks at Henry. 'Perhaps I should talk with you at another time, Rector.'

'Forgive us, Mrs Edwards, please continue,' Henry says.

She takes a sip of wine then rests her goblet on the table. 'Judith is from King's Norton district.' Her eyes flick to me. 'As you were, Mrs Wolfreston. Judith's news has been preying on my mind—you being the rector's wife and all.'

I grip the table.

Henry says, 'What on earth is this about?'

'It seems Mrs Wolfreston's *Catholic* mother has been arrested for recusancy and is being held in King's Norton gaol. Her father is—'

'Stop!' Henry says loudly. Then, more quietly, 'Mrs Edwards, you must stop.'

Candace's hand is on my shoulder. Faces cluster around me. Mrs Edwards is saying something to Charles. I have to get away.

I push through them. Henry tries to take my arm, but I stumble towards the library.

There I press my face against the window. Outside, the copper beech is skeletal in the twilight as it was when my mother was here. She must have decided, in her quiet way, to stop complying with my father, his church and with all that borders and curtails her.

Peg is lighting a fire. There are muffled voices in the hall. George, his high voice clear and full of care, is asking, 'What is wrong with Mamma?'

Middy's face peers at me around the door but I cannot even go to him. I stand surrounded by my books, rooted in this room where I last saw her.

I don't remember her ever leaving this room during those desperate weeks, but she must have.

On the last day, I woke to find her standing by the window, smiling.

'You always knew what you wanted, Frannie,' she said. 'You always wanted to be Boudicca. Do you remember you used to play with your brother Joseph, and when he wanted to be the king you would say, "No, I am older than you so I must be queen. You must wait till I die."' She laughed then, just as she used to.

'Joseph will inherit everything from Father, so he will have his way in the end,' I said. 'He used to dance with you, Mamma, remember?'

'We had some good times, didn't we?'

'Yes, Mamma,' I said. I felt so happy that she was there with me.

She looked out at the tree, her face awash with light.

'What is it, Mamma?'

'The tree is budding. Spring is here.' She opened the window wide and in her strong, sweet voice she quoted: '*Good Lord, how bright and goodly shines the moon.*'

'*The moon? The sun! It is not moonlight now,*' I countered.

'*I say it is the moon that shines so bright.*' She laughed.

'*I know it is the sun that shines so bright,*' I returned, and we laughed together.

That afternoon she told me that she had received a letter from my father summoning her home.

'Don't go, Mamma—stay here with me,' I pleaded.

'Your winter is over.' She kissed my cheek. 'You will get better, angel. This will pass, and you will be fine.'

I hear the creak of the door and turn to see Henry entering the library. I can hear Candace in the hall, speaking in hushed tones with the boys. Henry asks if I want to talk with her, but I shake my head. I do not want to be comforted. I am rigid with fear. I am layered full of a guilt that will not ease.

Henry's eyes search my face. 'We will go and see your mother as soon as we can arrange it. Do you wish to stay at Hazelmere?'

I smell burning, a sour-sickly odour.

'Frances?'

The logs settle in the fire and sparks fly up the chimney. The smell is not that of the logs here in the library of Statfold House; it is a remembered smell. In this dim room, it could be the fire in my father's study.

Inside me, there's a turbulence; a stirring of something that I can't bear.

'No.' I grind out the words like salt. 'We will stay in King's Norton.'

Part 2

'I see a woman may be made a fool,
If she had not a spirit to resist.'

WILLIAM SHAKESPEARE, *THE TAMING OF THE SHREW*, ACT 3, SCENE 2

12

After a fitful night, we leave the house early, before the boys are awake. It has been raining all night and the dawn sky is a thick veil of drizzle. Sam's heavy buff coat is slick from the rain as he sits atop the Broughtons' old carriage. Henry and I climb inside and sit on its narrow seats. I press my head against the glass and peer through the rain at the grey smudge that I know is Peg standing by the back door. She has agreed to stay at Statfold House with the boys while we are gone.

As Statfold disappears behind the trees, I already feel choked and uncomfortable in the cramped space. I stare out of the tiny window, wondering how my mother is coping in a small, dark cell. She has never liked the darkness. She always kept her bedroom shutters open to let the moonlight in.

'Frances,' Henry says.

I glance at him. His eyes are hooded with tiredness. He's been wanting to talk to me since last night, but I've been avoiding it. I was grateful that he stayed up late organising the affairs of the parish with Charles and Tom Dyer so that he might take the rest of the week off.

'I need to ask you something.'

'You're tired,' I say. 'You should try to sleep.'

Henry removes his hat and pushes his damp hair back from his face with his gloved hands. Then he gazes at me; he's not going to let this lie.

'Why would Mrs Edwards call your mother a Catholic and not a recusant? She didn't say your mother was a recusant. She was deliberate in her words.'

My eyes dart to the slot that the carriage's passengers use to address the driver. I wonder if Sam can hear us.

'I don't know, Henry.'

He peels off his gloves. 'So, you have no idea what's behind this accusation?'

I shrug. 'When I was young, she taught us some prayers, but my father put a stop to it. And we always went to church, Henry. My father saw to that.' I glance at him. 'I would not have considered marrying you if I thought there was such an issue with my mother,' I say, quietly.

The look on his face chills me, but he says nothing.

I turn away and wipe the window with my cloak. A solitary tree stands surrounded by sodden pastureland. It reminds me of the tree on the hill where Joseph and I used to sometimes hide. The tree where . . .

My heart beats faster, thudding so loud that I can hardly think.

'Frances,' Henry says, 'how can you say that?'

Under my cloak, I place my hand over my belly. I count slowly under my breath. I am aware of my lips moving, and Henry watching me as if he doesn't know me anymore. Frowning, he looks away, but his hand reaches for mine. The warmth of his hand comforts me and slowly, slowly the thudding of my heart begins to ease.

Eventually, despite the continuous jolting, and the worry pressing on me, I fall asleep against the side of carriage. I dream that I am in a boat bobbing gently in the waves, but then the boat begins to lurch violently in the swell. I look around frantically for something to hold, trying to secure myself. When I wake, rain is pounding on the roof, and I am clutching the side of the carriage. I am alone.

I shove the door open and stumble out into the downpour.

There's a sound of rushing water nearby and the rumble of distant thunder. The horses stand miserably beside the rutted road. Beyond them, Henry is standing in the ford of a wide, fast-flowing stream, his curly hair plastered to his face. Sam, holding a long stick, wades towards the middle of the crossing.

The water rushes past in a torrent, splashing white over some stepping-stones a short way downstream. I know this place. We are not far from the Hazelmere turning. King's Norton is a just few miles ahead. I must have slept for hours.

Sam hoists the stick into the water and steadies it against the rushing current. 'I think we can make it,' he shouts.

Henry turns and, seeing me, calls above the noise of the torrent, 'Get back in the carriage. We're going to cross the ford.'

It is late afternoon when, wet and bedraggled, we drive into King's Norton. As a child I admired this town; the striking black-and-white buildings framing the green, the spire of St Nicholas' piercing the sky, showing the way to heaven. But now I see it with war-weary eyes. What I see is the blood of hundreds of soldiers killed on this green by their own countrymen in an unnecessary war.

'Stop at the inn,' Henry says to Sam through the slot.

'But we need to go to the gaol first,' I say, touching his arm. 'I want to see my mother today.'

Henry shakes his head. 'We need to find lodgings for the night. It'll be dark soon.'

The inn is a long, two-storey building with a courtyard and stable at the rear. While Henry talks with the owner about lodging and stabling, I wander into the adjacent dining room to warm my hands by the fire. It is wood-panelled and contains several tables, all of them scraped and marked from constant use. Light from the late afternoon sun shines through the far windows, giving the room a worn but pleasant look. A heavy-set young woman in a blue dress wipes the serving bar with a cloth. Behind her are jugs of ale and port. She looks me up and down, her eyes crinkling as they settle on my belly. 'You've had some weather.'

'Yes,' I say, holding my damp skirt out towards the fire.

'It's a bit early for dinner, but I can serve you a cold cut of ham with cheese and vegetables now or there will be a hearty mutton stew ready in about an hour.'

My voice shivers with cold. 'We're going out again in a minute. We'll eat later.'

She pours some dark liquid into a cup and brings it over to me. 'Here's a daub of port to warm you.' She pulls a chair over towards the fire and gestures for me to sit. 'Rest here for a minute, ma'am. You look chilled through to the bone.'

'That's kind of you,' I say numbly.

I take a sip of rich, dark port. A burst of heat spreads from my throat to my chest. I become aware of just how frozen my extremities are; my fingers and toes are numb, and my ears are stinging. I have been cold for hours. I swill the port around in the cup. Suddenly, I hear my mother's tender voice inside me say, *Remember, Frannie, you can't look after anyone unless you first look after yourself.*

Henry and I walk in the fading sunlight to the magistrate's office, which the innkeeper told us lay at the end of the high street, beyond the gallows. It's a single-storey building next to the court-house. Behind it is the gaol.

I take Henry's arm to steady myself as we climb the few steps up to door.

The duty clerk, who is stationed behind a desk, looks up as we enter.

Henry gives his name and asks if Alice Middlemore is being held here.

The duty clerk opens a ledger and runs his finger down the entries. He stops and reads aloud. '*Alice Frances Middlemore, fifty-seven, of Hazelmere.*' He looks up. 'Is that her?'

'Yes,' Henry says.

'She was arrested on the seventh of October so has been here almost two weeks. There is a fine outstanding . . .' He trails off.

I nudge Henry, who takes out his purse. 'Can we see her?'

The clerk closes the ledger and stands up. 'Visitors are allowed after the morning market.'

'What?' I say too loudly. 'We've been travelling all day to get here. Please let me see her.' My hand reaches towards him beseechingly. My fingers brush his tunic sleeve.

The clerk steps back, eyes widened in disapproval.

Henry lays a warning hand on my arm.

As the clerk walks past me towards the front door, my body is trembling so hard that I think I might faint.

Henry takes my arm. 'Come, Frances. We'll sort this out in the morning.'

'Sir,' the clerk says, holding the door open. He is careful to look only at Henry. 'Ask for the magistrate's clerk in the morning.'

As he closes the door behind us, I pull away from Henry's grasp. I run around to the side of the building where there is a courtyard and stabling. There is a back door with a guard standing by it. Attached to the larger building is a smaller one with barred windows. I stare at them, wondering if my mother is there.

The guard fixes me with a stern look. 'You're not allowed here.'

I feel Henry's hand on my elbow. 'Come away,' he says, tugging my arm.

My legs move, but I feel somehow disconnected from them. I am aware of people passing in the dim light, but their faces are blurred, their voices a ringing noise.

I pull my arm away. 'Let me go, Henry. If we had gone straight there, I could have seen her today.'

Henry stands in front of me, his black hat hanging from one hand. His other hand rakes through his hair.

'I know,' he says. 'I'm sorry. You'll see her in the morning. And I'll make the payment and we'll get her out.'

We stand looking at each other. The rain has started up again, seeping into our cloaks, but we don't move. I'm aware of people looking at us as they hurry past.

'Let's go and get some dinner, Frances.'

I want to scream at the unfairness of it all. Instead, I touch my belly under my cloak and breathe in slowly through my nose.

'All right,' I mumble.

13

The next morning, we return to the gaol. Henry pays a visiting fee, and while he waits to see the magistrate's clerk, I stand in the short visiting queue. When it is my turn, the guard unbolts a large wooden door which leads to a dark corridor. It is quiet, apart from the sound of someone coughing. We pass several doors before he stops and unlocks one.

'Ten minutes,' the guard says as he pulls the door closed behind me.

The only light in the narrow cell comes from a high, barred window. My mother sits on a bench in the corner, huddled under a shawl.

'Mamma?'

I move closer.

'Mamma, it's me—Frances.'

Two sunken eyes peer at me. 'Frannie?' She tries to stand but falls back onto the bench. I sit beside her and embrace her.

'My dear Frannie,' she murmurs. She gazes at my face, studying it as if it were a tapestry. 'I hoped you would come.' She coughs—a dry, hollow hack.

It's been a few years since I have seen her, and I can't believe how much she has changed. She is grey-haired and thin. Her eyes are so pale they seem transparent.

I take out the potage that I brought from the basket. My mother sips the warm broth, her hands cupping the pot. When she is finished, she gives a little moan and reaches out to touch my cheek. 'I knew you would come.'

'I should have come before this. I should have—'

'Hush now,' she says, and coughs again.

'We need to get you a doctor,' I say, my eyes scanning the damp cell, landing on a pile of putrid straw in the corner. 'What happened, Mamma?'

She gazes at me. 'I . . . Your father, he . . .' She covers her mouth with her shawl.

'Tell me, Mamma, please. I want to help.'

She says no more. Her face is impassive, a familiar mask that slides into place like a deadbolt in a lock.

'You're trembling Mamma.'

'My hands are a little cold,' she admits.

I take off my damp travelling cloak and begin to drape my warm shawl around her.

'No, Frannie,' she protests. 'You need that.'

She tries to give the shawl back, and I stare at her hands—those scarred, raw hands that she always keeps hidden. They look sore and fragile, so stark against the rough stone walls and the iron bars on the small window, that I want to cry.

'I have another shawl at the inn, Mamma.'

She lets me wrap the shawl around her, lifting her chin like a child as I tuck it about her.

'I knew you would come,' she says again, her eyes shining.

Further along the corridor, a bolt clangs against metal.

I wrap her in my arms and hold her so close that she feels like a part of me. I want to understand what has happened, how I can help her, but there's no time for that now.

The cell is dim, but high on the wall near the window is a patch of warm sunlight.

'*How bright and goodly shines the moon,*' I say, staring at it through my tears.

I feel her face crease against mine as she smiles. 'No,' she whispers. '*I know it is the sun that shines so bright.*'

'Oh, Mamma.' I clutch her tighter.

The patch of light fades as the sun retreats behind a cloud.

'It's all right, Mamma, we're going to get you out of here,' I say. Then I brace myself, for I will need all my strength to let her go.

Outside, I wait for Henry, pacing back and forth, unable to stand still. My mother was even worse than I had feared. Her cough worries me. I scan the street, looking for an apothecary sign. Perhaps if the woman at the inn has some honey, I can make a paste up for her.

The town crier calls that it is twelve o'clock. An old woman is making her way towards me. She is hunched over so far that her face looks straight towards the ground. Over her arm, she carries a basket.

'Frances!' Henry runs down the steps of the magistrate's office, his face pale. 'There were hearings this morning, so I had to wait to see the clerk. How is your mother?'

'Not well,' I say. 'She has a bad cough. Did you speak to the magistrate? When will they release her?'

He doesn't answer.

'What is it, Henry?'

He glances at the magistrate's office, drawing his cheeks in. 'The fine is too high. Your father will have to pay it.'

'I have a few shillings,' I say, taking out my purse.

'No,' he says, placing his hand on mine. 'It's not enough.'

There's a constriction in my chest as my heart thuds.

The old woman tries to pass us. She twists her head sideways and looks at me. Her eyes are bright, inquisitive. 'Afternoon,' she says, as I step aside.

I breathe out slowly, watching her pass, trying to steady myself. 'How much is it, Henry?'

There's a sickly hue to his face as he says, 'One hundred and twenty pounds.'

A strange laugh comes out before I can stop it. 'No,' I say.

His eyes have that beaten look that he has after a burial. He looks along the street towards the spire of St Nicholas'. After a moment, he turns back to me. On his face is a peculiar expression that I don't recognise.

'How can she have such a high fine? Have you told me the truth of it?'

'I know as much as you do. I need to think, Frances. I'll see you back at the inn. We can talk there.'

He strides up the street, leaving me standing among the people hustling past the magistrate's office. Stuck like a rock in a stream, I watch Henry weave between the country women and shopkeepers, his black hat conspicuous among the light linen hoods and shafts of bright cloth. I wait till he's out of sight. I feel trapped, and I have no idea what to do.

14

The sun is low in the sky as we leave King's Norton. The road is deeply rutted, and we are jolted around so much that I have to grip onto the side of the carriage to stay on the seat. My satchel slips off the bench and something clangs onto the floor in the dark. With the next large jolt, Henry moans and curses as his head hits the roof. I turn away from him, a small part of me glad.

We had argued earlier, in our bedchamber at the inn. Henry insisted that we must visit my father in Hazelmere immediately to understand what had happened. I told him that we had to remain in King's Norton as I'd promised my mother I would return in the morning. He countered that we could be of more help to her if we had a better understanding of the situation. I refused to leave and suggested that he go on his own to Hazelmere and that I stay at the inn.

Henry wiped his hand across his brow and said, 'Frances, we are going to see your father. We are going to find out what your mother has done.'

I sank onto the bed then, dropped my face into my hands.

He sighed deeply. 'Why don't you want to see your father?'

I had no words to answer him.

We turn off the rutted road onto a smoother one that passes through the woods. I lean my head against the window, peering into the darkening twilight, searching for familiar landmarks, but there are only shadowy lines of trees. Now and then a small clearing appears, but as soon as my eyes ease and I start to relax, trees encroach again.

Henry murmurs to Sam through the slot. His voice is low but I hear him say that the road is too slow, that it is not safe to continue, that we should stop for the night at the next place.

I keep my eyes trained on the trees, for I know there is nowhere safe to stop at night in the woods. Blinking, I wipe my misty breath from the glass once more. There is something out there, I'm sure of it.

Slowly, as if an illusion, thick black fists emerge from the tops of the sprawling branches, then two tall straight fingers point towards the sky.

Silhouetted in the moonlight, the tall chimneys of Hazelmere loom above the dark bulk of the house.

'We're here,' I whisper.

The house is in darkness, but as we approach the front door opens and a figure emerges holding up a lantern. A woman stands hunched near the open doorway, scrutinising us.

'Who be there at this late hour?' she calls, voice hoarse and chiding.

'It's Frannie,' I say, stepping towards the circle of lantern light. 'It's me, Nance.'

She squints at me. Her mouth is clamped so tight her lips have disappeared into a mass of wrinkles. Her eyes flicker in recognition and her body sags in relief. A tirade of admonishments follows.

'Good God in heaven! What were you thinking, travelling at night in these times? You have me all worked up. Tell your man to take the horses round to the stable yard. Come in, then.'

She's still talking loudly as we follow her along the flagstone hallway. 'Go into the kitchen where it's still warm, Miss Frannie, and then I'll light a fire for you and make up a bed.' Nance casts a wary eye at Henry. 'The kitchen is good enough for you, I trust, sir?'

'Nance?'

She turns.

'Is my father in bed?'

She stares at me with wide eyes. 'No. He's not here. He's gone to your brother Joseph's.'

'When will he be back?'

She shrugs. 'He said he'd be back tomorrow.'

As Nance hurries up the stairs, I gaze around the hallway. There is a narrow walnut table on one side, and on the other several hooks with a wide hat shelf above. At the foot of the staircase, there is a portrait of my father. He is elegantly dressed and wears a brown wig. It must be a recent portrait as he looks older than I remember. His long face and aquiline nose give him a superior look. I touch my own nose self-consciously as I look at the painting.

In the kitchen, scents of nutmeg and cinnamon mingle with the dried lavender hanging from the mantel. The pale blue flowers hang in thick bunches, but between them I spot a posy of delicate red anemone blooms. They have been dried carefully in the dark to preserve their colour.

My fingers tremble as I ease into the chair at the end of the table—my mother used to sit here and work. She would write up her recipes while talking to Nance, and she would tie the cut flowers with wool.

Henry gives my shoulders a squeeze. His mood has improved now we have arrived and the horses are being stabled.

'There now. You don't even have to see your father tonight. And this is far more comfortable than the inn,' he says, looking around the kitchen.

As I watch Henry poke the kitchen fire into life, memories seem to spiral from its embers: Nance filling the wooden bathtub in front of the fire while I shivered in a wet, muddy dress. The dress crumpling into a heap at my feet while Nance peeled off the linens that were stuck to my skin. My father roaring, 'Where is she?' and the water choking in my throat, so that Nance had to clap my back and say in my ear, 'Breathe, Miss Frannie, breathe.'

'Your father will be happy to see you,' Henry says.

'He will not,' I say, a shudder passing through me.

Nance bustles back in and busies herself heating up some potage. She keeps turning from the cookpot to look at me.

I glance over at Henry. He's settled in a chair by the fire with his eyes closed.

'I saw my mother today, Nance,' I say.

She pauses in her stirring to look at me. 'Is she all right?'

'She has a bad cough.'

Nance turns back to the pot.

'She needs some warmer clothes,' I say.

Nance doesn't turn around. Her shoulders heave a little. 'I'll look those out for you in the morning,' she says, her voice sounding muffled, as if she has a cold.

Nance ladles the steaming potage into two bowls.

'I'll go and check on that fire in your room,' she says, heading towards the door.

'Nance?'

She turns, her hand resting on the doorhandle.

'What happened to Mamma? Why didn't she go to church?'

Nance's eyes flit to Henry, whose chest is rising and falling with his gentle snores. She opens her mouth to answer then, as if thinking better of it, sighs. 'You'll have to ask your father,' she says.

As the door closes behind her, I dip my spoon in the potage. It's far too hot to eat. As I wait for it to cool, I gaze around the kitchen at my mother's things. Her work apron with ivy leaves embroidered on the pocket hangs from a hook next to her worn, brown work shawl. On the shelf nearby stands her brass mortar and pestle. Next to it is her gardening book, *The Profitable Arte of Gardening,* a piece of card projecting from a page, marking the last plants she was looking at. Below the shelf are the boots that she wears around the garden. They are unbuttoned, open, and there's a crust of mud around the soles. They lie apart, one boot on its side, as if they've been taken off in a hurry.

I put my hands over my face and begin to sob.

15

When I wake the next morning in my old bedroom, the shutter is open and the light shines on the old quilt my mamma and I stitched. Henry is already dressed and sits on a chair, tying his boots. As he stands, he looks at me.

'You're awake,' he says.

I sit up, pulling the quilt over my arms.

'I'm going to walk over to the chapel after breakfast.' He adds, 'To talk to the rector.'

'Shouldn't you wait till we've seen my father?'

He shrugs. 'It won't do any harm to find out what the rector knows.' He bends to kiss my forehead then leaves, closing the door quietly behind him.

I push back the quilt and smooth my shift against my belly, staring at it, making sure it's still there, that I haven't dreamed it. I cup my hands around the bump. Henry held me last might, his arm wound around my belly, unaware. I could have told him then, but I heard his breathing deepen, felt his arm grow heavy, and the moment passed.

I glance over at my clothes, which are laid over the other chair. The skirt of my travelling dress is fringed with mud and smattered with dirt. Sighing, I get up, take a clean dress from the trunk and put it on. Folding my soiled dress over my arm, I walk into the hallway. As I pass my mother's room, I hesitate. Then I open the door and step inside.

My mother's bedroom is at the rear of the house. The window overlooks the fields and the long strip of grass that runs down towards the river. She had a seat built into the mullioned box window so that she could sit there as she read, catching occasional glimpses of the water through the trees when she looked up. I imagine her there now with her head bowed over a book, her lips moving silently as she recites the words to herself, her blonde hair hanging loose over her shoulders.

'You all right, Miss Frannie?' Nance says. I turn to see her standing in the doorway. 'You look as white as them linens.'

'I'm fine,' I say.

'You'll want some breakfast.'

'No, I'll sit here for a bit,' I say, looking at the window seat. 'The house seems very empty without her.' The clothing chest in her room is closed, I notice, and the bed is bare.

'That it does,' Nance says.

I lay my travelling skirt on the bed and sit on the window seat. I hold one of my mother's cushions against my chest. It smells of lilac and elderberry, like the woods at the end of summer. I bury my face in the cushion, breathing in the scent of her, letting my tears soak into the fabric.

Sniffing, I stare out of the window until I hear the door close, and I know that I am alone. I let my eyes follow the edge of the garden to the path that leads down to the stony bank, where Joseph and I stood the first time Mother took us to cross the stream. Fearful, we cried as she waded right across to the other side to show us it was safe. She came back again smiling. 'Be brave,' she called.

'*Our doubts are traitors, and make us lose the good we oft might win, by fearing to attempt,*' I murmur, quoting William Shakespeare as she had then, and often afterwards. The rhythm of the familiar words on my lips brings a stillness to me that I have not felt for days.

I plump up the cushion and, as I place it with the others along the back of the seat, I notice a large moth. I brush it away, but it doesn't move. I stare at it, wondering how it came to be stuck there. I touch it again, lifting the tip with my nail. It's not a moth, I realise—it's a corner of parchment.

A sudden thud startles me. Nance has returned and has dropped a load of kindling and logs onto the hearth, preparing to light a fire.

'Just leave that, Nance. I'll come downstairs.'

She puts one hand on the fireplace and levers herself slowly to standing.

'I'll lay those clothes out for you then, Miss Frannie.'

She opens the chest and takes out two dresses, laying them on the bed near my dress.

'I think that dark blue woollen is best,' I say. 'She'll also need another shawl. I left mine with her.'

Nance reaches into the chest for a shawl and puts it with the dresses.

'Now come down and get a bite to eat. Your mother wouldn't want you to be sitting here getting melancholy,' she says.

I pick up my skirt and follow Nance downstairs.

The kitchen is warm and smells of bread. Nance ladles out potage and hands me the bowl. I breathe in the familiar smell, wondering how it is that my potage smells a little different even though I follow my mother's recipe.

I eat hungrily. Nance stands near me watching, as she used to when I was a child. I look up at her, but as soon as my eyes meet hers she turns away, busying herself with some small task.

As I'm rinsing my bowl in the wooden basin, the back door is flung open.

Henry comes in, muttering under his breath. He pulls off his cloak and forces it onto a hook so hard I fear he'll rip it.

I glance at Nance.

She lifts my travelling skirt from the back of the chair. 'I'll clean this for you,' she says, and takes the clothes brush and the skirt outside, closing the door behind her.

Henry sits at the table, pulling off his muddy boots. His hair looks wild about his head and his face is puce, as if he is going to burst.

'Bloody man,' he fumes, shoving his boots aside.

'Who?' I ask.

Henry sits back in the chair scowling. 'The rector.'

Outside the window, Nance is bent over, brushing my skirt in short, rapid strokes.

I pull out a chair and sit down beside Henry.

He taps the table. 'I introduced myself to him, told him where I was from and that I wanted to know about your mother's church attendance.' Henry eyes are wide with indignation. 'He didn't even invite me in. After I walked through the deep mud around that chapel. Kept me waiting outside like a serf.' He breathes out through his nose. 'He's new apparently—a young man, about twenty-five.'

'You were younger than that when you took over Statfold.'

He puffs his breath out. 'I wasn't rude.'

I pick up Henry's boots and set them beside my mother's under the shelf.

'What did he say?'

'He told me he couldn't help me.'

'So my mother never spoke to him?'

'He said she came to him once, complaining about the actions of a woman in the parish, but that was the only conversation he's ever had with her.'

'What about their recusancy record?'

Henry shakes his head. 'He said they've only started it a few weeks ago.'

I walk towards the fire, rubbing my hands, trying to make sense of this. I turn towards Henry. 'So if they only have a few weeks of evidence, why is the fine so large? And why is Mamma in gaol?'

He rakes his hand through his hair. 'That's what I'd like to know.'

The long clock in the hall strikes two. Henry sits opposite me by the fire in the main room. He is reading one of my father's books: *His Majesties Declaration to All His Loving Subjects, Occasioned by a False*

and Scandalous Imputation. I have a copy of Chaucer open on my lap, but I am unable to concentrate and find myself staring at the tapestry on the wall adjacent to the dining table. It shows a country scene at harvest time: women bearing baskets of apples, men scything crops. My mother was fond of it as it shows men and women working together.

The corners beyond the dining table are far from the window light and are moody with memories. I turn away, focusing on the warm flames of the fire, but slowly my eyes are drawn back towards the dining table. I recall my father banging his fist on the table so hard, his bowl and spoon jumped. My mother stood up quickly, her chair falling to the floor. Her hands shook as she looked at him. I thought she would shout out, but she picked the chair up and quietly left the room. I wanted to go with her, but my father's heavy frown prevented me. I looked at Joseph, but he was staring into his bowl.

'Frances,' Henry says, startling me.

'What?'

'You're miles away.'

'We shouldn't have come here, Henry. I want to see my mother today and we're running out of time.'

'We need to talk to your father. You know that.'

He sighs, opens his book again and begins to read. 'You know Charles's stubborn belief in his divine right as King is the root of all of England's problems,' he says without looking up.

I glance over at the table with all the empty chairs around it. My mother said something to my father just before he hit the table with his fist. I squeeze my eyes shut, trying to visualise the scene.

My mother is wearing her dark grey bodice with the cream lace shawl collar over. Her pretty face is downcast and she's tipping her bowl to reach the last of the potage with her spoon. And she's smiling, but it's the tight smile she reserves for when she is displeased. She tilts her head towards my father. 'But you know I can't go to King's Norton now,' she says.

I stand up abruptly. 'I'm going for a walk, Henry.'

Henry looks up. 'Do you want me to come?'

'No.'

Trembling, I walk into the long, cold hallway. I take my cloak from the hook and pull it around me. Outside, the wind stirs the leaves. It's too cold for a walk. I glance up the stairway, wondering if I should go and sit in my mother's room before my father returns.

The sound of horses' hooves breaks the silence.

Nance comes running from the kitchen. 'That's your father now,' she says, hurrying to the front door to meet him.

I have noticed that many times I react to certain events by flying into action, moving swiftly, almost instinctively—my body doing what needs to be done. But now, as I wait for my father to dismount his horse, hand the reins to the stable boy and come towards the house, I am completely motionless. The only movement is my heart pounding in my chest, its beat loud in my throat and in my ears.

I watch Nance talking to my father while trying to keep pace with his long stride. My father stops, his gloved hand moving to his mouth as he takes in what she is saying. He rubs his chin, a slow movement back and forth. He looks away towards the trees then, eyes narrowed, he looks at the open doorway, where I am still standing inside by the coat hooks.

His pace towards me is slow, careful. He takes his hat off as he steps inside. His cloak is covered in mud, his skin grey from the journey, but his eyes are bright.

'Frannie.'

'Hello, Father,' I say, my words faltering.

His eyes crinkle and jowls of sagging skin appear. He looks as if he might cry. He mutters, 'Father?'

A sharp pain jabs my breastbone. I have always called him Papa.

16

Henry eases into a comfortable chair by the fire in my father's study, but I hesitate near the door. When my father arrived home this afternoon, he shook Henry's hand and asked politely about the parish, and the ages and health of George and Middy. Then he asked Henry to excuse him, as he wanted to take a bath. He would meet us in his study before dinner. He made no mention of my mother and steered his gaze carefully away from me.

I look around the study. The three wooden chests where my father keeps most of his books are lined along one wall. Adjacent to the desk, which still sits in front of the tall, mullioned window, is a well-crafted oak casement displaying my father's best books. The books are arranged in the traditional way with their spines facing inwards, chains locking precious manuscripts in place. It's a practice I have moved away from as I have acquired more books with the titles on the spines. I lift up my father's copy of Harpur's *The Iewell of Arithmetick*. This book had always resided on the corner of his desk as he referred to it so frequently.

My father clears his throat. He stands in the doorway with his chin raised, assessing us.

He is a little greyer than the portrait in the hall, but he is also more handsome in life—less severe than the portrait artist seemed able to capture. He again offers Henry his hand, which Henry shakes heartily, and then turns to me.

'Frannie,' he says. 'You are looking well.'

He gestures for me to sit by the fire as he walks over to his desk.

'We went to the gaol yesterday,' I say. 'I saw Mamma.'

He nods several times, as if he is trying to take this in.

'She cannot stay there,' I tell him. 'She is not well.'

Henry shakes his head at me to stop but I can't.

'You must get her out of there, Father.'

My father's eyes are glassy in the candlelight as he sits down at the desk. He motions again for me to sit. I stay standing.

He looks past me to Henry. 'What do you know of all this?' he asks.

'Very little, sir. We learned of your wife's incarceration from a neighbour a few days ago. Yesterday I spoke to the magistrate's clerk in King's Norton, but he gave few details.'

'Well,' my father says in a flat voice, 'I will tell you what has happened as well as I am able.' He brushes his hands over the clean desk as if sweeping away crumbs. 'You may as well sit, Frannie, there's nothing you can do tonight.'

He looks absently at his desk, waiting for me to sit. With a simmering glance at Henry, I reluctantly comply.

'The commissioner's men came some years ago with a covenant to sign. You will have seen these covenants declaring loyalty to parliament, denouncing Rome?'

'I've heard of—' Henry begins.

'I signed gladly,' my father interrupts. 'But,' he adds acidly, 'I would have had no choice in the matter anyway, as refusing to sign would have meant some of my land would be sequestered.' He lifted some papers from a drawer and placed them on the desk. 'I anticipated that, as I had compounded with the recusancy commissioners in this way, they would turn a blind eye to your mother's refusal to attend church.'

'Father . . .' I begin, but he glares at me and I fall silent.

My father fidgets with the quill and ink. His fingers shake. Seeing me watching, he taps the papers into a neat pile.

'This worked for a while, but it seems now that the recusancy law has been tightened that is no longer the case, and so she was arrested.' His jaw fixes into a hard line. 'There is a fine to pay. One hundred and twenty pounds.' He lays his hands on the table and looks at us to gauge our reaction. Observing our lack of surprise, he says, 'So, you know already?'

Henry leans forwards in his chair. He says softly, 'The rector told me this morning he had started the recusancy record only weeks ago. Why is the penalty so high, sir?'

'Because she hasn't gone to church for several years.'

My breath catches. I grip the arms of the chair to steady myself.

I glance at Henry who is staring at my father, his eyes narrowed in question, his mouth slightly open.

'But she always went to church when I was at home,' I say. 'How could you let this happen, Father?'

'I didn't "let this happen"; I tried to reason with her, but you know how stubborn she can be. And you know she prayed in the old religion,' he says, too loudly. 'Don't pretend otherwise.'

I stare at the fote-cloth covering the ash-stained flagstones in front of the fire. The seam between two of the narrow strips of plain-weave cloth has unravelled, leaving a gap wide enough to fit your hand through. Why would my mother suddenly stop going to church after all those years? It makes no sense.

Henry looks appalled, as if he is caught in a room with a plague that might infect him. Any earlier sympathy Henry had for my father seems to have disappeared.

My father is dipping the quill absently into the ink. Dark spots drip onto the blotting parchment.

'Why haven't you paid the fine?' I ask.

'It is not that simple, Frannie,' he snaps.

I sit back in the chair, startled by his inability to control his temper in front of Henry.

I stare at the gap in the fote-cloth, wondering when the hole appeared. My mother is particular about repairing things.

My father sighs audibly. 'They are saying she is a Catholic and has no intention of repenting. They intend to take my land from me.' He puts down the quill and crumples the blotting parchment. 'We will end up paupers.'

As I watch him wearily stroke the damp hair from his forehead, an unwelcome pang of pity stings like salt on my tongue. I have never seen him look so defeated. I search for some words of reassurance, but each thought is countered by the futility of it all. This government has never shown leniency towards supporters of the King, or to Catholics, or to women who disobey their husbands. There is no hope except to pay.

Henry looks helplessly between us. I know that he finds the friction between my father and me unbearable.

The only sound is the crackling fire and the dull plod of Nance in the hallway.

After a few moments Henry says gently, 'If you pay the fine, sir, they must surely release her, regardless of the land issue.'

My father recoils as if he has been burned. 'I've worked all my life for this land. I cannot give it up that easily.' He looks away from Henry as if disgusted by him. He stares past us both into the fire. After a few moments, he says, 'I've been talking with Joseph. We've been trying to work out how to secure her release without losing the land.'

'Father, there is no time for delaying. Mamma's been in prison for nearly two weeks already. She is sick with a bad cough.'

My father continues to stare into the fire, his mouth closed sternly.

I take a deep a breath and continue. 'She's been a good wife to you. She's the mother of your children. Please, Father, I'm begging you: pay the fine and have her released!'

He turns to me, his expression both angry and hurt.

The door opens and Nance comes in.

'I've set up the supper table for Mr and Mrs Wolfreston, sir,' she begins, only to retreat hastily when she sees the look on my father's face.

My father stands up, steadying himself against the desk. He picks up the papers and tucks them under his arm.

His voice is cold as he says, 'You were taught to be respectful, Frannie. This lack of decorum does not serve you well. Have supper and we can discuss this in the morning, when you are calm and rational.'

'Father, I—'

Without looking at me, he opens the door and closes it behind him.

I look at Henry, but he will not meet my eyes.

'Henry?' I say.

He turns slowly and gives a look that makes me shudder.

In a low voice he says, 'I feel like I don't know you, Frances. You're snapping at your father as if it's his fault your mother is in gaol. Your father isn't the one who's broken the law.' He stands up. 'And another thing—you knew your mother still prayed in the old religion. Your father said so.'

The sharpness of his tone surprises me and I make a sound, almost like a laugh.

'Henry, please let me—'

The door slams before I finish the sentence.

17

I dream that night of a wild horse galloping, thundering over hills and through shallow rivers, splashing up wings of spray. The heart-beat pummels, loud and strong. A rapid beat: *thud-ump, thud-ump, thud-ump, thud-ump*. The pounding continues as we weave through trees, past battlefields, past churchyards. The horse doesn't stop, and I realise that I cannot stop it. I am a part of it; the horse is part of me.

As I wake in the half-light, the beat is still pounding inside me. I reach for Henry, but he is not there. The bed appears untouched on his side, as if he had not been to bed at all.

We had argued again last night, in aggravated whispers. I told him that my mother only prayed alone in her room, that outside of it she always behaved like a true Anglican. Henry seemed to believe me, taking my hand in his. But then I suggested that my father wasn't being truthful with us, that he was hiding something. Henry said I was showing signs of madness, and that if my mother had obeyed my father then there would have been no trouble. I rebuked him for taking my father's side, and for saying that my mother has been foolish. 'You cannot say that until she explains,' I insisted, but even as I said the words, I knew that part of me also thought she was foolish. But he had turned away then, inching as far from me as the bed would allow.

In the dim, shuttered light, I rise and get dressed, loosening the ties on my shift so it is not so tight. The buttons on my skirt are straining but will do for another week. Finally, I pin my blue shawl so that the ends hang in low points at the front. Satisfied that no one can see my belly, I take the wooden comb and untangle the knots in my hair. I picture Candace's beautiful blonde curls as I quickly plait my own plain brown hair into a heavy braid that hangs down my back.

Downstairs, I notice that my father's cloak and hat are gone. There is no one in the warm kitchen, but there is broth simmering on the fire. I give it a stir—it is a thin variant of last night's stew.

Outside, Nance is walking with a bowl, sprinkling meal for the fat hens that flutter and cluck around her. She steers them carefully away from the green, where two drying linens are laid out like shrouds. Jackdaws loiter behind the hens, keeping their distance from Nance. On the ridge of the stable roof are several more, cawing. As soon as Nance steps away, the daws will swoop down among the hens and fight for the grain.

'Nance, where is Mr Wolfreston?'

She looks up. 'Oh, he's getting the horses ready. Says he's leaving soon. He was looking for you.'

We must be leaving for King's Norton straight after breakfast.

'And my father?'

She turns the bowl upside down, letting the last of the crumbs fall. 'Gone for a walk, Miss Frannie.'

Flustered, I take the narrow path to the stable yard to find Henry. A jackdaw swoops down and lands on the path ahead of me, fixing me with its pale eyes. Shooing the bird away, I hurry along the path. The jackdaw flies ahead some yards and lands on the path again. I bat my arm to ward it off, but it lands once more, blocking my way. 'Blasted bird,' I mutter, skirting around it through the long, dewy grass.

The stable yard is half full of stacked hay.

The Broughtons' small carriage, dusty and spattered with mud, stands in the middle of the yard, where Sam left it two nights ago. Near the trough, a man is wiping down a sweat-covered horse while Sam leads Lady, who whinnies and flicks her tail.

'Where is Mr Wolfreston, Sam?' My voice echoes in the small courtyard.

'He is in the stable, readying Merlin,' Sam says, touching his hat as he passes. He leads Lady towards the harness and begins hitching her up.

In the stable, Henry rests his head against Merlin's neck. He is talking softly but Merlin spots me and snorts.

'Ah,' Henry says with a sorrowful smile. 'How did you sleep?'

'Well,' I say. 'I'm sorry about last night, Henry.'

He tugs Merlin's rein and says, 'That's all right.'

Merlin's hooves clop against the cobbles as Henry leads him over to the carriage. He gives the reins to Sam and reaches out to take my hands. His own hands are red, swollen with cold. As he looks at me, I notice his right eye twitch as it does sometimes when he is worried.

'Listen, a letter came from Charles Broughton this morning,' Henry says, nodding towards the man near the trough.

'What's happened? Are the children all right?'

Henry takes a folded note from his coat. 'Yes,' he says. 'But it seems there is an urgent matter in Statfold I must attend to.'

He hands me the note.

I read it quickly. It is very brief.

Henry,

A parish matter has arisen, and Lichfield is aware. Don't delay your return.

Charles

'What can it be?'

'I don't know, Frances, but it must be important. In saying that Lichfield is aware, Charles is warning me that the bishop knows of it.' He nods towards the horses. 'I've given it some thought, and it's best if I go back now with Sam, then he brings the carriage back here in a couple of days.'

I look at Sam, who is already sitting atop the carriage wearing his buff coat, eyes gazing ahead as if he cannot hear us.

'Please wait, Henry. A day or two will make no difference. Let me see my mother today and then we can talk this through.' I squeeze his hands, trying to make him listen.

But he's looking at the house, scanning the long upper windows as if someone may be watching. I follow the direction of his gaze, but I see no one there. His eye twitches again, and I realise that he can't wait to be gone from here.

'I am needed in Statfold, Frances.'

My hands fall limp by my sides. 'So, you are leaving me here to deal with this . . . this awfulness.'

'I have no choice. If I don't leave now, I will not make it home before nightfall.' He rubs his hands together. 'I will send Sam straight back for you.'

'I cannot manage this . . . my father . . . on my own.'

'You're strong, Frances. You know you are.'

'But . . .'

'Talk to your father. Listen to what he has to say. I promise you he has your mother's interests at heart.' He kisses my forehead then climbs up next to Sam. 'Take care, my love.'

Henry's cloak flaps in the wind as they set off towards the forest. He looks briefly back with the pinched face of a troubled conscience. Then, without even a wave, he turns away.

Aching with disappointment, I watch the carriage till it is swallowed up by the ash trees and the rumbling of its wheels can no longer be heard.

18

My father looks up briefly from his newsbook as I enter the dining room. 'You look pale this morning, Frannie. Eat something.' He gestures to the chair beside him and continues reading.

Nance's beef broth is warm and comforting; her sourdough bread is light with a firm crust. As I sit quietly beside my father, sipping the salty broth, my thoughts keep returning to Henry. He thinks I am strong, that I can cope with everything, but sometimes I need his help. I break a piece of bread and let it fall into the dark broth. I glance at my father, his face so stern as he reads. He is quite unlike Henry, who always wants to know what I have been doing. But this, sitting quietly without conversing, has always been my father's way.

Slowly, I begin to relax.

I notice my father's face is still flushed from his morning walk and his hands are red with chilblains.

'I will make you an ointment for your hands—from fern and grease,' I say.

He gives a thin smile. 'Your mother would normally . . .' He clears his throat. 'Perhaps you can prepare some things for your mother to make her more comfortable.'

'They're already laid out.'

'Of course,' he says.

I lift my spoon to sip some more of the broth, feeling that perhaps Henry is right. I should give my father a chance.

'Did you want to talk about the fine before we go into King's Norton?'

His eyes blaze as if the question has offended him and I have no right to speak to him so.

My spoon shakes in my hand. After all these years, he still affects me as if I were a child. I lay the spoon down, careful that it makes no sound.

He raises his newsbook again and glares at it, making a pretence of reading.

After a few minutes of uncomfortable silence, I say quietly, 'I will get those things for Mamma and bring them downstairs.'

He nods without looking up.

Nance has laid my mother's clothes at the foot of the bed over the trunk. I start to fold them and then glance over at the window seat, recalling the corner of parchment. Quickly, I close the bedchamber door, toss all the seat cushions onto the floor and examine the window seat. There's a narrow gap the length of the seat about three inches from the wall below the window. I try to lift the seat up, but I cannot shift it. I drop to my knees. Tucked underneath the lip of the seat are two tiny bolts. I undo them carefully and ease the lid upwards.

It's a shallow space. On the left side there's a folded blanket that I remember Mamma used to wrap us in after we were bathed. I stroke the worn, pale wool. On the right-hand side is a small pile of books. The corner of the top book is turned up. I smooth it out and read the title: *The Man-Woman*.

Footsteps in the hall make me spring to my feet. The lid slips from my hand and crashes down with a thud.

'Frannie!'

I shove the cushions back into place as the door opens.

'What was that noise?' my father asks, looking around the room.

'I w-was . . .' I stammer and point to my mother's dress and shawl draped across the chest at the foot of the bed. 'The chest lid slammed.'

He looks at the dress for a moment then walks to the window. I feel a moment of panic, wondering what I should say if he lifts the seat.

'Your mother sits here,' he says, looking back at me. He places his hand on the seat.

I hold my breath.

'There is such a pretty view of the river from this window.' He sits and points over the fields of wheat stubble. 'They are going to take the land, Frannie, no matter what I do.'

The morning sun on his face shows every sleepless night, every concern.

'Can some be given to Joseph to protect it?'

He gives a slight shake of his head. 'Time is against us. Your mother's refusal to comply is overriding all logic and leniency.'

'I don't understand. She can't comply if she is in gaol.'

'And she will not when she comes out,' he says fiercely.

I lift my mother's dress, breathing in the faint scent of lavender. My mother has always tied sprigs of lavender to the inside of the chest to ward off moths.

'Perhaps this awful experience will make Mamma see the error of her ways.'

He is staring out of the window. 'Always the optimist,' he mutters.

'I mean that she must be given the chance.'

He looks at me, his eyebrows raised almost comically. 'Your mother knew that I could lose everything, but she still refused to go to church. I have begged. I have pleaded. I have ordered her to go.'

I sit heavily on the bed. My swollen belly looks obvious to me, and I pull my mother's dress over it. I glance at my father, but he has not noticed.

He brushes his hand against the window seat, sweeping something away. 'This is humiliating for me,' he says.

'I know,' I say softly. This house, this land, is everything to him; without it he is nothing, nobody.

He continues sweeping at the cushion and it occurs to me that perhaps he can see something protruding from the gap.

He stops sweeping and turns his steely gaze towards me.

A tightness crawls though me like the screw turning on the napkin press. He knows, I think. I sit frozen on the edge of the bed.

'I thought I could rely on you, Frannie.'

I swallow hard, wondering what to say. It is hardly a deceit—I have only just realised myself that there are books under the seat.

'Joseph and I discussed it, and we believe that if we can persuade your mother to sign an oath denouncing the Catholic faith, then we can plead that there is no case for land sequestration. We might also be able to get the fine reduced.'

I stare at the fire. The logs have shifted, suffocating the flames, and smoke is seeping into the room.

'Frannie,' he says.

I turn to him, wondering how to respond. I can't imagine my mother agreeing to this.

'I need you to convince your mother to sign.'

'No, Papa,' I plead. 'I can't. You or Joseph should do it.'

He shakes his head. 'She will listen to you, Frannie. You must talk to her. It is our only chance.'

19

The sun is high overhead as we set off for King's Norton. My father, a satchel slung over his shoulder and a blanket roll containing my mother's clothes tied behind him, rides his grey mare. I follow on his other horse—a gentle old mare with liquid brown eyes. As we enter the dim forest path, my horse takes up a trot behind my father's grey. The sunlight blinks between the trees, the contrast between dark trunks and shafts of light dazzling. Ahead, my father's body rises and falls in the saddle, the blanket roll bouncing with the horse's gait. I glance to the side, and the alternation of light and shade makes me dizzy.

'Father,' I call. 'Wait till I get the measure of this horse.'

He slows his horse to a walk. The dull clomp of the hooves on the mud track resounds through the trees. We ride on in silence. There's no bird call or even a breeze. Everything is still, except for us.

When I was very young my father once told me that Hazelmere had taken a large bite from the forest, and that we had to watch that forest or it would swallow Hazelmere up again. For many nights I woke with nightmares about monster trees gobbling the land. Mamma told him,

'George, you have frightened her.' Papa laughed and said, 'You have too much imagination, Frannie. Hazelmere will always be here. I will never give up this land to any man or any tree. I promise you that.'

My father looks back at me. 'You used to be good on a horse.'

'I am just tired, Father.'

He waits until I am level with him then looks me up and down. 'Are you sick?'

I feel my face redden. 'No.'

My cloak hides my shape, but I sense that he suspects something.

'You will put my proposal to your mother as we agreed?'

'Of course,' I say dully. 'But I can't force her to accept it.'

'She will,' he says. He kicks his heels and his mare walks ahead, although the path is wide enough for us to ride together.

When we arrive in King's Norton, I follow my father along the busy streets towards the magistrate's office. We tie up the horses and unload the blanket roll.

A woman passes and our eyes meet briefly. She is elegantly dressed, with a bright blue lining to her dark hood—perhaps the wife of a merchant. She takes in the horses, the bundle that I'm carrying. Then her eyes widen as if she recognises my father. She looks quickly away. With a dry throat, I climb the three steps to the office. At the door, I glance back. The woman is watching—judging me.

Inside, my father pays the visiting charge then stands aside.

'Aren't you coming in?' I ask.

He grimaces. 'It'll be better if you go alone. Once she's signed the oath, I will take it to the sheriff's officer.'

I gaze along the corridor, which is busy with people. He has waited until the last moment before telling me that I would be speaking to my mother alone. I take the satchel from him and join the queue. I wonder if my father has even visited my mother yet. Surely he must have. I have to shake off this anger towards him—I don't want my mother to see me agitated.

When I reach the head of the queue, the dour guard nods in recognition. He opens the heavy door to the gaol. I wait while he locks it, then follow the guard down the dark corridor, the smell almost choking me.

Another woman is in my mother's cell, slumped in the corner with hay piled around her. She reeks of ale and piss. My mother sits on the bench, looking from me to the woman as if things could not get any worse.

'They brought her in during the night. They threw her in the corner, poor soul.'

I wish I had my mother's ability to see the good in everyone. I can't help but turn my nose up.

I take out the bread and ham and, while my mother eats, I show her the clothes I have brought. When she has eaten a little, I help her into the warm clothes and wipe her face and hands.

'That's better,' I say, forcing a smile; she looks so frail that I want to weep.

'What's troubling you, Frannie?' she asks, picking up her bowl again.

'I'm just sad because you are in here,' I say. 'Mamma, will you tell me why you stopped going to church?'

'We can't talk now,' she says, nodding her head towards the corner where the woman lies.

'But we must. I can't help you if you won't confide in me.'

Her chin quivers. She stares resolutely at the door as if she expects it to burst open.

'I hope Nance is looking after you. Did she put you in your old room? Oh, and have you seen the tapestry in the dining room? It is made from the most delicate of silk threads. It depicts the River Thames on its path through London to the sea.' She looks up at the window, as if suddenly remembering something. 'We walked by the river there, didn't we, angel?'

I nod and she says, 'Now tell me about my grandsons.'

I talk about George and explain that he has Henry's looks but that his temperament is like that of Joseph. She asks what books he likes to read.

'His favourite is Montelyon,' I say, and she smiles.

'And what of Middleton?'

I cannot bring myself to use the common word for Middy.

'He is . . . he is not quick to learn, Mamma. He speaks only a few words.'

'And in the village, is he treated well, Frannie?'

'Yes,' I say. 'Mostly he is tolerated kindly, but he will always need someone to look after him.'

She takes my hand and strokes it. 'We don't know what lies ahead, angel.'

The woman in the corner stirs, swears and kicks out with her foot, as if something has bitten her leg.

'I would like to see the boys,' my mother says.

'You must come and stay with us as soon as you are free.'

As I look around the cell, her eyes follow mine, widening slightly as if she has remembered where she is.

'You trust me, Mamma, don't you?'

'Of course, Frannie.'

'And you know the most important thing is that you are freed,' I say, my fingers resting on the clasp of the satchel.

She looks weary and begins to cough. The sound is loud, echoing off the cell's stone walls. I realise with dismay that I have forgotten to bring a paste.

The woman stirs again. 'Leave me be,' she cries. 'Begone!' She cowers further into the corner. 'Get him away from me . . .'

'You are safe here, madam,' my mother calls gently. 'There's no man in here.'

'Guard!' the woman screams, thrashing out at something before her. 'Guard!'

There's a thud of boots and a clang of bolts. A voice from the corridor shouts, 'Stop that squalling, woman!'

The guard enters, swearing. He casts a look of disgust at the woman moaning and writhing in the corner then says to me, 'You need to leave now.'

'But my father is coming . . .'

I stop abruptly, feeling my mother press hard on my hand.

She shakes her head at me. 'Do as he says, Frannie.'

I kiss her cheek. 'I'll be back as soon as I can.'

The guard ushers me out and slams the door shut behind me. I am still standing alone in the corridor when I hear the woman in my mother's cell shriek in pain—a response to a blow. Another blow, this time followed by a low moan. I stand there frozen, not knowing what to do. Then I contemplate what might happen if the guard emerges from the cell and realises that I have heard what he has done. I hurry along the corridor, my heart thudding.

My father is pacing outside. As he sees me, he gives a hopeful look, then his expression changes. 'What's happened? You look like death.'

'There was some commotion with another woman in the cell and I was sent out.' I swallow. 'The guard beat the woman, I'm sure of it.'

'Is your mother safe?'

'I think so, but I don't know. She told me to leave.'

'Did she agree to sign the oath?' he asks, taking the satchel from me. He opens it and takes out the papers.

'Papa, what are you doing? You need to go and make sure that Mamma's all right.'

His eyes seem to bulge as he scans the papers, and his face contorts so that I barely recognise him as my father.

'Why aren't these signed?' he demands.

'There was no chance even to talk of it with her.'

He thrusts the satchel back at me. 'Stay here.' He rushes into the clerk's office.

Several men approach the building. They stand talking at the bottom of the steps as if they are waiting for someone. I press my back against the wall. My hands are shaking so much that I have to grip my arms. What if my mother has been hurt? She's so close but I can't get to her. Fear overcomes me so that I cannot think. A tear runs down my cheek.

Oh, I cannot bear to show weakness in front of these men. To steady myself, I dig into my pocket for a leftover scrap from the bookshop in Tamworth and run my fingers over the vellum, picturing my books, imagining letters imprinting themselves onto my skin and into my soul. Words come to me from *Julius Caesar*, the play Joseph and I had read with our mother when we were children. '*O constancy, be strong upon my side; Set a huge mountain 'tween my heart and tongue! I have a man's mind, but a woman's might.*' I repeat the lines over and over.

Moments later my father strides towards me, glowering. He casts a sideways glance at the men and mutters, 'You can go in again in a few minutes.'

He wipes his muddy boots in the grasses nearby, sending dandelion clocks floating around us like snow. He looks at me, holding my gaze so intently that I want to look away but dare not. 'We are all relying on you to get this done, Frannie. Next time, there will be no time for pleasantries.'

'Feeding her and getting her into warm clothes are hardly pleasantries,' I say through gritted teeth.

My father shows no sign that he has heard me as he unties his horse from the hitching post. I watch as my father talks softly to her, wondering how he can show such gentleness to his horses and so little to us.

Back inside, the dour guard grunts at me to follow him. As soon as he opens the door to the long corridor, the unsettling sounds of heavy coughing can be heard coming from several cells. Someone is banging on a door, and from my mother's cell the woman who had been beaten moans pitifully.

I look at the guard, but he waves me on. He stops outside a different cell.

'This is not my mother's cell.'

'She's been moved,' he says gruffly and opens the door.

This cell is smaller and has no bench. My mother sits huddled on the freezing stone floor, her fresh clothes already dirty.

I look at the guard. 'There's nowhere to sit.'

He gives a shrug. 'I'll get a stool. Bang on the door when you're ready to go.' He pulls the cell door shut, locking me in.

'Mamma,' I say, kneeling beside her. 'Mamma, did he hit you?'

I take the small flask from the satchel and hold it up for her to drink.

She touches her head. 'He pushed me.' She takes a sip of the ale. 'I'm glad you're here.'

'We have to get you out of this gaol,' I say.

She takes another sip and leans her head against the wall, her breathing laboured. Her breath has the sour smell of sickness.

'I'm cold,' she says, pulling her cloak around her.

I move quickly. I take out the paper, set the ink bottle on the floor and fumble in the satchel for the quill. My hands are shaking as I flip the satchel over and lay the paper on it. I dip the feather into the ink, spilling drops onto the stone.

My mother watches me. 'I'm worried about you, angel. You don't look like yourself.'

I hold out the quill. 'Mamma, I have a paper here for you to sign then Father can pay the fine and you will be released.'

'What paper?'

The putrid stench of the cell, of sickness, crawls over me. I am desperate to leave before it reaches the baby. 'It doesn't matter. We need to get you out before—'

'The magistrate mentioned no paper.' She tries to sit up straighter. 'What is this, Frannie?'

I smooth the page with my hands. 'It's an oath of abjuration. It swears your allegiance to the government and—'

'And denies my faith in the Catholic religion.' Her eyes hold mine, burning into me.

I look away. 'Father says it's the only way to get you out, Mamma,' I whisper. 'He needs you to sign it so he can negotiate with them. They will take the land if you do not sign.'

She pushes the paper away. 'There is not enough light to read this. I cannot sign what I cannot read.'

'I have read it, Mamma. It is a commitment in writing to attend service. There are no practical restrictions beyond that. And you know that we all have to attend anyway . . .'

'That's enough, Frannie.' Her voice is fierce. 'That is enough,' she says, her chin straining up towards the window set high in the wall, as if searching for a way out.

I observe her beautiful face in the dim light, the soft wrinkles around her narrowed eyes, her lips drawn tight in defiance.

'Mamma,' I say softly, hoping to reason with her, 'there are people being arrested all over the country. There is a woman in Statfold, Hannah Smythe, who ministered to me when Middy was born . . .'

My mother's eyes shift, meeting my own.

'She's in trouble because she doesn't go to church. And it's me who is tasked with recording her absences from church. It troubles me greatly, Mamma. Yet she won't let me help her.'

'Have you talked to her?'

'I have tried, Mamma. I have tried to make her understand that she must go to church but she will not come.'

'Is she Catholic?' my mother asks quietly.

'I don't know—I don't even know her true name—but I think she's hiding something.'

My mother is quiet, her head tilted in thought, her skin pale and translucent in the light.

'She will tell you nothing unless she trusts you,' she says.

'What do I do to earn her trust?'

She looks down at her hands, which are clasped tightly. Then she fixes her eyes on me. 'You must listen to her. If you listen, she'll confide in you. And if she does, you mustn't let her down, Frannie.'

I wipe my eyes. She is talking about us.

My mother watches me silently. Her gaze is unwavering as my breath quickens.

'Don't let her down,' she repeats.

I look down at my mother's hands. My face burning, I reach out and take them in mine. She tugs them away, but I pull them gently towards me, feeling the rough, dry skin of the scars. As I clutch her hands tightly, an acrid smell surrounds me. I stare at her, feeling suddenly overcome.

She gazes at me with wide, pale eyes. 'It's all right, angel,' she says. She pulls me towards her and wraps her arms around me. I lay my head on her shoulder. We hold each other for a few minutes, then my mother releases me, placing a tender kiss on my cheek before she sits back against the wall.

I wipe my face as Mamma carefully tucks her hands back inside her shawl.

Outside, the distant cry of a pie seller pierces the silence of the cell. 'Hot pies, two a penny, just two a penny.'

We listen as his calls come closer, then move further away.

'Life carries on,' Mamma says.

Sniffing, I pick up the quill and paper. With a trembling hand, I hold out the quill. 'I promise you can trust me, Mamma. Now will you please sign the oath?'

She stares down at the paper then she looks up at me, searching my face desperately. Tears form in her eyes.

Her voice is fragile when she speaks. 'Frannie, my love, I need you to do something for me.'

'Anything.'

'I need you to go back home and look after your children.'

'But, Mamma, I need to get you out of here first.'

She surveys my face as if memorising it. Then she shakes her head. 'I need you to go home, angel,' she repeats, her voice soft but her expression resolute.

'Come home with me then. Think of it, Mamma. You could read all the books you want. We could walk together in the hills. You could see your grandsons. Just sign this damned paper and you will be free.'

She squeezes her eyes shut and her lips move silently. When she opens her eyes, she looks at me sternly and says: '*I see a woman may be made a fool, if she had not a spirit to resist.*'

My fingers tighten on the quill. The ink forms a black pool on the oath before I snatch the feather away.

'Go home, Frannie.'

'No, Mamma. I will not go until you are free.'

She stares past me to the corner, where a pile of straw masks the excrement but fails to mask the stench. 'I wish you would do as I say, my daughter,' she says quietly.

I hold out my hands, hoping she will take them.

She does not respond. Her eyes have hardened into the familiar, closed look reserved for my father when he used to come home late from King's Norton.

'I will go, if that's what you want, Mamma.'

She nods. 'Tell your father that he will have to talk with me himself. He has avoided me long enough.' With glistening eyes she adds, 'Go quickly now, Frannie, and be safe.'

20

It's raining again. We take the track through the woods back to Hazelmere. My father rides ahead of me: far enough to convey his anger, but not so far that he loses sight of me among the trees. I keep my eyes on the track, urging the reluctant mare around the deepest holes and ruts. It's painstakingly slow. The sickness I felt earlier this morning has subsided, but my mother's words keep returning to me. '*I see a woman may be made a fool.*'

There was a hungry look in my father's eyes when I walked towards him outside the gaol. I handed the paper back to him and watched as he examined the splodge of ink where her signature should be. 'Mamma said you must ask her yourself,' I said, expecting that he would rush into the gaol and demand to see her.

Instead, he folded the papers and, taking his satchel from me, placed them inside. Then he fastened the clasp and busied himself getting his horse ready.

I could tell by his calm demeanour that he had known all along that she would not sign. He had made a fool out of me. They have had an argument, and neither of them will tell me the truth of it.

And now, despite my declarations, my mother thinks I have taken his side.

With each glint of light that penetrates the gloomy forest, I catch sight of my father's black cloak in the distance. I have no desire to close the gap between us. I tell myself that I will return tomorrow and tell her the truth, that Father forced me to ask her. But did he force me? I could have refused. I should have refused. Once again, I am caught between them, like a rope fraying under their pull.

I slow the horse, delaying the return to Hazelmere as long as I can. I resolve to apologise to my mother. I will start again. I will tell her of the baby; perhaps that will help mend the breach between us.

When I reach the clearing, my father is already in the stable yard waiting.

He takes hold of the reins when I am near. 'There's nothing more you can do here. In fact, you are a distraction. You should go home to Statfold.' His voice is as cold as steel.

I slide off the horse and steady myself against her shoulder. 'Father, please . . .'

'You can stay until your husband returns with the carriage. But you are not to visit your mother again. You are only making things worse.'

He turns from me and I call out, 'What will you do now?'

'I will talk again to Joseph. We must protect as much as we can.'

'But what about Mamma?'

'Your mother is my concern, Frannie, not yours.' My father hands the reins to the stable boy and strides to the house without a backward glance.

I cannot face going back into the house when my mother is not there, so I pull my shawl around me and stride out through the garden at the back of the house towards the woods.

I push my way through birch, elders and rambling bushes that have grown over the trail. Thoughts of my mother crowd my head, and I can almost hear our laughter echoing among the trees. Yet nothing feels as it did then, when we innocently played our games; the woods are darker now, forbidding.

A wood pigeon coos and I jump. My heart is beating fast as I stride, unwilling to linger in the trees yet not entirely sure where the path is taking me. A distant chime makes me stop. It sounds like a church bell, but it cannot be, for Nance told me that the Hazelmere bell had been melted down for cannon. I stand, listening. The only sound is the swish of the long grasses at the edge of the wood.

Stepping out from the shade of the trees into a meadow, I am bathed in sunshine. In one direction, the field slopes down towards Hazelmere village. In the other, the field climbs gently to a hilltop, where a solitary oak tree is dropping the last of its leaves in the wind. Just beyond the tree lies the hollow where I used to hide. It can only be seen from the branches of the oak tree. Of course I've come here. I always came here.

As I set out for the tree, a volley of birds rises up from the grasses near me: the air becomes alive with their calls, their wings loud as flapping sheets. As they gain height, they soar and spin, their wings glistening silvery-ash flickers in the autumn sun. An ache carves through me as I recall my mother sitting in my father's study, her face caught in disbelief as she realised what was about to happen. I push the scene away and force myself to keep walking until I reach the tree.

Panting, I gaze up at the gnarled trunk. This is the place where Joseph and I would come when our father was angry. We would climb up and sit on the lowest branch of the oak tree and survey our kingdom. The squirrel hole in the trunk, where we used to hide treasure, is still there but much higher now. I stretch my arms as far as I can reach but I can only touch the underside of the branch.

There's a burned odour in the air. I scan the field and the distant chimneys of the village houses but can see no smoke. I wipe my mouth, trying to remove the bitter taste of charred earth that seems to surround me. I look around, feeling uneasy. I can almost see Joseph sitting there, his back against the tree, his sooty hands clasping the field flask, his breath rasping from running. He drank from the flask until it was dry. He held it upside down above his head, catching the last drops. 'I saved it,' he said, pointing to a book with a cover so singed and blackened that it made me cry all over again.

My breastbone aches as I gaze at the tree, trying to remember what happened to that book. Nothing more comes to me.

In the distance, the church tower is swathed in dark cloud. I recall the misery in my mother's eyes when she asked me to leave today. I feel numb, empty. Even the babe inside me seems to have recoiled from me.

I walk down the hill and back into the wood. I have done no good coming back here. I should have given my mother more time to consider the situation instead of blurting out my father's wishes so. She trusted me and I let her down.

Rain starts to spit as I leave the woods. I hold out my hands and watch the drops fall, dissolving the dirt on my hands into rivulets.

I start as I look up and see Nance's face looming before me.

'Lord help us, what are you doing out here, Miss Frannie? I've been looking everywhere for you.'

'I let her down, Nance.'

Nance takes my arm and leads me through the rain into the kitchen. She pulls off my cloak and my sodden shawl. Tutting, she guides me into a chair by the fire, below the dried lavender tied with blue wool. Water boils in a pot and Nance stirs in crushed camomile stems. She mutters to herself, 'All these years and nothin's changed.'

'Drink this,' she says, spooning the herbal brew into a bowl.

I cup the bowl with both hands and sip slowly.

The kitchen is dim. Thunder rumbles in the distance. Rain lashes the glass. Nance sighs as she watches it. 'That's all we need.'

I gaze into the fire, wondering what will become of my mother now.

'She trusted me, Nance, and I let her down.'

Nance places the back of her hand on my brow. She pats my arm and says soothingly, 'You didn't know what you were doing. You were just a girl, Frannie.' She picks up my shawl and cloak. 'I'll hang these up to dry. You sit there and let that fire warm you through.'

'A girl did you say, Nance? I was talking about today.'

Water drips from the sodden cloak onto the stone flags as Nance stares at me with a puzzled look. It was the same way my mother had looked at me.

'What do you mean, Nance?'

She shakes her head briskly and looks down at the puddle around her feet. 'Now look at the mess on this floor,' she says.

She twists and squeezes the wet cloak over a tub then drapes it over a wooden chair and dries her hands. 'If you ask me, it's best to leave the past in the past,' she says.

'But what about recently? You must know why she doesn't go to church anymore.'

'I'd best be closing the shutters against this storm.' Nance hurries into the hallway.

The kitchen cat looks up, uncurls from her corner next to the woodpile and fixes me with her wary amber eyes, as if I have caused trouble. My head aches. I look for solace in the fire which crackles and spits under the cookpot, but all I can see in the flames is the hurt in my mother's eyes.

21

I wake as Nance opens the shutters, letting the dappled sunlight into my old bedroom. She moves around the room, straightening my clothes. She picks up the jug of water that she has left by the door and places it on the washstand.

'Thank you, Nance,' I say, my voice gravelly.

'That horseman of yours came back at first light. He must have been driving all night.'

I push back the covers to get up, but Nance stops me. 'Where are you going?'

'I have to see him.'

Nance tucks the covers back around me. 'He's asleep in the stable; you'd best leave him be awhile.'

'Did he have any message from Mr Wolfreston?'

'He didn't say.'

Nance doesn't meet my eye and I know she doesn't want me to ask her any more questions. The back of her hand rests on my forehead. Satisfied that there's no fever, she says, 'Stay in bed till the house heats up.'

I nod my assent. My arms and legs feel weighty, and I would rather avoid any further conversations with my father.

Sam doesn't stir when I open the stable door. Still splattered with mud from the journey, he's lying under a blanket near Merlin and Lady. I step quietly over to Lady and rest my head against her shoulder, breathing in her warm sweaty smell and listening to the comforting sound of her heartbeat.

Sam's hair is pushed back from his face. The last few weeks of Peg's food has softened his features, but he still has a fierce look, even in sleep. One of his hands is draped protectively over his satchel. I recall the day he took the Du Bartas from it and presented it to me with a flourish, and find myself smiling. I wonder what books he has in there now. The only book I have with me is my old *Licia*, a book of poems from 1593, which I found lying in the bottom of my trunk. It must have been there for some time for I have not missed it.

I take a soft step towards him.

Sensing movement nearby, he lunges towards me.

I reel back, gasping.

He holds his hands out in apology. 'Mrs Wolfreston. Sorry . . . I've been driving all night.'

'I know, Sam. I didn't mean to disturb you.'

Sam's hair has fallen over his face again. He rakes it back and takes a gulp of ale from a jar. I notice a curving scar on his neck below his left ear. A war injury, I assume.

'Sam, did Mr Wolfreston give you a letter for me?'

He sets down the jar. 'No, but he gave me a message. He said he couldn't leave the parish. Told me to tell you that you should come home.'

'What's happened?'

His face looks tense. He draws in a breath as if he's about to speak then exhales. 'There . . .' He falters. 'Mr Wolfreston said to tell you that the boys are well.'

I give him a sharp look. 'You were about to say something else. Has something happened in the village?'

His eyes flit about uncomfortably.

I feel my face grow warm. 'Mrs Edwards,' I mutter in disgust.

Sam smooths his hand over Lady's shoulder and adjusts the blanket around her. 'I don't know,' he says. 'I just heard something that I won't repeat. But people know about your mother.'

My stomach heaves and I reach for the stable wall, brace myself against it. I'm breathing hard, panting as if I have run across the fields.

Sam moves quickly, pulling out the milking stool and making me sit.

So, the villagers know. I rest my hands on my swollen belly and try to calm myself.

Sam is talking but I can barely hear him for the pounding in my ears.

'Mrs Wolfreston?'

Sam is staring at my hands, and I know he is taking in my condition.

'Mr Wolfreston said we are to leave tomorrow.'

'Tomorrow?' I say.

Merlin's ears flicker.

My voice shakes. 'I need to see my mother one last time before we go.'

'At the gaol?'

I picture her hunched in that filthy cell. 'Oh.' The word comes out like the low painful moan of an animal. I need to see her, but she won't see me. Lady's tail flicks unhappily, and I am unable to stop my tears from falling.

Sam sits on the stacked hay nearby, leaning against the stable wall, staring ahead rather than at me. I feel ashamed of myself for weeping in front of this man. What must he think of me? I inhale the humid stable fumes and remember how far the horses have travelled in the last few days, pulling the heavy carriage. And they must do it again tomorrow.

I sniff back my tears.

Sam reaches into his pocket. He removes something and silently hands it to me.

It's a piece of raw, smoky parchment from Mr Townsend's printing press. It's been folded over twice. I unfold it, examining the single word written in long loopy scrawls:

Mama

'Middy gave it to me for you,' Sam says with a hint of a smile. 'He's a good lad.'

Warmth surges through me as I study the beautiful, misspelled note my son has crafted. I wipe my eyes with my handkerchief and compose myself as well as I'm able.

'Thank you,' I say, smiling at him.

I stand and walk outside to the stable yard. I can see in the slow way he moves as he follows me out that Sam's exhausted.

'When you've rested, Sam, I'd like your help with something.'

His eyebrows arch in question.

'When I was young, my brother and I used to hide things in a tree on the far side of those woods,' I say, pointing. 'There's probably nothing there, but I would like to look anyway.'

'Of course, Mrs Wolfreston.'

While I wait for Sam to feed and water the horses, I busy myself in the kitchen, sorting through my mother's boxes of dried herbs and roots. She has always kept a range of medicines and has a well-thumbed copy of *The Profitable Arte of Gardening*, which lists the healing properties of each herb. I caress the leather cover with fondness. Inside the back pages she has added some of her own recipes, which I have copies of at home. Here I find, written in my mother's hand, which is more delicate than mine, a recipe for coughs. I recall my mother holding my hand and pushing the back of the spoon on the chopped herbs to show me how to crush them just the right amount. I crush some now, together with a piece of honeycomb, to make a thick paste for her to chew. It will put a coating on her throat and ease the cough. I wrap it in greased parchment. I also make up some more ointment for my father's chapped skin.

Nance's face creases pleasantly as she watches me.

'It's a tonic to see you working there like your mother, Miss Frannie.'

The rare compliment from Nance makes me smile, but she doesn't notice. She glares out the window, rushes to the door and pulls it open.

'You'll wash before you step foot in this kitchen,' she says, looking up at Sam.

She points at the bucket on a bench near the water trough. Sam takes his time washing his face and hands, then dunks his head right into the water and throws it back. Nance passes him a drying cloth.

She had earlier berated me for inviting him into the kitchen to eat. She is suspicious of Sam, as she is with most people. As he sits eating potage in the warmth of the kitchen, she watches him closely, as if she's expecting him to steal the bowl.

'Thank you kindly,' he says, smiling at her when he's finished.

It's his charming peddler's smile again, and it disarms her. She nods at him.

He turns to me and says, 'I'll wait for you outside, Mrs Wolfreston.'

'Where are you going with him?' Nance asks as I wrap my shawl around my shoulders.

'Over to the old oak tree. I'm looking for something.'

'Take the stable boy. He knows the land round here.'

I had thought of that, but I if I find anything, I want no gossip about it to reach my father. 'Sam's all right, Nance—he saved Middy's life.'

Her eyes widen. She looks doubtful but says nothing more.

I trek back through the woods and across the field, Sam following with a short ladder. When we reach the tree, he leans the ladder against the trunk, climbs it, and hoists himself onto the branch I indicate.

'The squirrel hole is there,' I say, pointing.

Sam lowers himself to lie on the branch and peers into the hole. He looks dubious.

'The hole is deep,' I call. 'Just put your hand right in and feel around.'

He puts his hand just inside, grimacing as he then thrusts his hand in among the soggy leaves and animal droppings.

'Well?' I say.

'Nothing,' he replies.

I look over the empty field and sigh. What a fool's pursuit. I knew there was little chance of finding anything, but I am very disappointed.

'Wait—I can feel something.' Sam withdraws his hand and holds up a mud-coated object.

He climbs down from the tree, kneels and wipes the mud from his find in the long grass.

'That old thing!' I say, recognising the grubby old flask Joseph carried everywhere.

Sam wrestles the stopper off, sniffs it and then tips it over. Nothing comes out.

'It might clean up,' Sam says, holding it out to me.

My stomach heaves in response. 'Throw it away, Sam,' I say, turning away in disgust.

Before I retire for the night, I quietly open the door to my mother's room. Swathes of moonlight fall on the oak floorboards. The bed is unmade and my father's doublet lies on the chair by the fireplace. My breath quickens. I scan the room, fretting for a moment that he is there in the shadows. But the room is empty. I close the bedroom door and tiptoe to the window seat.

Outside, eerie shadows fall across the garden—a witch's hat, a cat and the cat's long tail. I know they're the summerhouse, the outhouses and the path snaking beyond, but I still shudder. I cannot feel my mother's presence in this room as I could only a few days ago and that concerns me.

Underneath the window seat, I find the two small bolts. Slowly, silently, I release them.

Hearing the creak of floorboards, I hesitate. I creep to the door, ease it open a crack and peer into the hallway. A figure is climbing the stairs. The candlelight throws a huge shadow on the wall.

I hold my breath as the shadow comes nearer. My heart beats faster. Then my pulse steadies as I realise it is Nance. I recall Joseph, who use to slip upstairs before me. He would watch for me coming then, when I was very close, leap out and make me scream. I never understood why he liked to do it. But as I watch Nance, who is unaware that I am watching her, I feel a certain excitement. Nance pauses. She looks around as if she has heard something. Then she hangs my scarf over the handle of my door and retraces her steps.

When she's gone, I return to the window seat. I throw off the cushions and ease the lid up to rest against the mullioned window. I hold the candle over the cavity, but save a few cobwebs, there is nothing to see. The blanket and the books are gone.

I stare into the empty space. Then I recall my father watching me as he sat on the window seat; what a fool I am for alerting him to the presence of the books.

Pulling one of my mother's cushions against my chest, I sit down on the bed. I close my eyes and try to visualise the books I'd seen. The spines of two were coloured, one blue and one brown. There was also, I think, a thin playbook in the pile—but which was it? I saw part of the title of one book: *The Man-Woman*. My fists close in frustration. What books were here and was the singed book that Joseph found among them?

I push my nose against the cushion, trying to capture the scent of my mother, but I cannot.

I place the cushions back on the window seat and return to my room.

22

In the grey smudge of half-light before sunrise, Sam loads my trunk onto the carriage. I take a last long look at Hazelmere's familiar small windows and long chimneys, knowing that I will never willingly return to this house. I heard horses at midnight, but if it was my father returning, he has not risen to see us off. I wonder if he and Joseph have managed to devise a new plan. I hope they will remember to save my mother as well as the land.

My eyes are drawn to the staggered row of holly trees with their plethora of red berries. Mamma planted them to distinguish the garden from the woods without fencing in the land. She hates fences. Swallowing hard, I place my satchel inside the carriage.

'Miss Frannie, wait.' Nance bustles over with a large basket of food. I help her lift it through the carriage door. 'There now, that's done,' she says, sounding relieved.

I smile at her. 'What's in there—half a hog?'

She glows red. 'A cheese round . . . and pies for your little lads,' she says, smoothing down her apron. Her eyes flash up to Sam. 'And you'd better hurry along,' she tells him. 'You can't be driving in the dark with Mrs Wolfreston.' She squeezes my hand. 'Glad to see you, Miss Frannie. You take care.' She nods towards my belly.

I startle Nance with a sudden embrace.

She responds by holding me as if she doesn't want to let go. 'Get on with you,' she mutters, still clutching me.

I climb into the carriage. As we drive away, I press my face against the window. Nance stands in front of the house with her shawl pulled about her. She remains there after we reach the woods. I glimpse her through the trees, her hand caught in a wave.

The sky is pink over King's Norton as we approach, jolting along the ruts from the recent rain. A shepherd steers a flock of black-faced sheep across our path as we near the town square, where merchants are preparing stalls. We are surrounded by aromas of warm bread, corn broth and mincemeat pies. Sam must be tempted by the delicious smells, as he calls through the slot to me to ask if we can stop, but I tell him there is no time.

We continue through narrow streets until we reach the magistrate's office. Sam helps me down. Several people pass with baskets, going about their business, with little attention being paid to me or the Broughtons' carriage. Life continues on while my mother is incarcerated only a few feet away. I want desperately to free her, but my wanting makes no difference.

The building is quiet inside. A squat guard whom I do not recognise points to a bench near an open door on the right and calls out, 'Visitor.'

Inside, leaning over some documents at a desk, is the dark-haired man, wearing the sheriff's colours. He must be the man I saw my father talking with a few days ago—the sheriff's clerk.

He looks me up and down then signals me into his small office. 'How can I help you, ma'am?' he asks.

'I would like to visit my mother, Mrs Alice Middlemore.'

He subdues a laugh. 'It is far too early. Come back later, after the market.'

'But I have to return to Tamworth today. I cannot wait or we won't make it home by nightfall. Please, I need to see my mother before I go.'

I take some coins from my purse and hold them out. 'I can pay.'

He looks at the coins unmoved. 'I can't do it,' he says.

I wonder if I should delay the journey until I have seen her. But I have only the coins I offered him, not enough to stay at an inn.

'Will you give her something from me then?' I say, placing my basket on his desk.

He watches while I take out bread, honey paste, soap, a linen, a book and a candle. 'This is not a guesthouse,' he says. 'You may leave food, nothing more.'

Disappointed, I begin to return the items to the basket. As I pick up the book, I hesitate. 'Please, my mother is a good woman. This book will comfort her whether she has a candle to read it by or not.'

His eyes meet mine and he takes the book from my hand and reads the title. '*Licia*.'

I nod. 'It is a book of verses about love.'

'I know what it is.' He opens the book, and his eyes flicker up at me as he sees a note tucked inside the cover. 'And this?'

'Just a personal note to explain . . .' The words catch as I cannot say the rest. 'Read it, if you care to.'

I look over towards the gaol, my heart sinking. She is so near, yet I cannot reach her. There is no threat or plea I can make that will have any effect.

When I look back to the clerk, he is watching me, taking in my black dress, shawl and travelling cloak. There is not a hint of colour about me today.

'I'm a minister's wife,' I say.

'A minister's wife who is fond of sonnets,' he says with a sceptical laugh. 'And your mother is in here for what reason?'

'Recusancy,' I say, wary of his tone.

He fixes me with his steely eyes and I look back at him, waiting for his laugh.

He places the book near the bread. 'I will ensure she gets these,' he says solemnly.

I study his face for traces of sarcasm but none are evident.

'Thank you,' I say. I pray that he is a man of his word.

Outside, the biting wind whips through my cloak. I shiver, but I cannot move. I cannot leave her. I will return to Hazelmere and wait until she is released. I'll write to Henry's mother, asking to borrow money until my father can pay. But even as the idea emerges, I realise that it will never work. My father is too proud to accept charity.

Sam's call cuts through the bitter air. 'We have to leave, Mrs Wolfreston, or we won't make it to Statfold before nightfall.'

Without looking back, I climb into the carriage.

23

My heads whirls with guilt and recriminations. Despite the cold draught in the carriage, I begin to perspire and feel light-headed. I throw open the slot and yell to Sam to stop.

I clamber out of the carriage. Again, I am sick. Afterwards, I slump against a tree, waiting for the waves of nausea to pass.

I catch sight of Sam hovering nearby, anxious to be on the road. We have barely left King's Norton. My spirits sink at the prospect of lurching and rolling in confinement all day.

'I won't be a moment,' I say, wiping the damp hair from my face. A long tendril of hair has escaped my heavy plait. I tuck it behind my ear and stand up. There's nothing to be gained by staying here.

The carriage door is wide open. I retrieve my hat and tie it on then slam the carriage door shut.

'Give me a hand up,' I say, with my foot on the high driver's step.

Sam's dark eyes widen but he extends his hand. 'Ready?' he asks, when I am sitting beside him.

I nod and Sam urges the horses on.

Low cloud presses down on us as we pass several fields where the crops have rotted. It is a depressing sight. I lower my eyes to the horses' silky ears and listen to the soothing clop of their hooves. The breeze cools my face. Slowly my head begins to clear.

Ravaged brown fields interlaced with sweeps of common pastureland gradually give way to meadows and low rolling hills. A cluster of farm buildings appear on a hill with pinpricks of sheep below. It is a beautiful sight, but there's no respite for me in it. Beside me, Sam has his eyes locked straight ahead. He hasn't uttered a word. The only sounds are the rumbling of the wheels, the clop of the horses and the occasional snort from Merlin.

A hawk hangs above a meadow. It circles several times, plummets and swoops into the grass. My heart hovers. It emerges with its claws empty. I release a long breath.

'Are you from around here, Sam?'

Startled by my voice, his fingers twitch against the reins. He glances at me, blinking in the light.

He looks away a moment, as if deciding how much to tell me, or whether to tell me the truth. 'Near Winchester, like I told Mr Wolfreston.'

'That's a long way south.'

He nods. 'I was up here with the army. I've been roaming around since April—that's when the army stopped paying.'

'I thought Cromwell was trying to convince the government to pay the army's wages.'

'Don't trust that man.'

'I thought he was on the side of the men, that this was the point of his New Modelled Army.'

'There's only one side Cromwell is on.' He gives the reins a flick. 'And that's his own.'

His lack of caution makes me smile. 'Is that why you left the army?'

'I thought I'd stand a better chance on the outside. An officer signed me off on account of my leg.' He stretches out the leg as if it's not a real part of him.

He takes the reins in one hand and points to a house in the distance. 'I can tell you which of these big places will feed you and speak to you like you're a human, and which one of these ba—' He checks himself. 'Which of the gentlefolk treat you like an animal,' he finishes.

'So, what of the Egertons' place over Derby way?' I ask, for I know they are relations of Candace.

'The cook will let you have a wash and a drink.'

I stare at him, disbelieving.

He laughs loudly. 'She likes me. Told me to stop by anytime.'

'So, we could just drive there, see the house and go around the back to the cook.'

'Well, I can—but I'm not sure about you; seeing a clergy wife in that Puritan garb might send them all into hiding.'

I laugh aloud, the sound carrying over the swishing grasses. 'I hate wearing black,' I confess. 'I prefer green and blue.'

He's smiling now and I am struck by how a smile can transform a face. I feel comfortable talking with Sam and yet I feel uneasy under his gaze, as if he can somehow read my thoughts. For a moment, I wish that Henry was more like Sam.

I pull my cloak around me and tuck it under the seat, aware that he's watching me, supressing a grin.

'So, tell me, Sam, how did you learn to read?'

'My uncle taught me.'

'Your uncle?'

He nods but offers no more.

'How did you get into selling books?'

'Started buying the penny stories when I had spare. Sold them on after I read them.'

'And the Du Bartas?'

His eyes grow distant. 'I told you about that before.' His face is impassive, and a silence falls between us again.

'What about you?' he asks eventually, his eyes fixed between Merlin's ears. 'Who taught you to read?'

'My mother. She read verse and stories to my brother and me out in the fields and in the woods.' A warm smile spreads through me, but my voice cracks. 'There's something wonderful about reading outdoors. I spend so much time indoors, but I prefer to be outside.' As I say it, I realise that my mother hated to be tied to the house; she was always at the window like a bird waiting to escape.

He looks sideways at me. 'That's why you sing.'

'What do you mean?'

'You sing when you are working in the orchard.'

'Do I?'

He nods and his lips curl up a little at the sides.

I touch my face, surprised that no one has ever mentioned this to me. I can feel heat rising in my cheeks that it is he who has noticed this. I change the subject quickly. 'It says in the *Mercurius* that the Royalists are planning to free the King and help him make his way to France.'

'Yep,' he says, flicking the reins.

'It might not be a bad thing to have him out of the country,' I say softly, watching Sam for his reaction.

He pushes his hat back and sighs. 'They'll never let him go to France.'

'Why not?'

'Because he'd likely return with another, bigger army.' He looks at me evenly. 'Your history books will tell you that.'

A tightness grips me again. It is difficult to fathom what can be done with an unpopular king who has been removed by parliament. Yet what good is a country without a king?

We're approaching a hill and the horses slow. Sam pulls his hat low as if he wants me to stop talking. The horses' hooves plod up the steepening slope. The wheels jar against the ruts in the road and I grip the side of the carriage.

'They say war is likely to start again,' I say, trying to take my mind off the jolting.

'Hope not. Bloody pointless war, neighbours fighting neighbours.' His lips form a hard line. 'And for what?'

My body shudders. I can't answer his question. I have long thought the war a sorry waste of lives.

At the top of the hill, Sam stops the horses. The hill falls away to a lake that follows the curves of the valley. The water is so perfect a mirror that the trees and sky seem to be both above and below us. I breathe out slowly. The bruises and sores from riding, the discomfort of the jolting carriage rides from Statfold to King's Norton to Hazelmere, all seem to ease as I bask in the serene beauty of the scene.

A stillness surrounds me. I allow myself to believe that the guard has given my mother the book and that she is holding it close, knowing that I love her. I resolve to talk with Candace. Perhaps her father may know someone who can help plead my mother's case. Nestled among these low hills, their reflections more exquisite than any silk tapestry, I am hopeful.

Sam's eyes shine as he gazes across the valley. I am touched to realise that, despite all he has been through, he still sees beauty in the world.

'It's so lovely,' I say. 'Why did we not come this way before?'

'It's slower, but I heard that soldiers were moving on the main road. They'd likely slow us down.' His grip tightens on the reins as he speaks. It's a small movement but it tells me that he is worried.

'They would not bother us, would they?'

He shrugs. 'Who knows?'

We descend the hill and follow the road through the woods that surround the lake. Willows and laburnum droop here and there over the path. It must be a magnificent sight with the blossom in spring. 'I'm glad we came this way,' I say.

The horses walk at a steady pace.

'Sam?'

He looks at me, a frown creasing his forehead.

'When we get home, I will return the Du Bartas to you. It will be my gift to you for saving Middy.'

'No, Mrs Wolfreston, I sold it to you fair and square.'

'But I want you to have it. It was given to you.'

'No,' he says, looking ahead over the horses. 'I won't take it. I have no need of it.' After a few moments he adds, 'Anyway, I'm glad it's you that has it. You care about books more than anybody I've ever met.'

The road forks and we turn northwards along a narrower road. In the distance two cottages come into view: a hamlet where we can rest and water the horses.

Sam says, 'What did you hope to find in that tree?'

My shoulders slump as I look at him.

'Was it a book?'

The air seems heavy now, humid. I murmur, 'Yes,' then gaze out over the fields, hoping he will cease his questions.

'What was it called?' he says.

'I can't remember, Sam. It was an old one of my mother's. I'd hoped it might be in there.'

'Strange place to hide a book—animals would eat it. Why would someone put it there?'

I grip the skirt of my travelling dress as I recall my father's study, where charred parchment flew in the updraft of the fire and my mother's fingers reached into the flames for her precious book.

'Mrs Wolfreston? Are you all right?' Sam's urgent voice draws me back to the present.

'Yes,' I say, trembling. 'Just get me home, Sam. I want to see my boys.'

Part 3

'Say, that the sense of feeling were bereft me,
And that I could not see, nor hear, nor touch,
And nothing but the very smell were left me,
Yet would my love to thee be still as much . . .'

WILLIAM SHAKESPEARE, *VENUS AND ADONIS*

24

There is something strangely comforting in the architecture of Statfold House tonight. The plain brick facade is dark and sombre in the fading light. The lawn edged with tidy hedge is as orderly and serious as the house. Only the rambling vines climbing around the door break up the straight lines.

The door opens as we approach. George and Middy come running with Henry striding behind them.

'Mamma,' Middy calls, a crack in his voice.

In a moment, I have my arms around my boys, my face pressed against their sweet, plump cheeks. They smell of soap, and their clean hair falls over my face.

'We've had a bath,' says George proudly.

'I know,' I say with a little laugh. Oh, how I have missed them.

Peg is smiling as she lifts Nance's basket from the carriage. 'Welcome home, Mrs Wolfreston.'

I look up at Henry, who is watching me with the boys but has not stepped forward to greet me himself.

'How is your mother?' he asks. 'Is there any news?'

I shake my head slightly.

He is regarding me strangely, as if he is not pleased to see me.

'What's wrong, Henry?'

His eyes slide to the boys and I can tell that whatever he has to say to me cannot be said in their presence.

'It's cold, let's get you inside,' he says, but then he turns away, calling to the boys to return to the house.

George runs behind his father, but Middy takes my hand. 'Mamma back,' he says.

Another new word, I think as I lean down to kiss him. 'Yes, Middy—Mamma's back.'

After I've tucked George and Middy into bed, I return downstairs to the library, where Henry is sitting at the desk preparing some papers. He doesn't look up as I enter the room.

I am unused to this coldness from Henry. I look over his shoulder at his sermon. He has underlined a section: *Small farmers rely on strips of common grazing land. When landowners enclose common land inside their fences, it creates paupers. It is selfish. It is not godly.*

'That's strong, Henry. The farmers will like it.'

He looks up at me, his brown eyes stern. 'There are some who will not.'

'Who? Who is thinking of enclosing their land in Statfold? Not the Broughtons?'

He lays down his quill. 'The Dawsons are fencing around their land.'

'But why?'

Henry is not listening. He takes my hand and looks at it. Slowly, he twists the wedding ring on my finger.

'What is it, Henry?'

He looks up at me then, his brown eyes on mine, searching for something, until I am completely unwoven. I am so unsettled that I have to pull my hand away.

'What on earth is wrong, Henry? Please tell me.'

His voice cracks. 'Is there something *you* need to tell me?'

'What?' I am mystified. I stare at him, confused. 'I don't think so.'

He stands up and rakes his hands through his hair.

'We're both too tired for this,' he says. 'We'll talk tomorrow.'

He leaves the library, pulling the door shut firmly behind him.

I clasp my arms to my chest, listening to his footfalls on the stairs, perturbed. The last few days have been so fraught, I have not considered Henry. Questions and worries crowd into my mind. I had thought perhaps there was an issue with the parish tithes collection until Sam mentioned some gossip about my mother's situation. But that would not cause Henry to behave in such a way. Would it?

My arms are shaking as if I am still in the jolting carriage. I sink onto Henry's still-warm chair. The baby flutters against me like a butterfly caught in a net.

I was sure of Henry's love before, but his opinion of me seems to have changed since my mother's arrest. He used to share his thoughts with me. Or is it my love that has altered? In my darkest moments, when I am most alone, it is not Henry I think of but my mother.

. . . Love is not love
Which alters when it alteration findes,
Or bends with the remover to remove:
O no; it is an ever-fixed mark,
That lookes on tempests, and is never shaken;
It is the star to every wandering bark . . .

I recite of one of my mother's sonnets silently. My breath steadies. My heart calms. I have to stop abruptly; my mother knows all the lines but I do not.

I stare at the rows of books that I take such pride in, such comfort from. Each one a tiny salutation to this woman.

I reach for *The Taming of the Shrew*. I open the book and turn untrimmed pages looking for the familiar lines. But the words on the page jar. This book is not *The Shrew*, I realise.

I look at the title. I am holding the second edition of *Venus and Adonis* that Mr Townsend kept especially for me.

I stare at the fire and suddenly recall my mother sitting by the fire in my father's study. She had recited from *Venus and Adonis*, her eyes gleaming, her pale hands clenched in her lap.

'It shall suspect where is no cause of fear;
It shall not fear where it should most mistrust;
It shall be merciful and too severe,
And most deceiving when it seems most just;
Perverse it shall be where it shows most toward,
Put fear to valour, courage to the coward.'

With shaking hands, I place the book back in its place on the shelf. She had asked me to look after that book.

I take the candle sconce into the dark hallway. The light flickers on the oak as I climb the stairs of the sleeping house. I blow out the candle and open the shutters. Before me, the moonlit cross rises out of the trees like the hilt of a sword.

My hands cup the baby growing inside me. If it's a girl, will she fail me as I have failed my mother? I sit on the edge of the bed, shivering, hot tears coursing down my face.

I wake in the half-light. Henry has already gone. He did not touch me in the night. His hand did not search for mine and, finding it, clasp it tight as if to assure me we were still strong together.

I dress in the cold bedroom, loosening the ties on my day-slip a little more.

In the kitchen the fire is roaring and crackling, but the room is not yet warm. Peg still has her cloak on. The leftover bread and the pies that Nance baked are spread out on the table surrounding the basket. She looks at me with a worried frown.

'Morning, Mrs Wolfreston,' she says with what seems a forced cheeriness.

'Is Mr Wolfreston at the chapel?'

She rubs her cheek absently and says, 'Tom Dyer mentioned they were off to Lichfield to see the bishop.'

My mouth falls open. Before I can stop myself, I say, 'The bishop—why?'

She looks uncomfortable. 'He didn't tell me, I'm sure.' She takes the pies into the larder and puts them on a cool shelf.

I wonder why Henry hasn't told me. His behaviour last night was strange and yet he'd asked me to return home in haste.

'We're running low on candles,' I say, changing the subject. 'I'll go into the village and get some this morning.'

Peg colours from her neck up. She removes her cloak and hangs it behind the door, smooths her apron, then turns, picks up a pan from the fire and rests it on a skillet.

'I'll get them candles for you shortly, Mrs Wolfreston,' she says obligingly without looking up.

I stare at her. Why would she offer to do that when she has only just walked from the village?

'Is there something wrong, Peg?'

'You'd best be resting after your long journey,' she says. 'That's all.'

The door opens then and Middy and George come in. Relief spreads across Peg's features. 'Breakfast for big boys,' she says, then: 'Oh, Mrs Wolfreston, there was a letter today. I left it in the library.'

As the boys settle down to their breakfast, I go into the library. The pages of Henry's sermon are still on his desk. Beside it is the letter, ripped at the seal. Thinking it must be another note from Charles, I unfold it and begin to read.

My dearest Frances,

I hope your mother is well and your trip was comfortable.

I have some news that may interest you. Please visit me as soon as possible on your return.

Your loving friend,

Candace

Why has Henry opened my letter? I wonder, examining the broken seal. It may be his right as my husband, but it is not how things usually are between us.

I re-read Candace's note, trying to make sense of how oddly everyone is behaving. Candace wants to see me urgently; Peg doesn't want me to go into the village; and Henry, who was angry with me last night, has read my letter. I will have to go see Candace and find out what's happened while I was at Hazelmere.

25

After breakfast, the boys and I walk to Broughton Manor. The grey stone manor house has been the home of Candace's family for more than one hundred years. It is regarded as one of the grandest houses in Staffordshire, with its steeply sloping roofs, long windows, a dovecote and two summerhouses in the grounds. Candace mentioned that her father has commissioned the building of another, larger house in Hertfordshire, nearer to London. When it is complete, Broughton Manor will become a dowager house that Candace may one day inherit provided she does not marry. Charles will inherit the new house.

The boys run towards the walled kitchen garden through a vine-covered arch that George calls 'the tunnel'. It is their custom, when I visit with Candace, to wear themselves out in the gardens and then find their way to the kitchen, where the cook plies them with ham and cake.

I make my way up the drive to the front door, which has a knocker carved in the shape of a horse's head; I have always admired it.

A young maid opens the door.

'Is Miss Broughton at home?' I say. 'She asked me to call.'

The maid shows me into a large room with an enormous stone fireplace bearing a Tudor arch above its hearth. 'Wait here, ma'am,' she says.

I am not usually received in this room, so I survey it with great interest. There are several tapestries hanging on the walls depicting scenes from Chaucer's *Canterbury Tales*. Silk threads glisten in the light from the three tall, east-facing windows. I run my hand over the curved back of the daybed and onto the sumptuous purple velvet. It is a room for entertaining important guests. The young maid has unwittingly mistaken me for someone of importance.

The windows overlook a side garden with lawns that run down towards a summerhouse of proportions that make the one at Hazelmere look like a hut. Beyond this, a small natural pond lies nestled in a grove of trees. A man stands adjacent to the pond. Tall, with dark hair and with a pointed beard, he wears a travelling cloak and is holding his hat in his hand. He is looking down as if lost in thought. Suddenly he looks up and stares directly back at me. I step back from the window abruptly and bump into a side table. A vase topples, and I lunge to catch it.

I am still holding the vase when Candace enters the room. I set it back on the table, embarrassed.

'Frances!' Candace says. 'I am glad to see you.' She embraces me, then leads me to a daybed. 'Let's sit here,' she says, patting the velvet. 'How was your visit to King's Norton? Did you see your mother?'

'I did,' I say, trying to smile but finding it impossible. I shake my head and add, 'It was difficult to see her held in such conditions.'

My friend's green eyes are full of concern. 'So she is still in prison?'

'Yes,' I say. 'My father is trying to organise her release.' This is not a lie, but it does not feel entirely truthful either. 'It's not easy for him, though. The fine is large and he's worried that his land may be sequestered. He does not wear this worry well.'

She takes my hand, and we sit for some moments. 'How is your mother coping?' she asks softly.

My heart drums against my ribs and I can hear my breath quicken. She must think me heartless to leave my mother so. 'I am worried about her health,' I admit. 'She has a cough. But there was no more I could do for her.'

'May I ask, how much is the fine?'

'One hundred and twenty pounds.'

Candace gasps. 'My goodness. I was not expecting it to be so much.' She puts a hand to her mouth; she seems to be on the verge of tears.

Before she can say anything more, the young maid enters the room. 'Mr Brydges was hoping to see you before he leaves, miss,' she says to Candace.

'Oh . . . yes. Of course. Please show him in.' As the maid leaves the room Candace looks at me and says, 'You have so much to concern you, Frances . . . You must remember to look after your health.'

The door opens once more, and a man enters carrying a small book.

Candace rises. 'William,' she says warmly. 'How sorry I am that you must leave us.' She gestures to me. 'Let me introduce you to my dearest friend, Mrs Frances Wolfreston, before you go. She is the wife of our rector, Henry Wolfreston.'

William gives a little bow. His features are similar to those of Sir James, but his dark colouring and heavy brow give him a grave, contemplating look.

'I'm sorry to interrupt, Candace. I came to return this.'

'This is William Brydges,' Candace tells me. 'I believe I mentioned him to you? We have been reading Du Bartas's poems about Creation.' To William she says, 'It is Frances who lent me the book.'

'It's a great pleasure to meet a book collector.' His voice is so deep that it seems to make the floor vibrate. He holds out the Du Bartas to me. 'Thank you for this, Mrs Wolfreston. It has been a pleasure contrasting it with John Donne's works.'

'I'm glad you enjoyed it,' I say. 'I haven't yet read all the poems myself.'

I take the book, relieved to have it returned. I stroke the smooth cover, with its familiar scent of leather, wondering why each book comes to mean so much to me. I imagine the officer who treasured it, and how in thanks for his life he must have persuaded Sam to take it.

'. . . as Candace mentioned that you have an extensive collection of verse, I thought it might interest you.'

I look up at William. His mouth has a hint of a smile and his dark eyes gleam as if he were amused. I realise that he has been talking but I have not been paying attention.

'Yes, Frances has a wonderful collection,' Candace says sweetly.

I glance at her gratefully. 'You are most welcome to peruse it, Mr Brydges,' I say with a brief smile.

'You are kind; perhaps next time.' He looks at Candace, his expression perplexed. 'Well, I have intruded on you long enough. I will take my leave, Candace.' He bows again then smiles at me. 'Enjoy the book, Mrs Wolfreston. It is a treasure. I would not part with it, if it were mine.'

As the door closes behind him, Candace turns to me, a hand on her slim hip. 'I know he can seem foreboding, but he is a dear cousin of my father's.' Her green eyes flash. 'I did not credit you with being conceited.'

'What do you mean?'

'You might have at least expressed some gratitude for the offer, Frances, even if it does not interest you.'

I gape at her. 'What offer?'

'He invited you to visit Bridgewater. His aunt was the first Countess of Bridgewater, Lady Frances Edgerton. She collected many excellent books, mostly of William Shakespeare.'

'Oh no,' I say, reaching for the back of a chair. 'I didn't hear him.'

'Did not hear him?' Candace looks surprised. 'He has a voice that is impossible to ignore.'

Flushed with embarrassment, my shoulders slump as I sink onto the chair. 'Oh, I am sorry, Candace. I haven't slept well all week. I can't seem to concentrate.'

The young maid enters with a jug of ale and some cake. Candace walks to the window while the maid pours the ale.

'Frances,' Candace says, 'it is an honour to be invited to the Bridgewater estate—an honour that no one would refuse. What must William be thinking?'

'That I am deranged, I should think.'

She sits down in a chair beside mine. 'I meant what he must think of *me*. He intended for me to accompany you there, Frances.'

I exhale slowly as I realise how much this visit meant to Candace. I touch her hand by way of apology. 'I should not have come,' I say.

She attempts a smile. 'I invited you,' she reminds me.

The ale is strong. I place the cup down and take some cake to counter the bitterness. 'What did you want to talk to me about?' I ask, wiping the crumbs from my lips.

She tilts her head. 'To meet William before he left.'

'What about this parish business?' I ask steadily.

She shakes her head. 'What business is that? I don't know anything about it, only that Charles wrote to Henry. Why? What has Henry told you?'

'Nothing. But he has gone this morning to Lichfield to see the bishop.'

'That's peculiar. Charles has gone to Lichfield too.' She frowns. 'It is likely to do with the tithes. Money is usually at the root of all problems.'

'That is so.'

An awkward silence falls between us.

We sit for a few moments. I touch my belly, wondering if I should mention my condition to Candace.

She gazes at the Du Bartas lying on the table as if contemplating something.

'Will you continue teaching the Kavanagh boys to read, now that you've returned?'

'Yes, I'll send word to their mother.'

She nods. Then she says decisively, 'I'll write to William. I will explain that you have been distracted by family matters and that you misunderstood his invitation. He will ask you again soon, I am sure.'

I wonder why she is so keen that I visit Bridgewater.

'Thank you.' I smile wryly. 'But I cannot go anywhere at the moment, I'm afraid. I have to look after the boys, and I am too worried about my mother to enjoy social calls.'

Candace bites her lip. 'I'm so sorry. I should have realised.'

I pat her hand. 'It is all right. I am thankful. But perhaps you should go to Bridgewater without me? You would enjoy seeing the book collection and William would enjoy your company.'

'It's not what you think, Frances.'

'What is it then?'

Her cheeks glowing pink, she stands up abruptly, brushing at her dress. 'Now you must come down to the kitchen. I have something that the boys will love.'

26

I feel heavy with disappointment as we leave Broughton Manor and walk along the curving drive towards the edge of the village. Candace seemed so preoccupied by this William Brydges that she seems not to have properly registered my distress about my mother. I was hoping she might offer to help resolve the situation.

As we reach the small hill above Statfold, I gaze at the view over the watermill and the village pond. Just beyond, the chimney of Hannah Smythe's cottage is visible among the trees.

I consider visiting her, as my mother exhorted me to listen to her, but I'm too tired to walk along the long, narrow lane to her house today.

Something catches my eye and I turn to the other side of the pond. It looks like the Hardings' barn door has just been closed.

'Let's go down through the village, boys.'

George pushes back the ferns to make a shortcut down the hill. Middy follows behind, carrying a puppy in his arms. It is the runt of a litter from the Broughton hounds. Middy hasn't taken his eyes off it since Candace tucked it into his arms in the kitchen.

As we reach the watermill, John Patterson and his boy are unloading sacks of grain from a cart. I bid him good afternoon. He tips his hat in response and swings a sack onto his back. He seems to shrink under the weight of it, but he trudges into the mill. His boy, a fair-haired lad, follows with the next one.

Middy sets the pup down on the grass and he and George drop down beside it, laughing as it waddles and sits. It is a sweet little thing. It may prove its worth when it grows. I slip my windblown hair under my hat and rest my hands on my hips as I watch them. The door of the barn squeaks, and Jane Harding steps out carrying a bundle. She glances over at me and I wave. Jane hesitates, nods, and then ducks inside her cottage.

The barn door swings wide in the wind, revealing a man in a red neckerchief. He's looking around as if he's sizing the place up. I wonder if the forge is being rented out. The village needs a smithy, but that would leave the Hardings without a home, for the smithy would need the cottage.

Squinting back at Jane's house, I glimpse her at the window. When she notices me watching, she turns away. I look around, wondering if Grace is about. There are three villagers at the well behind me, talking. Mrs Brown lowers a bucket into the well, then looks up and catches my eye.

'Good day, Mrs Brown,' I say pleasantly.

The women stop talking. Mrs Brown responds politely, but immediately busies herself heaving up her bucket. The other women look away.

My skin tingles and I have the sense that there's something I'm not seeing. I look around, but the village is still save the pull of the bucket from the well and the gentle movement of Jane's barn door in the wind. The only sounds are the swish of the water over the water-wheel and the pup's snuffling in the grass.

My hair feels damp and burdensome, like a weight pressing on me. Clouds are scurrying from the south-west. There's a storm coming. At my feet, the puppy whimpers.

'Let's go, boys,' I say, eager to be gone from here. 'Middy, I'll carry the pup now.'

I tuck the puppy inside my cloak. Its wriggling warmth comforts me. I imagine how this new child might feel in my arms. I push the thought away—there's a long way to go yet.

The storm strikes as we near Statfold House and icy rain hits our faces as we run the final yards. Peg throws open the door and we hurry inside before she slams it shut again.

Rain drums on the windows. It runs under the back door onto the kitchen flagstones. Peg chases it with a mop.

'Go check all the windows are closed,' I shout to the boys. Raindrops seem to bounce off the cobbles in the stable yard. The stable doors are bolted, and I wonder if the horses are inside. 'Did Mr Wolfreston make it home?' I ask.

The room is so dim now, I can barely see Peg shake her head. 'And Sam?'

'I haven't seen him since this morning.'

'Where is he?'

Peg shrugs.

I smile to myself. She's never warmed to Sam.

'I came back through the village, Peg.'

She stops mopping and lifts her head to look at me. 'Idle tongues and idle minds, that's what,' she says.

The pup is shivering. I pull off my wet cloak, wrap the pup in my shawl and sit by the fire cradling it.

'They're all shut,' calls George as the boys troop back into the kitchen. He drops into the chair opposite mine and rubs his hair with a drying linen.

Peg catches Middy as he reaches for the pup. 'Let me dry you first.'

As soon as Middy is free, he kneels beside me and gazes at the pup adoringly. Laughing, I give him my warm seat and the pup to cradle.

Even by the window, it is too dark to read, so I light a candle and sit at the table with Grey's Almanac. I make notes in the margins of each page of the days I have missed: Middy's new pup, the return of the Du Bartas, the money spent on candles in the last two weeks, how many jars of preserves were made. As the storm eases, I read aloud a story from the almanac about a boy who stole apples from a farmer. George and Middy laugh at all the attempts of the farmer to catch the lad in the act. Even Peg's shoulders shake a little as she stirs the stew. She enjoys it when I read aloud, although of course she would never say so. As I close the book, I notice that the rain has quietened and the room is brighter. Outside, snow now tumbles and gusts.

I lean against the window, peering out. 'Lord have mercy. I've never seen snow this thick.'

'What is this, Mrs Wolfreston?' Peg is beside me, holding a hessian sack. 'I found it in the bottom of that basket you brought home.'

'Oh, that's a cheese for the boys,' I say, remembering Nance's comment.

Peg's eyes widen. She holds the sack out towards me as if it contains vermin. 'That's not cheese.'

Peg watches me as I take it, a half-frown still lingering on her forehead. Her close observation makes me wary, so I open the sack a little and peek inside.

There's a rectangular package tied carefully with blue wool—the same kind my mother uses to tie up the lavender to dry. My hands begin to tremble.

'Would you heat some milk for the boys and the pup, Peg? I'll be in the library.'

The library is frigid. Snow is piled against the bottom of the window and the copper beech is a shadowy outline among swirling flakes. As I pass the shelves of books and lay the package on Henry's desk, my heart pounds. I recall my mother sitting on the floor of that dim cell.

I loosen the wool and unwrap the cloth. Five books are bound together with a piece of twine. The title of the top volume is obscured by a piece of parchment. I quickly untie the bundle and pick up the folded note. It reads simply: *For Frannie*. The handwriting is my mother's.

I stare at the brief note wondering what instruction my mother gave Nance about these books. Could she have known she would be arrested? Perhaps someone tried to warn her as I warned Hannah Smythe. But why would she want me to have them now? Unless . . . I clutch my mother's books against my chest and sob.

My eyes are swollen and my throat aches when I finally stop crying. I place the books on a shelf. I cannot look at them yet. Then, wiping my face, I take a deep breath and return to the warm kitchen.

Peg watches me as I lift a basket of plums onto the table, sniffing back tears.

'You all right, Mrs Wolfreston?' Peg asks.

'Of course,' I say, removing the stone from a plum and cutting the flesh into slices, preparing to make a preserve.

Later, as Peg cuts some bread for the boys, I stand at the window watching the snow, biting my lip. I wrap my arms tight around my chest, remembering the strength of my mother's embrace.

27

In the middle of the night, I wake to a banging. I pull on a shawl and run down the stairs to find Peg, who decided to stay overnight because of the snow, already standing behind the oak door.

'Who be there?' Peg calls.

'It's me,' Henry calls.

I open the door and pull him inside.

He stamps the snow from his feet, while I pull his sodden woollen cloak from his shoulders then usher him towards the fire that Peg is stoking.

'Tom has set out for home. We put the horses in the stable.'

'Heat some food, will you, Peg?' I ask. 'He's chilled through.'

Henry's hands are so stiff and sore from the cold he can't even pull off his boots. I tug at them then rub his frozen feet vigorously.

'I thought you would stay in Lichfield or Tamworth,' I say to Henry.

'We got lost before we even reached Tamworth. Had no choice but to keep moving.' His eyes are rimmed red, his voice hoarse.

'Well, you're home now,' I murmur.

His eyes rest on me, but he looks away before they soften. He's still troubled. I wish he would talk to me, tell me what he's thinking and feeling.

I drape a blanket around his shoulders, letting my hands rest on him a moment.

He takes a long draught of ale, gazes into the fire. 'The bishop has ordered an investigation,' he says.

I inhale. 'I'm sorry, Henry.'

'What?'

'I went to the village today and no one would talk with me. They must have heard about my mother too.'

He pulls the blanket around him and leans closer to the fire. 'The trouble is not to do with your mother,' he says.

I frown. 'Well, what is it then?'

He stares at me wide-eyed, as if he can't believe I don't know. 'The recusancy record,' he says.

As I gaze at him, I can feel my mouth falling open.

'You deliberately omitted Hannah Smythe's name from the recusancy records. Everyone knows. Mrs Edwards has made sure of it.'

'Oh, that . . .' My voice falters. 'I couldn't find her in the birth register. I wanted to check the Rivermead records before committing her name into our records.'

Henry brushes some invisible snow from his leg. He looks at me and I can see that he doesn't believe me.

'Her house is in the parish. Tom Dyer could have confirmed that, if you'd asked him. I could have confirmed that, if you'd asked me.'

Doubt fills me. 'I meant to,' I say.

'Well, you didn't, and now the bishop thinks I'm up to something.' His voice is calm, but his eyes are burning with anger. 'What were you thinking, Frances? You know the woman hasn't been to church for years.'

He returns his gaze to the fire, as if he can't bear to look at me.

I stare at the flames too, but I am unable to feel their warmth.

'We have nothing but this parish, Frances,' Henry says. 'And those records are in my name. When you write anything, you are writing in my name, not yours.'

My heart is beating like a bird's—so rapidly I can barely sit still. My mother's predicament has consumed all my waking hours; I'd assumed I would have time to fix the records.

Peg bustles in with a bowl of steaming potage for Henry. He dips bread into the stew and eats as though he is starving.

'What will happen to Mrs Smythe?' I say quietly, as Peg closes the door.

'The sheriff's men will take her.'

'But we've only been keeping recusancy records a few weeks. How can they?'

Henry wipes the last of the bread around the empty bowl and chews it slowly. Then he looks over at me as though I am a child.

'Mrs Edwards told the bishop that Mrs Smythe has been a recusant for years and that you have been shielding her.'

'But that's not right, Henry,' I say, my voice quivering. The baby lurches, surprising me. I wrap my arms around my belly protectively. 'I visited her to tell her to come to church.'

Henry looks at me, his brown eyes dark. It's clear that nothing I can say will appease him.

After a beat, I ask, 'What will we do?'

'I will have all the parish records corrected and readied for inspection. And you . . . you must not interfere with the proper running of the parish again.'

'But I have done everything for you all these years. What will I do?'

He thrusts his bowl away, pulls the blanket from his shoulders and throws it onto the chair. 'Stay at home, tend to the children, tend to the household affairs. You need only leave the house to come to Sunday service.'

'You are not serious?' I give an uncertain laugh.

He drinks the last of his ale. His eyes blaze at me. 'This isn't a game. We are under investigation. For God's sake, Frances, you must do as I say.'

28

The snow piled around the house is a comfort as it prevents me from going anywhere so I do not feel confined solely by Henry's orders. While Sam clears a path to the stable, Middy and George make circles in the snow as they drag the pup on a board around the garden, its long ears flapping in the wind. Henry walks back and forth between the house and the chapel, head bent with an unaccustomed rancour. He says no more to me than is necessary and then only about the children or household matters.

After they have tired of the snow, George and Middy settle down to their lessons. I help Middy with his writing, holding the quill with him while he scrawls the letters. His progress is slow but there is a little advancement. If it is a game, he learns better. If I write an A and hide it behind an apple, he can find it easily now. I wonder if this technique will also help the Kavanagh boys when they return.

The following day, the snow is too wet so the boys play in the warm kitchen with soldiers that Sam made from bits of old horseshoes. Peg watches them while she makes a pudding from preserved fruits, and I work my way through the pile of *Mercurius* newssheets that Henry bought in Lichfield. The King has been moved from New Market to Northampton. There are talks taking place at Putney, where is it seems the country's fate is being discussed, with the Levellers seeking a new constitution and the Puritans resisting. I read aloud some news that the parliamentary army are still petitioning to get paid and comment how cruel it is to take men from their families to fight and not pay them for months. Henry listens but he says nothing. It seems after four years of war and this last year of uneasy peace, there is still no good news.

It snows heavily again in the late afternoon, covering all the tracks and paths.

The next morning Henry and Sam take the boys to the village. As I stand by the leaded window watching the snow drift from the branches of the copper beech tree, melancholy grips me. The beauty outside cannot lift me. I feel like a prisoner in this house. My mother must have felt like this when my father watched all her movements. How lonely she must have felt much of the time.

To distract myself, I take all the infant gowns from the chest in which they are kept, intending to repair and ready them, but as soon as I hold the soft wool and inhale the milky scent, my heart pulses like a swift's wings. I lock them in the chest and flee from the room.

I sit alone in the cold library. I cannot even look at a book. Each seems to take me on a circuitous route back to my mother. I dearly want to see Candace. I wish I had asked for her help.

The next morning the snow begins to melt. The boys' footprints widen into dark holes tracking across the garden towards the chapel. I pace and peer through every window like a caged bird. It feels as if there's a hole inside me—as if there is a part of me that's missing and I don't work properly without it. And it's growing bigger.

I can bear the captivity of the house no longer.

I pull on my cloak and step outside. Taking in great breaths of air, I walk past the chapel, past the rowans and the fat yews. I push the churchyard gate against the snow, and squeeze through. My cloak billows behind me as I take in the trees and bushes, orientating myself in this white landscape of standing stones.

'Near the willow tree, by the brook that chatters . . . so it's not too quiet for her,' I murmur, a dull ache growing in my chest.

I trudge through the snow till I near the long trailing branches of the willow. The brook gurgles to my right, but it's impossible to see where the bank ends and the path begins. I count the gravestones— three up, two in—and trudge through the snow until I find it. My hand dusts the snow from the stone. Soft as petals from a winter rose, the snowflakes fall away, revealing the name etched in dark grey letters: *Charlotte Wolfreston*.

The ache sharpens, cutting across my throat and demanding tears that have already been cried. I picture her dark hair flying around her face, blue eyes indecisively freckled with hazel. Running; she was always running. And George and Middy chasing her as Joseph used to run after me. Charlotte had a temper as changeable as a smithy's flame, from gentle to raging, white hot.

It had snowed early last year. She seemed to have just a chill, not even a cough.

She was gone before we realised how ill she was. She was just four years old.

Henry and I didn't talk for a long time afterwards. What was there to say?

I don't know how long I have been kneeling in the snow, but I am shivering when someone touches my shoulder.

'Mamma?'

George stands knee-deep in the snow. 'I've been calling you, Mamma,' he says. He points back towards the lane.

A man bundled in cloak and scarves sits astride a grey horse plodding slowly along the icy lane. As he dismounts, fabric falls over his breeches and I realise it's a woman. With the wrestle of a scarf, Candace's face appears.

'Frances, I couldn't wait any longer to see you.'

'What are you wearing, Candace?!' I cry.

'I borrowed a pair of Charles's breeches,' she says, lifting her skirts to reveal them. 'Do you disapprove?'

'No, but some might,' I say.

She shrugs that worry away. 'Only if they see me.'

She arches her eyebrows and curtsies with her skirt held above her breeches. Middy and George can hardly contain their glee. Candace kisses my cheek and gives my shoulders a squeeze.

The boys run to get Sam to tend to the horse, while I tuck my arm in Candace's and we make our way back to the house.

'I am so glad you are here,' I say, looking at her lovely face.

I lead her to the library, where Candace browses among the books while I coax the fire back to life.

'Let's keep our cloaks on till the room warms,' I say.

Candace is looking at a small brown book. It looks well-used and familiar, but it is not one of my books.

'Where did you find that?' I say, rubbing my hands to warm them.

She points to the small pile of books half-concealed in a cloth at the end of a shelf.

I join her. There's a scent of old leather and of sweet, heavy lavender from the pile of books. In my mind, I am sitting with my mother at Hazelmere on the evening before I married. She had packed a trunk with quilts and tucked dried lavender in before adding the linens. 'It will remind you of home,' she'd said.

'These are my mother's books,' I tell Candace. 'I haven't had time to look at them.' The lie comes easily. I have had plenty of time to look through the books, but I can't face them.

'I'm sorry.' Candace looks worried as she hands me the small brown book.

'That's all right,' I say, finding a smile. 'This one is my mother's first catechism,' I say, turning to the title page where my mother's name is written in the margin in a child's hand. I run my finger over her writing, trying to imagine her as a child. Swallowing hard, I scan the pages, looking for any inscriptions or messages inside the cover, but there are none.

Candace is at my shoulder. 'What is it, Frances? Are you looking for something particular?'

'I think my mother told old Nance to give me these books, but I don't know why she would do that.'

She squeezes my arm. 'Perhaps she just wanted you to add them to your collection.'

'Perhaps,' I say doubtfully.

Candace picks up two more books. 'These look intriguing. *Hic Mulier: or, The Man-Woman* and *Haec-Vir: or, The Womanish-Man.*'

'I've read them,' I say, turning the thin books over. They are dated 1620. 'This one, *Hic Mulier*, is an acrimonious rant about women, particularly their immodest and assertive behaviour. The most heinous act, apparently, is to dress like a man.' I glance sideways at Candace.

She gives a satisfied chuckle and lifts her skirt to reveal the bottom of Charles's breeches. 'And the other?'

'*Haec-Vir* is completely different—and better written, in my view. It calls for women to have property rights and be recognised as individuals. It's a call for liberty.'

Candace says, 'Oh, I want to read that one, if I may.'

'Of course,' I reply.

As Candace picks up the next book in the small pile, my heart leaps and tears prick my eyes. The spine is worn smooth, but it looks in good condition. I wonder how it survived.

She holds it out for me to inspect it, but I cannot take the book from her. I cover my face with my hands. I take a few breaths, telling myself it's all right—that it doesn't mean anything is wrong.

When I look up Candace is peering at the book and then at me.

'What's wrong, Frances?'

My head spins and I sit. I breathe out slowly, trying to steady myself, but it is no good, panic is rising. My head feels hot, but I am shivering all over.

Candace places the book on the side table.

'What is it, my dear?'

I stare at the tiny volume of *Shakespeare's Sonnets* that my mother always kept in her pocket. 'My mother loves those sonnets, Candace. She can recite many by heart.' My breath is catching, breaking. 'Is there any message inside?'

Candace turns the pages carefully. She shakes her head. 'Not that I can see, but every page would need to be checked thoroughly.'

I take the book and breathe the oily scent of old leather. I turn the pages, searching for names, annotations or a message folded in between the pages. There is none.

I close my eyes, clasping the blue book against me.

'You look cold, Frances,' Candace says, leading me back to the fire.

The flames billow in the hearth as I sit clutching the little book of sonnets. I am aware that Candace is watching me, waiting for me to speak.

'I think she has sent them to me because she fears the worst,' I whisper.

'No,' she says firmly.

'But she always kept this book with her,' I say.

'Then she must have intended for you to have those books before she knew she would be taken to gaol,' Candace points out. 'Otherwise, how would they have come to you?'

I swallow hard. 'I don't know. Perhaps she told Nance she wanted me to have them when she found out she was going to gaol.' I stare at her, wondering if I should speak my mind.

'Tell me what's going on, Frances,' Candace urges.

'She's sick and I don't think my father is going to have her released in time. He is so angry with her, and I do not trust him . . .'

My voice falters. 'He wants her to sign an oath of abjuration so that his land is protected.' I stare out of the window, wondering if I should say any more. I turn and look at her. 'But she will not. And she can't be released until she does.'

Candace's eyes darken. She pulls the lace at her throat, her fist taut. 'Have you talked with Henry about this?'

A frustrated sigh escapes me. 'He is focused on this business with the register and Hannah Smythe. And that . . . that is all my fault, Candace.'

She sits by me while a gust howls in the chimney. The branches of the copper beech thrash and snow flurries past the window.

'We all make mistakes,' she says. 'That's what defines us as human.'

'Well, I am very human then,' I say, shivering.

She takes my hand to comfort me then gasps. 'You are frozen,' she says. She runs a hand down my arm. 'And you are wet through! Why did you not say? Let's get this cloak off . . .' She unties my cloak and eases it from my shoulders. Then she pauses, staring at my stomach. After a moment's silence she says, 'You stay here, dearest. I'll get Peg.'

She hurries from the room.

I let my head fall back against the chair and close my eyes.

29

My head feels dull and heavy when I awake in bed with blankets about me.

Henry dozes in a chair by the bedside, his chin wedged uncomfortably against his chest. His hand lies on the cover near me.

When I met Henry, he was eighteen but looked sixteen, with curly hair and cherub cheeks that blushed pink whenever I looked at him. I felt as though I were a prospective friend of his mother rather than a marriage candidate. As we walked around the garden at Hazelmere, my thoughts were filled not with Henry but of Tom Hughes.

Tom had a serious face but eyes that always seemed to hold the possibility of a smile. Whenever he passed, he would tip his hat and say, 'Mornin', Miss Middlemore.' I would nod at him, and say, 'It's a fine morning, Tom Hughes.' I loved watching his lips curve into a smile. I took to running down to the lane near the field where he worked. I would stand picking flowers or berries, waiting to see how his serious face lit up when he smiled.

In the winter he turned seventeen, Tom Hughes fell ill with a fever. He passed away before the doctor got to him.

I could not have married Tom—my father would never have consented, and I would not have been a good wife for a farmer. These things I always knew, but still I grieved for Tom. I always hoped to feel again as I did when he smiled. I never did. So, I settled on managing the accounts for my father, keeping the house records that bored my mother. When I was twenty-five, my father took me aside and told me that he had had an offer from Henry Wolfreston's mother. She said her son was in need of a strong woman skilled in managing accounts to support her son. That he would provide a good home for me. 'Joseph can manage the accounts for me and your sisters can perform your other duties,' he added as if to put my mind at rest.

The third time I walked with Henry, he asked me to marry him. I withdrew my hand from his and said, 'I will not make a good wife for you. I will not be quiet. I will not always do as you say. I . . . maybe I do not believe as strongly as you in the church, so will disagree with you on matters. You will not be content.'

His eyes scanned mine. He was not expecting this, I could tell. No doubt he had already been assured that I would accept his proposal.

I mumbled my apologies and strode to the summerhouse. I watched him walk back to the house, his head bowed as if deep in thought.

Later my mother came and found me. We sat in silence as the sky darkened and she pulled her shawl around her.

'He is a boy, Mamma.'

She sighed. 'I know he is not what you have dreamed of for a husband, Frannie, but he is a good young man.'

I put my hands over my ears but, as gently as a caress, she removed them and held them in hers.

'He will allow you to be yourself. He won't try to change you.' She gripped my hands tighter. 'This is your chance of a better life.'

When I stood to leave, she said, 'Listen to Henry tomorrow. Find out what it is that he likes.' Her eyes glinted as she nudged me affectionately. 'Do not judge him hastily, for you hate people who do that, Frannie.'

'You really think I can be happy with him, Mamma?'

'Yes, I do,' she said.

'Papa would be pleased.'

'No, he won't. Whatever he says to the contrary, he wants you to stay here and keep doing what you are doing. He expects you to refuse Henry Wolfreston.' She stared back at the house, her voice steady and soft. 'But if you agree, I will make sure he allows it.' Then she touched my cheek. 'You say so little these days, Frannie. Go find some happiness.'

I gaze at Henry now. There are faint lines near his eyes, and his beard has a strand of grey. His eyelids flutter in his sleep as if he is dreaming; his mouth twitches like a smile is trying to break free.

As if sensing my scrutiny, he stirs and opens his eyes. 'Frances— you're awake. How are you feeling?'

When I don't answer he takes my hand and moves his face close to mine. He kisses me but I don't respond.

'What happened yesterday?' he asks softly.

I shake my head slowly and pull my hand away. 'Yesterday? How long have I been asleep?'

'More than twenty hours,' he says, his brown eyes soft. 'George told me he found you kneeling in the snow in the churchyard.'

I look out of the window.

Henry's eyes follow mine.

We stay like that for some time, staring out beyond the chapel to the graveyard nestled among the yews. Charlotte never liked those shadowy yews.

'I cleaned the snow from the grave. I stayed there awhile.' My words disturb the silence like droplets rippling in a pond.

His shoulders hunch as his hand finds mine again. He studies my face, then his gaze settles on my belly. 'Why didn't you tell me about the baby?'

I close my eyes. 'I should have . . .'

'Candace told me. Well, she scolded me for not looking after you.' He smiles wryly.

A warm pulse rushes through me at the thought of Candace berating Henry. 'I have caused her a lot of worry if she argued with you. It's not in her nature.'

His smile widens. 'I'm not so sure about that.' He squeezes my hand. 'I want you to stay in bed for a few days, Frances. Peg said she'd stay and look after the boys.'

'But I need to see Candace. I think she or her father may be able to help with my mother.'

His eyes widen. 'That's your father's business. You shouldn't discuss it outside the family. We don't want the whole parish knowing that she has not gone to church for years.'

'Everyone probably knows already. Mrs Edwards is hardly discreet.

The woman hates me.' I sit up and throw back the covers. 'I cannot lie here when my mother is in gaol. I'm sure Candace will help.'

'There's nothing you can do now,' Henry says. 'Candace told me to let you know that she's leaving tomorrow.'

'Where is she going?'

He shrugs. 'I don't know exactly. She said it was a family visit.'

I wonder if she has written to her cousin William as she said she would, and his invitation to visit Bridgewater has been renewed.

Henry is watching me. 'Anyway, I don't think you should ride in your condition.'

'You don't care about my mother,' I say to him.

He looks hurt. 'Of course I care,' he says.

'Then *do* something.'

He puts his hand on the bedcover, inches from mine, then suddenly he retracts it.

'I'm sorry,' he says, standing up, 'but I can't interfere. I'll get Peg to bring you something to eat.'

He leaves the room and I stare at the closed door, feeling very alone.

30

A blanket of snow covers the harvested fields as I follow the boys towards the village. Middy takes my hand while George runs ahead, investigating dark spots in the snow for black ice. When he finds one, he calls back to me in his most serious voice, 'Watch this one, Mamma.' I shush George as we pass near the Dawsons' place. Mrs Dawson had sent for Henry this morning and he's more than likely still there; I don't want to alert him to our presence.

When we reach the village, I notice the Hardings' barn doors are wide open. Just inside, a man is working. He's about thirty, with long black hair tied loosely at his back. There's something oddly familiar about him.

As I approach, he looks up, his eyes bright as a blackbird's.

'Mrs Wolfreston,' he says, as if surprised, and then adds, 'Morning.'

I hesitate, wondering how he knows my name. Perhaps Jane has told him or perhaps he has guessed. I press my hand against my skirt, conscious that my black garb leaves little room for doubt.

'I'm the new blacksmith,' he offers, smiling.

'I can see that.' I watch as he examines a horseshoe and lays it on the anvil. 'Have we met before?' I ask.

'No, ma'am. I'm not from these parts.' His attention on his work, he nods to me as if the conversation is over. Without further warning, he strikes the shoe with his hammer. The baby squirms inside me and the boys cover their ears. I hurry them away.

I leave George and Middy playing with the Kavanagh boys, warning them not to wander, then I skirt around the pond to the narrow back lane that leads to Hannah Smythe's house.

The mournful-eyed cow is still tied to a stake by the door of the cottage, mooing plaintively. Hannah Smythe opens the door to my knock and steps aside to let me in. There is a welcoming fire in the hearth and in the corner, resting on a bed of straw, is a calf just a few weeks old.

'She was late born,' she says, waving a hand towards the calf. 'She's been sickly.'

As she closes the door, a heavy stench of cow hangs in the air.

'Do you bring the mother in here?' I ask.

'The barn roof has fallen into ruin, so I've had to have her in at night and during that last storm.'

'I'll tell Mr Wolfreston; we'll get you some help to repair the barn.'

She flashes me a look, her eyes narrowing suspiciously. 'What brings you out here, Mrs Wolfreston?'

I take a small jar from my skirt pocket. 'Peg told me you still have honey. I wondered if I could buy some?'

Moving as if her bones are stiff, she takes a pot from a high shelf and slowly, her thumb bent at an awkward angle, spoons the thick brown liquid into the jar.

'There,' she mutters.

I slide a coin across the table and the piece of ham I've brought.

She takes the ham but eyes the coin as if it's a bribe. 'The ham's plenty,' she says. 'And you could have sent your boy for the honey.'

'I wanted to talk to you, Hannah.'

She points to a chair by the table, and I sit down gratefully, unwinding my scarf, which feels tight on my neck.

There's a pot on the spindle from which she spoons thin brown broth into a bowl. She passes the bowl to me. I breathe in the rich, smoky scent of dandelion. It has a strong, slightly nutty flavour; she has boiled the roots rather than the leaves.

I put the bowl down with a satisfied sigh.

She stays standing, watching me, waiting for me to say something.

I clear my throat, feeling strangely nervous. How do you persuade someone to trust you? I try to remember how my mother used to talk to people, as she was a well-liked woman, but all that comes to me is the image of my mother crouched on the dirty floor of the filthy cell with her back against the cold stone wall.

'I saw my mother in gaol in King's Norton.'

Hannah's eyes flicker.

'She . . . well . . .' I falter, for I hadn't meant to mention my mother. 'It turns out she hasn't been going to church for some time. So, she's in gaol until the fine can be paid.' I swallow as tears press at my eyes. 'And she's sick—a cough that's going to her chest.'

Hannah sighs. 'I'm right sorry to hear that.'

I touch my throat, which is beginning to ache. 'I don't want that to happen to you, Hannah. I didn't write up your name because I wanted to give you a chance. Please—won't you tell me who you are?'

She says evenly, 'I'm Hannah Smythe, widow of John Smythe. We were married in Statfold chapel. Your father-in-law married us.'

'What was your name before you married? There's no record of your maiden name, your age or where you were born.'

Slowly, she spoons out dandelion broth for herself and sits in the only other chair, blowing on the broth to cool it.

Behind her, the bed is raised off the floor on a wooden frame and covered with a pretty bedspread of a dark cloth stitched around the edge of a pale green panel. At the bottom of the bed is a plain wooden chest, with a blanket folded on top. Under the only window is a wide shelf with two bowls and several herbs strewn on it. Rosemary and lemon thyme hang on hooks from the wall beside her tools and herb bag, and even more herbs hang from the wooden beams, among masses of drying lavender. The room would smell of lavender, but for the cow. It's a peaceful home, I think, as my eyes drift back to the bed she shared with John Smythe.

'It's a comfortable room, Hannah.'

She sips her broth steadily, not meeting my eyes. 'It were better kept when John were alive.'

'Is that why you stopped going to church?' I say softly. 'Because John died?'

She gives the briefest of nods.

'Tell me who you really are.'

'Why would I do that now, Mrs Wolfreston?'

'Because I might be able to help you.'

She says nothing.

'There's no other way out of this,' I tell her. 'Cromwell and the Puritans are fanatical. They will confiscate your cottage and put you in prison.'

Hannah gazes into the corner where the calf is idly chewing a piece of hay. The calf is white with a brown patch over one eye.

'What are you afraid of?' I say, my voice wavering.

She looks at me sharply then looks away again. Slowly, her hand runs over the rim of the empty bowl then, aware of me watching, she clasps her hands tightly. She closes her eyes and the lids flicker, as if memories are coursing through her.

She opens her eyes. 'John Smythe was a good man,' she says in a gruff voice, her gaze fixed somewhere over my shoulder. 'He had the fields beyond the lavender in them days, with flax and oats in them. I worked the fields with him before we were married. Did you know?'

She picks up a splintered log and pokes it into the fire. Then she sits on the low box near the hearth. Flames flicker, lighting her face so she looks brighter, more youthful.

'No,' I say softly, pulling my chair closer to the fire. 'I didn't know.'

'No one expected him to marry me. But he did.' There's a surprising pride in her tone. 'He never bothered me with questions—just took me as I was. There's not many that take folks as they are. But he did. That's what I always liked about him.'

She's quiet again, staring into the fire.

A faint moan escapes her. 'You see, there's things I haven't thought about for a long time. They've been locked away in a chamber in my mind, but now . . . well, it's like you've opened it and I can't seem to close it again. Things are coming back; things I don't want to be bothered with. John helped me forget those things, but you're forcing me to remember.'

Hannah's mouth twists as if she's in pain.

I bite back a question, remembering my mother's advice: *You must listen to her. If you listen, she'll confide in you.*

After a long silence interrupted only by a single bellow from the cow outside, Hannah speaks again.

'You ask me what I'm afraid of? You can't even imagine it. I can't go through it all again.' She looks me in the eye. 'I can't do it.' She drops her head.

'It's all right, Hannah,' I say in the soothing voice I reserve for Middy when he cries because he can't make himself understood.

She looks at me again, searchingly.

'It's all right,' I say.

'Everyone turns against me in the end. You will too, Mrs Wolfreston. In the last place, I had a home, I was about to be married, then it all went wrong. They tied me up and dragged me through the town. It was awful; I thought I would die.' Her voice cracks. 'I prayed to God to take me, but it went on and on. Then something hard hit me on the forehead and knocked me out.'

I clutch my knees, my whole body tight and tense, trying to understand what she is saying.

'What happened, Hannah?'

Hannah shakes her head and sits back on the low stool, wiping her eyes with her sleeve.

'Next thing I knew I was waking in my bed in the dead of night, clutching onto the sides of it for all I was worth. My head was spinning. I was shaking with cold and dripping with sweat at the same time.

And there were these visions coming and going in front of my eyes. People's faces, ugly screaming faces. I screamed out myself then.'

She rubs her right wrist with her left hand.

'I kept screaming. I couldn't stop. Then I heard my mam's voice, clear as a church bell, as if she were right there in the room with me. *Shush, Jenny wren. Shush.* I'd not heard that name for a long, long time. Jenny wren—that was what my mam always called me, Mrs Wolfreston.' Hannah pauses for a minute. 'I looked about the room for her, but I couldn't see her. The straw I'd stuffed in the window gap had blown loose and bits of straw were swirling around. Dancing they were—so many you could never catch them. I held up my hand to catch one. That's when I saw the blood all over my wrists and the sleeves of my dress. *Hush now, Jen.* I heard the voice again. But it wasn't my mam's voice. It was the widow Penny leaning over me. Her eyes were glowing yellow, like they were when she found out about her son William. *They'll kill you next time, Jen,* she warned me. And I remembered everything, then, and I buckled over and retched.'

Hannah talks rapidly, barely pausing for breath.

'The widow Penny—May was her name—was urging me to leave. *They'll come for you again. You need to leave, quickly.* She took me by the elbow and tried to pull me from my bed. But my strength was gone, and I rolled right back onto the straw. *Get up, Jen!* She was a small woman, May Penny, but she tried again—near wrenching my arm out of its socket. Still, I couldn't get up. I thought then I would die there. May Penny held a cup of ale to my lips. It spilled down my chin like I was a babe, but some went in. She made me sit up and drink the rest. Then she pushed me onto my side and said again, *Get up, Jen!*

'Every part of me was hurting, but I managed to haul myself up. The effort was almost enough to fell me all over again, but May Penny wouldn't let me rest. She shoved my shaking arms into the sleeves of a heavy coat: William's coat—it smelled of him. Then she wrapped a shawl over my head and tied a rope around my waist. *Hush*, she said softly. *Hush your crying now.* As she hurried me to the door, I took a last look around the place. My white goat was sleeping in the corner like a babe, my herbs were hanging drying above the mantel, my cap and my amulet were lying on the table. I took the amulet.'

Hannah stares into the flames and swallows. 'That was my mam's amulet, Mrs Wolfreston. I couldn't go without that.'

'How did you get away in the night, Hannah?' I ask.

'Well, at first I was glad to be out in the cold air, but I could barely walk. The widow Penny helped me till we reached the woods, but from there the path was so narrow that she had to go on ahead. I was so slow that several times I thought I'd lost her. Eventually I reached the river and saw that she was standing in it up to her knees. *Over here, Jen,* she called. But I wasn't getting into that black water.

'I waited as she disappeared through the curtain of a willow tree. A few minutes later she came back through the leaves pushing a boat. It was a flat-bottomed thing; it looked like a floating coffin. *It'll take you far from here and that's where you need to be,* she said. But I shook my head. I wouldn't get in that boat. Then she said, *'Twas my William's boat, Jen.*

'My legs and arms shook with fear but I crawled into William's boat. May Penny pulled the boat through the reeds into the deeper water. I looked at her old face, knowing I'd never see her or my home again. *Take my goat, May,* I told her. *She's a good milker.* And she said, *God be with you, Jen*. Then she pushed the boat out into the current.

'She stood there in the moonlight, waving. I was too scared to let go of the side of the boat to return her wave, so I just watched May Penny fade into the darkness. I loved her only son, and she sent me off in his boat.'

Hannah looks up at me. 'She was a good woman, May Penny.'

'Yes,' I say, watching Hannah wipe her eyes then rise and prod the fire.

After a minute or so I say gently, 'So your name is Jen.'

'That's right. It was Jen, and my mam always called me her Jenny wren.' Her face crumples into a sad smile.

'That's lovely,' I say. Then, without thinking, I say, 'What was your mother's name?'

Hannah straightens up abruptly. She walks over to the door and opens it, then busies herself untying the cow's rope.

'Hannah,' I say, following her, 'I'm sorry.'

'You'd better be going, Mrs Wolfreston. Looks like there's rain coming and I've got to see to this calf.'

The rain starts before we reach Statfold House. Soaked again, I run behind the boys to the back door and into the kitchen.

Peg sets down the apple pie she's taken from the oven and helps me with my cloak.

'It must be a wild one,' she says, eyeing my mud-splattered skirts.

'What?

'That babe,' she says, nodding towards the bump. 'It's got you running round the countryside in all weathers.'

My hands instinctively rest on my belly. For a moment, I wonder if the baby is affecting my judgement. My mood has certainly been low of late. I sit at the table for a while, breathing in the sweet aroma of apple pie, thinking of poor Hannah Smythe sitting on her own by the fire with all that lavender hanging heavily all around her.

'Peg, why do we buy lavender from Mrs Smythe, when we have plenty in our garden?'

Peg has that guarded look in her eyes again. 'I was told that old Mrs Wolfreston insisted on it.' She wipes her hands on her apron. 'Of course, if you want that to stop . . .'

The pup skitters into the room and tries to clamber onto my lap.

'No,' I say. 'I just wondered.'

31

There's a smart stone house just a mile the other side of the chapel, set back from the main village. The Edwards moved to this house when Mr Edwards handed over the running of their farm to his nephew.

As I open the gate, a black cat jumps down from its spot on the wall and walks ahead of me to the door. The cat darts into the hallway as soon as Jane Harding opens the door. Jane is covered in black spots.

'Chimneys,' she mutters, sweeping a hand down her apron.

There's a vigour about Jane that I like. I give a conspiratorial grimace.

She smiles and says, 'I'll tell her you're here.'

'I've told you not to go to the door looking like that, girl,' I hear Mrs Edwards mutter. She comes along the hallway, stick tapping on the floor.

'Well, well, look what the wind has blown in.'

I laugh, although I think she meant to be rude. I hold up a jar. 'I've brought you some honey, Mrs Edwards.'

Somewhat reluctantly, she invites me into a small but comfortable morning room. She takes a seat at the table and doesn't invite me to sit so I remain standing, eating the proffered humble pie.

She looks frailer in the morning light. Her hands grip her stick tightly, as if she's expecting trouble. After a few moments she gives an audible sigh and motions for me to sit.

'How are you, Mrs Edwards?' I say, removing my cloak and sitting on the horsehair chair. 'Have you had any trouble with the snow?'

'Not too much. I heard your husband found Robert Caldwell in a bad way.'

'Part of the roof of his house collapsed under the weight of the snow. They found him inside, trapped and frozen.'

'What does the doctor say?'

I shake my head. 'They're trying to keep him comfortable.'

'Hmm,' she says, looking at me with her uncompromising eyes. 'Well, it may be a blessing.'

'The Baxters also lost a part of their roof, but no one was injured.'

'What about Mrs Smythe? She's over that way.' Her tone lifts, and I wonder if she's hoping that Hannah Smythe has suffered some punishment for not going to church.

'Unaffected, I understand. The trees that surround her cottage seem to have stopped the worst of it. Actually it was Mrs Smythe I wanted to talk to you about.'

She stiffens in her chair as if bracing for an onslaught.

'I wanted to apologise to you for not keeping you informed about the parish records.'

'You don't have to keep me informed, Mrs Wolfreston. You are simply obliged to record the names I give you.'

I force a half-smile. 'Yes, you are right. In this case, I made a mistake. I couldn't find her name in the records and I wondered if the cottage was in Rivermead parish. So I left her name aside, while I investigated. Then, when I was . . . called away to King's Norton, I confess that I was so distressed about my mother I left the records incomplete and forgot about them until I returned.'

She raises her left eyebrow and looks down her nose.

'However, I wanted to let you know that neither Henry nor Tom Dyer had any knowledge of the mistake.'

'Really?' she says.

'Yes. Normally I am very reliable. They had no reason to doubt the integrity of the records.' I sigh and clasp my hands in my lap. 'It is a shame that our parish has to suffer this dent in its reputation on my account.'

'Are you blaming me for this?'

'No, of course not. It is unfortunate that I was distressed about my mother, but it is entirely my fault that the records were not up to date.'

She shifts in her chair and glances at the long clock.

'If I had followed your advice, Mrs Edwards, the records would have been correct.'

'Yes,' she says. 'That is exactly right.'

'And the reputation of this parish and its benefactors would not have been sullied.'

She purses her lips. 'I have only done what any loyal benefactor of the church would do.'

'Of course.'

I glance out of the window. A small patch of garden has been cleared—a green rug in an expanse of snow—and a robin hops and pecks at a piece of fat lying there. She has a heart then.

'And you were right to inform me of my mother's situation,' I say. 'I would not have seen her until much later, if you hadn't.'

She gives a conceited look.

'Henry and I would have preferred it if you had told us in private,' I add, 'but we understand that you meant no harm.'

She takes a cross-stitch frame from the ornamental table and picks at a loose stitch, to avoid meeting my eye.

I reach for my shawl.

'How is your mother?' she asks, her brow furrowed.

'Very poorly. I hope my father is able to get her out before . . .' I stop before tears come. I clear my throat and take a breath. 'Anyway, I didn't come here to . . . my mother is not your problem, or indeed this parish's problem. I simply wanted to say sorry.'

'What about Hannah Smythe?'

'I have done my best to persuade her to come to church.' I give her a tight smile. 'She has said she will come on Sunday.'

'Hmph, I doubt she'll be there. She's a sly one. I never knew what John Smythe saw in her.' She looks up at me finally. 'Or why you Wolfreston women insist on fawning over her.'

I tilt my head, wondering what she means.

But she has returned her gaze to her cross-stitch, applying the needle with a proficiency far superior to mine. 'The sheriff's men in our district are known to inflict the toughest of punishments. I hope you told Hannah Smythe that.'

My spine tingles—this woman unnerves me. I wrap my shawl around me and look about for my cloak. Several birds have joined the robin and are tussling for position.

'Anyway, as is my duty,' I hear Mrs Edwards say, 'I've told the bishop and I'll be going to see the sheriff as soon as this snow clears. You make sure to tell the rector that.' She leans forward, peering up at me as if searching for any objection in my expression. 'I do not hide my actions, Mrs Wolfreston. I am not ashamed of performing God's duty.'

To thine own self be true, I think wryly.

'I will let Henry know,' I say with the politest of smiles.

Jane Harding opens the front door for me and follows me out. She dips her hand in her pocket and takes out a piece of parchment.

'Grace asked me to give you this,' she whispers, pressing it into my hand. She turns to go inside.

'Jane,' I say quickly, 'what do you know about Hannah Smythe?'

She looks surprised. 'Nothing . . . she keeps herself to herself as far as I know. Some think her peculiar with all those bees flying about her, but my Grace likes her.'

She takes a step towards the threshold and I reach for her arm.

'Wait, Jane,' I say. 'Who is that new blacksmith?'

She pulls the door to and says quietly, 'His name is Jack. He's staying in the barn and paying me a small amount of rent from what he's making from shoeing.'

'Where is he from?'

She shrugs, her face fraught. 'I don't know. Good day, Mrs Wolfreston.' She closes the door.

As I walk home, my head is filled with questions. Where have I seen that blacksmith before? I must ask Henry about him. And what was Mrs Edwards implying about my mother-in-law? Perhaps I should visit Henry's mother when the snow clears, I think. It may be more expeditious than trying to get information from Hannah. Henry wouldn't want his mother to worry about the parish, but her knowledge could prove helpful. It is, however, the opposite of what my mother would advise. She would want me to listen to Hannah rather than seeking her story from others. I stop at the wooden gate, resting my hand on the frigid metal latch as the pain that accompanies any thought of my mother burrows into my ribs. What is it that my father has done to my mother that she will not do as he asks after all these years?

When I reach the lane, I remember the piece of parchment and unfold it carefully. Grace has drawn me a picture: a black cat with ears and whiskers. Underneath she has scratched in charcoal the letters C-A-T. The sight of the carefully spelled word fills me with such joy that I want to jump in the snow like a child. Grace Harding has started to read and write. No one, not even sour Mrs Edwards, can take that from her.

Trudging up the lane, I pat the parchment in my pocket. I will fold it inside a book. How wonderful to bring the pleasure of reading and writing to one little girl. It is a small success, one small word, but like each new word Middy acquires, it has a greatness about it. *Teach all your children to read*, you said, Mamma.

32

The next morning Joe Kavanagh and his brother John arrive in time for breakfast. Peg looks at me dubiously as I spoon out porridge for them, but as usual she keeps her thoughts to herself.

The boys have forgotten much of what they learned, so I start again at the beginning. It's not too long before they are making some progress. Middy sits beside them trying to scribble letters, but if my attention is on George or the Kavanagh boys for too long, he will wander off to the kitchen looking for the pup.

After the lesson is finished, George reads aloud a story from the almanac, while I review the boys' work and plan what to do with them tomorrow. The Kavanagh boys can write their names and read simple words like *cat* and *dog*. They are both trying hard, but neither is as clever as Grace Harding. What a pity Mrs Edwards stopped her from coming. As I watch the boys listening to George read, I decide to start reading *The Famous Historie of Montelyon* to them—a few pages each day. This will serve as a reward for sitting still and learning, and I know George and Middy will enjoy it too.

When Joe and John leave, George and Middy run outside to play.

Peg brings out a basket of apples and sets it on the kitchen table. Without discussion, we pick up knives and begin to peel them. I enjoy peeling fruit and vegetables, trying to get the thinnest amount of peel off, wasting as little of the fruit as possible. Peg looks content as she slices the apples and lays them on pastry. She adds figs and pears for sweetness, and saffron to give it a rich golden colour. Then we both lift and place the lattice of pastry on top and step back to admire it. It's a beautiful pie.

Suddenly, George throws open the back door. 'Mamma, come quick.'

Still in my apron, I run after him.

In the clearing at the bottom of the orchard, Hannah Smythe is standing among the bonfire ashes. She looks around as if she has lost something.

'She's been standing there for ages,' George says.

'Mrs Smythe,' I call.

She looks up, her face caught in an expression of grief. There are deep rings under her eyes.

'Come up to the house. Peg has a hearty lamb stew cooking.' I take her arm and guide her up the hill.

Inside, I help her into a chair by the kitchen fire. She looks small and out of place in the big kitchen. Middy gives Mrs Smythe a kitten to hold. She smiles and her eyes follow him as he joins George, who is tossing a spinning top on the other side of the room.

When I bring her a bowl of stew, she takes it gratefully. She eats, savouring every piece as if she hasn't had meat for a while.

'That was good,' she says when she is done.

I let her sit while I pick up the sticks that the pup has dragged over the floor and place them back into the kindling box. Then I sit opposite Hannah and, careful this time not to ask any questions, lift some threads I've been plaiting into a band for Grace Harding.

Hannah Smythe watches me work. 'You set me right off the other day with all them questions, Mrs Wolfreston,' she says. 'I haven't slept right since.'

'I'm sorry,' I say. 'You don't have to tell me anything else, Hannah.'

Her voice is low and gravelly. 'But I do.'

Peg, who is chopping vegetables, says loudly, 'I'll go and fold the linens, Mrs Wolfreston.'

After the door closes behind Peg, Hannah stares into the fire. 'Where was I?'

'In the boat.'

'That's right,' she says.

She's silent for a few moments, watching me plait the colourful threads, her breathing sounding shallow in the quiet room.

'After I left May Penny,' she says, 'I sat in that boat too scared to move in case I fell out. I could hear bats and owls screeching. I could see trees and shadows along the bank, but I couldn't see the moon. I remember that because I wanted to see the moon. I must have fallen asleep sometime, because I woke up. My eyes were sticky and swollen but I could see the pink sky, and I could hear a song. I recognised it. Then I realised it was me, humming.'

I stop plaiting and look at her. She's smiling to herself.

'I don't know how long I was in that boat. My head was heavy as an anvil, so I just lay there. I slept and woke and slept and woke.

Sometimes it was night, sometimes day. I didn't think about anything when I woke, just stared up at the sky.

'Then I woke to find the boat had stopped. It was caught in the rushes lining the riverbank. And I knew I had to get out or I would die.

'So, I climbed out of the boat and saw a narrow path, so I followed it. It wandered along the bank then climbed away from the river. It led me into the dark woods, and as the sun set they grew ever darker. I could hear the screech of bats and hear a rustling in the undergrowth and I was scared then; I thought I'd got out in hell.

'I didn't have another step in me, so I sat down under a tree. It was cold, a hard frost setting in around me. My head was sticky with blood. I said a prayer then to God. Asked forgiveness for my sins. Then I lay down to die.'

I lean forward to touch her hand and Hannah flinches.

Peg enters. 'I'll just put them pies in the oven,' she says.

I watch Peg without moving, without talking, fearing that if I do, Hannah might bolt.

The pies in the oven, Peg leaves the room again, closing the door behind her.

'Go on,' I say.

As if there had been no interruption, Hannah continues. 'Then someone was shaking me roughly. Each touch was like being prodded by a hot poker. *Get up—you can't stop here*, I heard a man say. I could hear myself moaning but it didn't seem like me. *Come on. Get ye up out of 'ere.*

'Then came a woman's voice, the sweetest voice I'd heard. *Stop that*, she said. And the man stopped shaking me. I felt the woman near me. She smelled like the lilac tree that grew next to my old cottage.

She eased the blanket back from my face, her hands tender and gentle. *It's a woman*, I heard her say. *Go get help*.

'She squeezed my hand gently, and I squeezed hers right back.'

Hannah wipes her face then, anticipating my question, says, 'It was Mary Wolfreston. And I was right down there in your orchard.'

I stare at her. 'My mother-in-law?'

She nods, satisfied by my surprise.

'Mary Wolfreston nursed me back to health. She rubbed ointment onto my wounds. She fed me as if I were her child. Her husband were none too pleased about it, but he let her be. Once I was up and about, she found me work looking after John Smythe. His wife had died and left him a widower.'

I put down the finished ribbon of plaited threads. 'Did you tell her what happened to you?'

She shakes her head.

'She never asked you?'

She rests her head back on the chair. 'No,' she murmurs. She gives a long sigh and closes her eyes.

I watch her, trying to understand why my mother-in-law would not question her.

'You all right, Mrs Wolfreston?' Peg stands by me with the poker in her hand. She cocks her head towards Hannah slumped in the chair.

I nod, looking around the kitchen. It's nearly dinner time. Peg picks up some bowls and carries them into the dining room. I stare into the fire, trying to figure what Mary Wolfreston might have known about Hannah and whether she'd ever mentioned anything to me. She had kept the parish records for her husband and then for Henry till I came. Had she somehow managed to hide the detail of the marriage record from her husband? Henry's father was a rigid man when it came to the records. So perhaps he knew about it too?

I feel a touch on my arm.

Peg says, 'Go get something to eat. I'll look after her.'

After dinner Peg and I quietly clear up the kitchen, while Hannah Smythe sleeps in the chair with the cat lying curled at her feet.

'Do you want me to stay?' Peg asks.

'No, you get on home, Peg,' I say.

I sit at the table, read a little and write up the almanac, noting that the Kavanagh boys came back to lessons today.

I stretch, my hands in the small of my back, then glance at Hannah. She looks exhausted, older than her years.

All this hounding of a person and I've been hounding her too, pressing her for information that is obviously painful to share. Unlike me, Mary Wolfreston asked nothing of Hannah Smythe.

Hannah shifts in the chair but doesn't wake. I decide its best to let her sleep. So I lay a thick shawl over her and go upstairs.

Weariness fills me as I climb the stairs. I open the door to the boys' room. They are fast asleep. The pup is curled in the crook of Middy's knee. I ask for God's blessing for the boys as usual, then glance quickly towards the door as I realise that I have made the sign of the cross, just as my mother always did when she blessed us.

When I reach our bedroom, I'm relieved to find Henry asleep as I have no desire to discuss Hannah Smythe with him. She is in my thoughts as I undress, and as I splash water from the bowl and wipe the day's dirt from my face. The marks on her wrists seem to encircle me, winding around me like ivy suffocating a tree.

In Tamworth some years ago, near the bottom of a lane that led from the church down towards the market square, I saw a small crowd of people pelting vegetables at a wall. One small boy was throwing pebbles. The crowd had formed a semicircle around a girl about fifteen years old. Her hands were tied to a tall wooden post. Her wrists were bleeding as she twisted and tried to turn away each time something hit her.

I throw more water on my face.

The girl's orange hair like a flame against the wood and her eyes wide with fear.

I sit on the bed breathing into the drying linen as I remember how I turned away: away from the girl's frightened eyes, away from the jeering crowd. I should have helped that girl.

I climb into bed. Henry wraps his arm around me, his warm hand resting on my belly. The baby kicks gently in response.

In the morning, Hannah Smythe is gone.

33

As the Statfold chapel bell chimes across the fields, summoning everyone to Sunday service, I sit as usual in the second row on the left with the boys either side of me. The front row, which is reserved for the Broughton family, is empty. Across the aisle from me, Mrs Edwards sits with her head bowed, her chin resting on her ruff. Her nephew and his wife sit on the far side of her. He is not her real nephew, but the stepson of a second cousin. As Mrs Edwards has no children, he will inherit after she dies. There's no love lost between Mrs Edwards and the younger women, and her nephew wears the fraught smile of a reluctant peacekeeper.

I turn around, looking for Hannah Smythe. Behind us are the Dawson family. After that the seating is free, but people tend to sit in the same place each week. The widows and paupers take up the rear rows, and if those are full, they must stand at the back next to the door. How it is that those with money are allowed closer to God—and the warmth from the vestry fire? Lord, help me, Henry's right: I am beginning to think like a Leveller.

The church bell stops. Everyone stands. There's no sign of Hannah Smythe.

I find my mind wandering again to Hannah Smythe during the sermon. How exhausted she had looked yesterday. I feel guilty for hounding her with questions when she's clearly suffered.

Middy taps my hand. When I meet his gaze, he looks unhappily at the ground. At first, I think he has dropped something, but then I hear it. The faint but distinct tap of my foot on the stone floor. My face burns as I fix my eyes on Henry.

At the end of the service, I follow Henry from the church. As I pass the rear rows, I notice Jane Harding smiling. She is blushing, pink as a plum. Sitting next to her, his hair shining in the light from the window, is Sam.

He looks up and our eyes meet. He gives a crooked half-smile. My pulse thuds in my throat.

'Hurry, Mamma,' George whispers as he pulls me outside.

I take my place beside Henry beneath the bare branches of a rowan tree and nod to each of the parishioners as they pass.

'Well, well,' Henry says, leaning towards me. 'Looks like the widow Harding is holding a candle for Sam.'

I shrug.

'You don't approve?'

'It's . . . hasty,' I say, trying to think of suitable response, while still unsettled by my response to Sam's smile.

He snorts. 'She needs a husband.' Then, as if that's the final word on the matter, he changes the subject. 'What do you think Mrs Edwards will have made of my sermon?'

I clear my throat; I can't recall the sermon.

'Go ask her,' I suggest, pointing to the corner of the churchyard, where Mrs Edwards is huddled in conversation with Mrs Dawson.

Henry strides over to the two ladies and, smiling, engages them in conversation. Just beyond the crowd wearing their Sunday best, I see Jane Harding, still in her black widow's shawl, talking to Sam.

A man with long hair interrupts them. As he turns to talk to Sam, I have a full view of his face—it's the blacksmith.

'Come, Frances,' says Henry, who has returned to my side. He takes my arm. 'You look as if you've seen a ghost.'

Mrs Dawson and Mrs Edwards, leaning on her stick, are both staring over at me.

I pull my cloak around me. 'I'm just a bit cold.'

As we walk back to the house, I remember clearly where I first saw him. He was there on that awful day of the bull-baiting in Tamworth. I was distraught over Middy, so my focus was not on my surrounds, but I'm certain the blacksmith was the man standing next to Sam as he handed Middy up to me in the cart.

After the noon meal, Middy tugs my hand to follow him into kitchen. He opens the back door and points. Hannah Smythe is standing on the green, clutching the amulet she wears around her neck, while the wind tries to pull the scarf off her head.

I walk to her, pressing down my skirts as my hair escapes its plait.

'Come inside,' I say.

'John wrote this note. Can you read it to me?' she says, taking out a piece of yellowed rough cut.

I take the card and read it aloud: *'Dearest Genie, For the sake of old times, I kindly ask you to look out for Hannah. She has helped me these lonely years. Your devoted friend, John Smythe.'*

She narrows her eyes. 'Is that it?'

'That's it.'

She snatches it from me and tucks it back into her skirt.

'Who is Genie?'

She doesn't answer, but paces around the drying green muttering to herself. I can't make out anything except, 'God Almighty.'

She stops in front of me.

'I'll tell you my name, Mrs Wolfreston, I'll tell you everything, but I don't want it in them records.'

My mother's words come to me clearly. *If you listen, she'll confide in you. And if she does, you mustn't let her down.*

I nod and we turn towards the house.

Hannah sits in the same chair in the kitchen by the fire. She sits and waits till the all the work is done and Peg has left.

I make a warm drink flavoured with aniseed, berries and honey, and pour it into two cups. Flushed with anxiety, I watch Hannah sip at it, hoping that she won't tell me something I'd be obliged to tell Henry or the sheriff.

Hannah sniffs the concoction. 'She had a way with herbs, my mother,' she says. 'People came from all around when something ailed them. They came to her more than they went to the doctor. That always made my mother laugh. She said Dr Laingborne was a sour, cantankerous man who told everybody they were dying and they must repent to be cured.' Hannah's eyes moisten as she remembers her mother. 'She'd help with their dying, and she'd help bring new babes into the world. Sometimes she'd hand me a new little thing, still covered in birthing muck, while she saw to the mother. She was delivering the afterbirth and she didn't want me to see that.' Hannah nods at me knowingly.

'Then this man came,' she continues. 'His name was Thomson. He was the sort of man who couldn't look you in the eye when he was talking to you. You know the sort, Mrs Wolfreston, I'm sure.'

She picks up the tea bowl then sets it down again without drinking from it.

'I'll get us some wine,' I say.

She gives a wan smile as I hand her a cup of wine.

'Well, he started it off. Every time something went wrong in the town, he blamed it on my mam. If someone's cow got sick, he'd say, *Wasn't she round here last week?* There was a boy who had fits. He'd had them since the day he was born, but Thomson insisted Mam had put a spell on him. Then he brought her sisters into it too, till every blasted piece of bad luck in the town was their fault. It ended with the three of them being fetched from their homes and dragged through the streets, with everyone shouting and throwing stones, turnips and the like at them.'

She stares into the fire, holding the cup of wine to her lips, her eyes heavy with tears.

The familiar pain starts in my breastbone, along with a sick feeling. I don't want to know any more.

As if sensing my apprehension, Hannah lowers the cup and looks at me steadily.

'Go on,' I murmur.

'I could hardly see, I was crying so hard. My uncle—my mam's brother—held my hand tight as he watched our neighbours abusing his sisters. Then it went quiet. Not a breath could be heard. I looked up and saw my mam and aunts standing side by side. Not crying or pleading, or anything.' She takes a deep breath. 'Then they hung 'em.'

My own breath catches in my throat. 'Like the Pendle sisters,' I mutter.

The Pendle sisters were from a town up in Lancaster. They were accused of being witches by a local landowner. I remember my mother telling me about it when I was a girl. She thought it a tragic case.

Hannah Smythe gazes at the flames. 'Aye, that were them. The Pendle sisters.'

'My Lord,' I say.

We stare at the fire awhile, not saying anything.

Hannah's face is red from the heat when she reaches for her amulet. She grips it firmly. 'I was sick with grief for my mam and those two aunties for a long time. They did nothin' but help people.' She shakes her head and her voice quivers. 'They had webbing inside their toes, you see, and they said that proved they were . . .' She trails off, sagging in her seat.

'Who looked after you, Hannah?'

'My uncle took me away. My name was changed to Jen Brown. I was only eight at the time, a skinny thing.' She adds ruefully, 'Still am.' She goes on. 'Then people found out who we were, and we had to move again. My name was changed to Coulter. I thought I'd never have a proper home, a proper life, but William Penny liked the look of me. He wanted to marry me, but he fell sick and died before we wed. A girl who'd had her heart set on him found out who I was. She said I was a witch, that I'd put a spell on him and when he tried to break free of it, I'd killed him.' Hannah's lips tighten.

'So, they dragged me through the streets to the square, and they put me in the stocks. I remember all the villagers screaming at me— they were people I knew. Women I'd helped with their birthing. People who'd bought my honey and herbs. They left bits of the ropes they'd tied me up with on my wrist and they cut right into my skin when I was in the stocks.' She pauses and rolls back her sleeve to show me the scars. 'Then they pelted me with everything they could lay their hands on: eggs, rotten fruit, dung. One boy even pissed on me while they all laughed. Finally it stopped, and I thought that was it.' She lets out a long, slow breath. 'But they left me there, and when it was dark, some of the men came back . . .

'The next thing I knew, I was in my hut. And there was the widow Penny—William's mother—shaking me and urging me to get up. She put me in William's boat and shoved me out into the night.' She sighs. 'And that was that.'

She drains the last of her wine and gets to her feet.

'They're hanging witches again around here. Pays well to find women to hang or drown, don't it?'

I stand up too, worried suddenly about the boys and Henry. What will happen to us if people find out about this?

'Cat got your tongue, Mrs Wolfreston?'

I stare at her, my mother's words ringing in my ears. *There's no such thing as witches, angel*, she had told me once. *They're just women being blamed for something or other.*

'I'm sorry I've reopened these old wounds,' I say.

Hannah smiles wryly. 'It's not your fault. You can't help being the sort that wants to put everything to rights.'

She pulls her shawl over her head.

'But you see, there's some things that happens to people that can't be put right. I knew this when I watched them hang my mam. It follows me around: lurks in the fields when the harvest's bad, at the village well when they see a changeling or hear some idle gossip about deformed puppies and strange-shaped fruit. I stay well out of the way, but it finds me anyhow. And once it finds me it grows as fast as a beanstalk till there's no Jen and no Hannah—just a conjuring of something out of their heads.'

She opens the door.

'Stay here till the morning, Hannah,' I say. 'It's not safe to walk so far in the dark.'

She clutches her amulet. 'I'll be right,' she says. 'No one comes near a witch at night . . . I suppose that's something to be said for having a reputation like mine.'

And with that, she disappeared into the night.

34

When Henry opens the shutters, I throw back the covers and get out of bed. I have been awake for hours, worrying about my mother and wondering whether to write to Joseph. I've also been trying to figure out what to do about Hannah Smythe. I wish I'd never asked her about her past. It's hard enough to carry the burdens from my own past.

'Are you feeling sick?' Henry asks, glancing up at me as he pulls on his shoes.

I realise that I've just been standing numbly by the bed. I feel reluctant to discuss my mother with him, and now I can't tell him the truth about Hannah Smythe.

Giving me a searching look, he says, '*Though men can cover crimes with bold stern looks, poor women's faces are their own faults' books.*'

'What do you mean?'

'You look troubled by something. I thought you'd like the quote. It's from Shakespeare's *The Rape of Lucrece.*'

'I know that,' I say, too harshly.

I turn away from his brown eyes, lift my day-slip from the chair and dress quickly.

My mind keeps wandering during the morning lesson with the Kavanagh boys. I can't rid myself of the image of the Pendle sisters standing on the gallows with Hannah looking up at them helplessly. I send Joe and John home early and take George and Middy out to get some fresh air.

I'd hoped physical activity would take my mind off my problems, but it's very windy outside, and the baby feels uncomfortable, so I return to the house. I decide to put away all the washed linens and bedding. On top of the pile is one of my shifts—too small for me now. I've been trying to work out how many months I have been with child. I think four and a half, but I can feel the baby kicking so it may be five or more. Though if it's five months, my belly should be bigger than it is. Perhaps the baby is a girl. I think of beautiful Charlotte lying in the cold earth. The first baby I lost was also a girl. Perhaps I have no luck with girls.

To distract myself from such morbid thoughts, I start sorting the linens on the dining table, near to where Henry is sitting.

Suddenly, there's a thundering of hooves in the lane. Henry stares out of the window then gives me a worried glance before reaching for his coat.

I drop an armful of linens onto a chair and follow him. Good news doesn't come at that speed.

In a commotion of shouting and dust, eight men in yellow tunics and round hats halt their horses in the lane in front of the house. Several of them have muskets strapped over their tunics.

'They look like soldiers,' I say.

'No,' says Henry. 'They're the sheriff's men.' He strides forward to meet them.

'Wolfreston?' a voice booms.

'Yes,' Henry says. 'I'm the rector here.'

A tall man with a grey-tinged beard steers his horse clear of the others. He's wearing a dark blue tunic with a yellow sash. He removes his helmet.

'We're looking for a Royalist captain called Grey,' he says. 'He has been sighted in Lichfield and Tamworth. Now we're searching all the eastern parishes.'

'What has he done?' Henry asks.

'Aside from being a traitor?' the tall man responds. 'He led a party that freed prisoners from the Lichfield garrison.'

Henry points down the lane. 'The village is that way.'

'We'll search around here first.'

'There's no one here but me and my family.'

Ignoring Henry's assurance, the tall man orders two men to search the house and barn, while another two are dispatched to the stable and orchard.

'Can you show me the chapel?' the tall man asks Henry.

Henry looks at me. 'Make sure the boys are indoors.'

I hurry towards the house.

'Where are the boys?' I ask as I enter the kitchen.

Peg, who is chopping vegetables, pauses. 'You sent them out to play,' she reminds me.

I peer out of the window. The barn door is swinging in the wind; the sheriff's men must be inside.

'Where's Sam?'

'I don't keep track of 'im, Mrs Wolfreston.'

Peg comes and joins me at the window.

'What are they looking for?' she says as we watch the sheriff's men.

'A Royalist captain.'

Peg snorts. 'There's only peddlers and paupers round here.'

I lift my shawl from the hook. 'I'm going to find the boys,' I say.

As I pass the stable, I glance inside. The men are still in there, searching the stacked hay. There's no sign of Sam. When I reach the small rise that leads to the orchard, I hear a man's voice calling.

'Where do you think you're going?'

He has a musket slung over his shoulder and a mean-looking mouth.

'I'm looking for my sons,' I say.

'Who's been sleeping in the barn?'

'The stable hand.'

'And where is he now?'

I shrug.

He stares at me as if it will compel me to say more. When I don't, he waves me back to the house. 'Your boys will be fine. Go back inside till we're done.'

Although I'm hardly reassured, the man gestures to the house again, with his musket this time, and I have no choice but to obey.

Shortly after the men have left, Henry returns.

'Did they search the house?' he asks as he comes through the back door into the kitchen.

'Yes,' I say.

He sets his hat down and sighs. 'They searched the chapel and the vestry. I tried to talk them out of it, but they were adamant.'

'I don't know where the boys are,' I say, unable to hide my anxiety.

'Send Sam to look for them.'

'Sam's not here.'

'Where is he?'

'I don't know, Henry.'

Henry looks concerned, but he says, 'Well, they'll come back when they're hungry.'

I shake my head. 'I'm going to look for my sons.' I leave Henry standing in the kitchen and hurry outside.

When I reach the rise above the orchard, I catch sight of George and Middy walking up the hill between the plum trees, the pup at their feet. 'Where have you been?' I demand. 'I've been worried about you.'

Middy's eyes widen, and for a moment I think they've been up to something, but George says, 'Getting fresh air, like you told us to.'

I exhale loudly. 'Well, stay near the house. There are sheriff's men about.'

The boys exchange looks.

'Yes, Mamma,' George says for them both.

While I'm writing in the almanac in the late afternoon, the boys sit near me, taking turns to toss the spinning top. Middy is completely focused on the game, but George is jittery, looking up at every noise.

Peg paces between the fire and the window, watching for Henry to come back so she can serve dinner. Suddenly she says, 'That's them sheriff's men back, Mrs Wolfreston.'

Outside, through the bare trees, I can make out a cart moving off, followed by several horsemen.

'I'll be back in a minute,' I say, pulling my cloak on over my shawl.

As I approach the lane, the party of sheriff's men passes, heading away from the village towards the Tamworth Road. Ahead, I see the cart disappear behind a tree; it looks like someone is sitting in the back. My heart quickens as I stare after them.

One of the horsemen at the rear turns his head to look at me—it's the man with the mean mouth. I pull my cloak tighter around me and look away.

I catch sight of Henry standing among the rowans. His face is so pale it makes me think of the whey after the curds have been removed.

I walk unsteadily towards him, buffeted by the wind. With each step, my heartbeat becomes faster, louder.

'There was nothing I could do,' he says, his face creasing as if he's in pain.

'Was that Sam in the cart?' I ask.

Henry shakes his head. 'Mrs Smythe.'

I gasp. Someone must have told them about Hannah. 'Mrs Edwards,' I mutter.

'No,' says Henry quietly. 'It wasn't her. Mrs Smythe handed herself in. I heard her tell them it was no one's fault but her own that she hadn't attended church; that she'd had a sore leg and thought she'd rest it.'

My heart is thudding so loudly the sound fills my ears. I picture Hannah standing on the green yesterday, gripping her amulet as if it were the most precious thing in the world. I should have told her it would be all right, that she could trust me. That we would sort it out together.

'Breathe, Frances,' Henry is saying. He takes my arm and leads me to the bench between the trees.

'It's my fault,' I say.

'No, it isn't.' His thumb traces soft circles on my hand. 'You're not responsible for her.'

I try to slow my breath. 'Did you talk to her, Henry?'

He nods. 'She asked if the boys would mind her cow and calf. I sent Tom to fetch them.'

I give a small moan.

Henry says, 'I tried to persuade the sheriff's men not to take her now. Told them I'd bring her myself tomorrow. But that damn man was determined.' He rakes his hair back with both hands. 'Why would she hand herself in like that? It makes no sense.'

I stare out between the bare trees towards Craggy Hill, which glows in the late afternoon sun. How desperate must she be to have done that? Perhaps she thought she might avoid an investigation that way.

My head falls against Henry's shoulder as we walk back to the house. He puts his arm around me. There is nothing I can do for Hannah now. I hate the way this life seems to suffocate women instead of helping them. It's all so hopeless. I want to bury myself deep and not have to think anymore.

Later, I stand by my bedroom window, staring out at the moonlight. The moon is a sliver above the shadowy trees. Everything is still. I think I hear the watchman in the village calling, 'All is well,' and the sound echoing across the millpond. But all is not well.

I imagine my mother sitting beneath that small high window in her cell, gazing up at the same moon. '*How bright and goodly shines the moon*, Mamma,' I murmur. If she is looking, she must surely feel my love and my wish for her to be strong.

I am about to close the shutters when I see movement outside; a shadow flitting. I peer through the glass but my view is obscured by trees. Then I see it again: something—or someone—is moving towards the barn.

'Henry,' I whisper.

There's a faint sigh behind me as Henry rolls over. I hold up the candle and stare at him. He's fast asleep.

I creep downstairs to the kitchen. There, I light the lantern, pull on my cloak and open the back door.

I walk quietly towards the barn, stepping on the grass to muffle my footfalls. I try the barn door and find it unlocked. I step inside and hold up the lamp.

'Sam?'

There's a creak and footsteps. Someone is in the stall at the far end.

'Is that you, Sam?' I say, walking forward. Hannah Smythe's cow turns her head to stare at me. I hold up the light. Looking around, I spot a shoe sticking out of the hay behind the cow.

'Who's there?' I call, making my voice as deep as possible. 'Make yourself known.'

The hay rustles and a fair head looks up.

'Middy!' I say. 'What on earth . . .'

Beside Middy, the young calf lies on a bed of hay, its eyes wide and blinking. Middy wraps his arms around the calf. To the side is Sam's blanket.

'Oh, Middy, have you been sleeping out here?'

He nods.

I sit with him next to the calf for a few minutes. Then I say, 'Middy, the cow will look after its calf. You must come back to bed.'

I lock the barn and take Middy back to the house. As I am walking upstairs with Middy's hand in mine, Middy says, 'Sam?'

I squeeze his hand and whisper, 'He'll come back to us soon.'

35

Henry is talking. He's telling the story of how Gabriel came to Mary and told her she was carrying the son of God. I am meant to think how happy Mary must have felt to be chosen in such a way, and usually I do, but this morning I find myself wondering if she felt sick in the mornings. She rode on that donkey till the babe was born. She must have been in agony. The Bible never mentions her discomfort. She is virtuous and silent, but she must have screamed during her labouring like the rest of us. I give a little snort at the thought of Joseph running for hot water and towels, for there were no women in attendance.

Suddenly conscious of the noise I have made, I look up to see Henry giving me a disapproving look.

I clear my throat and take out a kerchief. I am aware of people staring, but I gaze steadily at Henry. I watch his mouth moving but I don't listen to the words. I am sure he could have done more for Hannah Smythe. He could have told them that they must wait until the investigation is completed. He has that authority as the rector.

My jaw is clamped tight as I watch him. He could have done more for my mother, too. She thought him such a good man, raised by a strong woman. *He will allow you to be yourself. He won't try to change you,* she'd said. Yet, despite my rational arguments, he refused to persuade my father to act.

'*My tongue will tell the anger of my heart, or else my heart concealing it will break,*' I mutter under my breath.

Middy looks up at me, his blue eyes wide with alarm.

I reach for his dimpled hand. His little fingers wrap around mine.

At the end of service, I close the *Book of Common Prayer.* Middy takes it from me. He carries it carefully to the back of the chapel and stacks it on the table there with the other copies. There are only a few, for not many people can read.

I hang back, not wanting to talk with anyone. There will be no pleasant Sunday chatter from the rector's wife today. Sam waits at the rear door for Jane Harding and Grace. He returned early the morning after the sheriff's men came. When I asked him where he had been, he looked me straight in the eye and said, 'I was sick, and I stayed with Jane.' Embarrassed by his directness, I asked no more.

As if he can tell I'm watching him, Sam turns suddenly to look at me. He holds my gaze for longer than he should, his expression serious. Then Jane touches his arm, and the moment passes.

I feel annoyed as I watch them leave together, although I don't know why. I should feel happy for Jane. I place a hand on my belly and take a deep breath.

As I see the crowd in front of the chapel begin to disperse, I venture out.

Henry is talking to Mr Dawson.

'Mrs Wolfreston,' Mrs Dawson says when she sees me. 'There you are. My goodness, you're expecting.' Without pausing for breath, she says, 'Mrs Edwards is waiting for you on that bench over there. Her legs are bad today.'

I rearrange my mouth into a smile as she ushers me over, calling, 'Here she is, Mrs Edwards. I told you she was still inside.'

Mrs Edwards pats the bench and I sit down, leaving as much space as I can between us. Mrs Dawson stands awkwardly a moment, then—when it's clear that neither of us will speak in her presence—she moves away, though not so far that she won't hear every word.

'Good day, Mrs Wolfreston.'

'Good day, Mrs Edwards.'

She says nothing further, but gives me a hard stare as if waiting for me to say something. I return her gaze. Her eyes flicker and she looks away.

On her lap is a small sack. She removes a stiff yellowed parchment from it. 'John Smythe wrote this note to me before he died.'

She gazes at me; her expression seems caught somewhere between curiosity and anger. 'Hannah Smythe's had this all these years.' Her eyes glisten. 'All these years'—her voice hardens—'she kept it from me.'

'He must have held you in high regard to ask that favour of you.'

Her eyes widen a little. 'So, you know of his request?'

'Mrs Smythe asked me to read it to her just recently. That was the first I knew of it.'

'I knew John Smythe wouldn't go to his grave without thinking of me. He was something . . .' She hesitates, then adds quickly, 'It was before I met Mr Edwards.'

I recall the scent of wild roses and garlic growing in the lane in Hazelmere and Tom Hughes' violet eyes sparkling in the dappled light of the trees. He had been something to me.

She waves the note like a flag. 'I suppose this is meant to stop me from reporting her to the sheriff?'

I stand up. She has no concern for Hannah Smythe, just for her own self-importance.

'It's too late for that, Mrs Edwards,' I say. 'Hannah Smythe reported herself. She's in Tamworth gaol.'

'What?' she exclaims.

I leave her there, her mouth hanging open. I do not bid her good day or raise a hand of farewell to the hovering Mrs Dawson.

'What was that about?' Henry asks, following me from the churchyard.

I do not reply, and we stride in simmering silence till we reach the front door of the house.

'Frances!'

'Yes?' I say, taking off my cloak and tussling with the ribbons of my cap.

'You were blatantly rude to Mrs Edwards.' He stands in the doorway, demanding an explanation.

'She reaps what she sows. That woman rejoices in the despair of other women.'

He blows out his breath. 'She's an elder of the community and a benefactor of the church. You should respect—'

'Oh, leave me alone, Henry,' I say, thrusting my cloak onto the hook, and banging the library door shut behind me.

Henry and I sit in silence by the fire. We have kept our distance from each other all day. While Henry ate dinner with the boys, I sat at the kitchen table. Peg, red-faced and worried, offered no words of either query or solace. She moved around the kitchen, determined not to catch my eye.

'Why are you angry with me?' Henry says finally.

My head feels confused, cluttered and cross. I hadn't expected so direct a question.

'Hannah Smythe saved my life and Middy's. Whatever you think of her, Henry, we owe her. We should have done more to help her, to warn her.'

His face floods with colour. 'We did everything we could to warn people.'

'You set Mrs Edwards on Hannah Smythe's trail, when everyone knows she hates the woman.'

Henry turns to me, his nostrils flaring. 'I appointed a parish benefactor to an important role.'

'Without even discussing it with me.'

Henry makes a guttural sound.

We are silent again for several minutes.

'What else am I guilty of?' he asks.

'You could have insisted they left her here until the investigation was complete.'

'I tried, but she handed herself in. She admitted her fault. I told you that.'

I say nothing.

'What do you want me to do?' he asks.

'I want you to pay the fine and have Hannah Smythe released.'

Henry looks surprised. 'The church can't do that.'

'I'm not asking the church—I'm asking you.'

He shakes his head. 'If people find out we paid her fine, everyone will expect us to do the same should they find themselves in similar trouble.'

'No one would know.'

'Everyone would know. Anyway, I can't do it. I can't pay the fine for someone who refuses to go to church.'

Our eyes meet; there's a flicker of anger in Henry's gaze.

'Well then,' I say, 'there's no point in me telling you what else I want you to do.'

I start to stand up.

He puts his hand on my arm, his eyes full of concern. 'Wait, Frances. What is it?'

I resume my seat. 'I want you to help me get my mother out of gaol.'

He stares at me in disbelief.

'Henry, you said we would talk about this when I came home. So, let's talk.'

Without speaking, he pours two cups of ale and hands me one.

Then he sits back in his chair.

It's clear that he would prefer not to discuss the matter, but I wait, refusing to fill the silence.

After a few awkward minutes, he says, 'I know you're upset about your mother.'

I force myself to speak steadily. 'I am very unhappy that she is in gaol, when the payment of a fine would see her released. We could offer to lend money to my father.'

'We can't afford to pay one hundred and twenty pounds or even part of it. There's nothing we can do.'

'We could borrow from the Broughtons. There are many options we could consider if you truly wanted to help.'

Henry stares out of the window into the night. 'Your father should be able to afford it. He may need to sell some land, but . . .'

'You know he is refusing to act on her behalf. But she is my mother, Henry. She's your mother-in-law.'

He looks at me, his eyes narrowing as if he's wondering why I'm failing to understand. 'But she is his responsibility, Frances.'

A woman belongs to her husband, he means, just as I belong to him.

I place the cup of ale on the side table and look at him, aware that my eyes are flaring with anger.

'Why is it that men put money, land and just about anything before women? If I had the money, I would pay it tomorrow to get her out.'

'Well, you don't have the money, because you don't earn any, save a few pennies here and there on eggs.'

I stand up. 'Then I will just have to find the damn money, Henry,' I say, and I leave the room.

I go to the library. I stand by the window, staring out at the moonlit copper beech, nerves tingling as if something of my mother remains in the air. A cold draught from the window brushes my skin. The day comes back to me then, unfolding before me, unwelcome but refusing to be restrained any longer. It's as if it's always been there, waiting for me to be able to see it as it truly was.

It had been a sultry summer day. Nance was singing, *Rain, rain, stay away. Come again another day,* as she laid out the linens over the kitchen chairs because the grass was dewy. My little sisters were following her, getting under her feet, while I weighed the linens down with clean pebbles from the stream to stop them blowing onto the wet grass.

My father called, 'Frannie, come into the study for a minute.'

I ran smartish, for my father did not tolerate tardiness.

His question to me when I reached him was a simple one: 'What does your mamma like best?'

'Her books,' I said.

'And which are her favourites?' he asked, and I told him, listing the books that I knew Mamma loved.

He leaned his face towards mine. 'She must have a favourite among those.'

'Well, it seems like it's *The Taming of the Shrew*,' I said, 'but she prefers the old book of the shrew to Shakespeare's play.' But then I hesitated. I couldn't say that she loved her book of sonnets best, because I was the only one who knew she kept the little volume hidden in her skirt pocket.

My father's eyes bore into me.

I lowered my gaze.

'Tell me, Frannie.'

'She likes *Venus and Adonis* best,' I said, and he sat back in the chair and smiled at me.

'Good girl.'

A little while later, I was in the yard helping Nance with the chickens when my father called for me again. Nance seemed bothered by this, I remember now, for she glanced at the house then said urgently, 'Run and play, Frannie.'

But I didn't dare to disobey my father, so I went inside.

My throat is dry, and I swallow, trying to force the memory away. But my mind will not allow it. I rub my palm against my skirt, trying to rid it of the feel of Father's clammy hand as he tugs me towards the fireplace.

Before my eyes, I see pages burning, each one torn from my mother's playbooks and dropped one by one into the fire. Words deform, fuse and wither into the flames. The leather covers singe and hiss as they burn with a rancid odour that seeps into every part of me. My mother is watching in silence, blinking with disbelief. With every blink of her eyes, the hurt deepens. And my father watches her like a tutor punishing a student for refusing to learn.

My breath judders as I let the last of the memory be. There's no more it can do to me.

I wipe the mist of my breath from the glass. The moon shines through the branches of the copper beech. I take a deep breath and exhale slowly through my nose. Mamma told me that the beech tree is queen of all the trees and that the very first books were written on strips of beechwood.

'I see a woman may be made a fool, Mamma.'

I gaze around the library at the hundreds of books standing quietly on the shelves like an army of words that has served and can be called on to serve again. I run my hand over the copy of *Venus and Adonis* that I bought from Townsend. Printed in 1599, it's the oldest work of Shakespeare I own. I place it on the desk with a sigh.

'I didn't stand by you then, Mamma,' I say. 'But I will now.'

36

Heavy grey clouds hang over Tamworth Castle as the cart trundles into the town. I have no stomach for the market square, so I tell Sam to turn towards the blond stone of St Editha's church. On the way we pass the courthouse, a wood-framed building above the butter market. The building has been damaged and there is a large prop holding up one of the walls. Behind it is the gaol, where Hannah must be. I have four shillings in my pocket: not enough to pay Hannah Smythe's fine.

We pass the church and turn into a street that runs near Townsend's.

Sam ties up the horses as close to the bookshop as we can get the cart. It's still a walk down a narrow lane with the trunk, but Sam calls to a young lad to mind the cart and another, bigger lad to help him with the heavy load. So, we set off, a rector's wife, a scruffy soldier and an urchin in procession down the cobbles.

A bell rings as I open the shop door. There's no one around, just the faint smell of tobacco in the air.

'Put the trunk down over here, Sam,' I say, walking towards the back of the shop where the books are. 'Can you wait outside?'

I climb the stairs and quietly open the door to the printing room. Mr Townsend and another man are standing next to the press.

'Mr Townsend?'

The men look up.

'Mrs Wolfreston,' Townsend says, smiling broadly. 'What a pleasure on such a dull morning.'

'I've brought some books to show you.'

He raises his grey eyebrows then, asking the other man to excuse him, wipes his hands and removes his ink-splattered apron.

'What is this about, Mrs Wolfreston?' he asks, as we walk downstairs.

'I need to sell some of my books,' I explain. 'I thought you might like to buy them.' I open the trunk and lift out a few books. I hand him the book of Du Bartas' poetry.

He turns it in his large hands, inspecting the printer's mark, then flicks through the pages slowly, reverently. 'This is a fine book.'

'I have many others. Hundreds, in fact.'

Next I hand him the *Venus and Adonis* quarto that I bought from him and several playbooks that I bought in London. Opening one, he runs his fingers across my name, which I have written on the title page. 'Frances; that's your name, is it?'

'Yes,' I say softly. 'And there's these too . . .' I place Lloyd's *The Practice of Policy* and Raleigh's *The Prerogative of Parliaments in England* on the table near him. 'I bought these in London some years ago. There are several more in the same set.'

He picks one up. 'These are good books.' He lifts his head to look at me. 'Why are you selling these?'

'I want to raise some money . . . to help someone.'

'Do you mind me asking who?'

A lump grows in my throat. I turn and gaze out of the window.

'It must be someone you care for,' he says, 'for I know how much these books mean to you.'

I touch my lace square to my eye.

'There's a woman in the village, Mrs Smythe, who is in prison, and I want to pay her fine. She's a good woman.'

He nods. 'How much is it?'

'Six shillings.' I clear my throat. 'So, will you buy them?'

He indicates a chair by a bookshelf, 'Sit down, Mrs Wolfreston. I'll get you a drink.'

I sit on the leather-covered chair and fold my hands in my lap. It is embarrassing to have to ask for help. When I was organising the books into piles last night, it seemed so straightforward. It was obvious to me that Townsend would want to buy my books. It is an impressive collection; everyone who sees it says so. I look out of the window onto the narrow lane. Sam is standing opposite with the urchin lad beside him.

Mr Townsend hands me a small draught of wine. He brings a chair and sits opposite me, watching as I sip.

'I need some money, Mr Townsend.' My face burns. 'It's for my mother. I need to pay part of a debt,' I say.

He nods sympathetically, his eyes watching me steadily as if he knows I am not being honest.

A faltering breath escapes from me. 'You know about my mother?'

He tilts his head towards the front of the shop. 'Men talk when they're smoking.'

I look around for somewhere to put the wine cup, trying to push down the suffocating shame.

Mr Townsend takes the cup from me. There's a rattle in his chest as he sighs.

'Your books are mostly old, and well-used. If you sold them, you would receive only fraction of the price you paid for them.' He takes another labouring breath. 'But I can't buy any of these. Most of my customers are men and I can't sell any books with a woman's name on them.'

I stare at him, winded by his words.

'I'm very sorry,' he says.

I stand and, with my head lowered, take the books I'd shown him and start cramming them back into the trunk. The titles jump out at me as if emphasising my folly: *The Constant Maid*, *The Comical Revenge*, *A Quip from an Upstart Courtier.* I shove the last books in and bring down the lid of the trunk with a bang.

'Mrs Wolfreston . . .' Townsend says softly.

I shake my head. 'Selling the books was a silly idea. They have so much value for me that I didn't think through the resale price.' I look up at him, trying to smile.

He is holding out a handful of sovereigns in his ink-stained hand. 'Let me help you,' he says.

I cover his open hand with mine and gently push his fingers into a fist around the sovereigns. 'Thank you for your kindness, Mr Townsend. I really am very grateful to you. Good day.'

I leave him standing there, and I rush out to the lane, tears stinging my eyes.

37

I walk back up the cobbled lane to the cart, followed by Sam and the urchin lad carrying the trunk between them. The boy groans as they hoist the trunk onto the back of the cart. Sam gives each lad a penny and they walk off grinning. I watch them till they turn out of the lane. Each paid the same, but the bigger lad worked much harder for his penny. I exhale long and slow, my hand resting on the trunk. Life is unfair and that's a fact.

Sam watches me as he readies the horses. I pretend to check the lock on the trunk.

'You all right, Mrs Wolfreston?' he asks.

I sigh. 'I tried to sell him my books, Sam. But he wasn't interested.'

He looks along the lane, as if searching for some response. Then he looks back at me, his brow furrowed. 'Why are you selling them?'

'To get my mother out of gaol.'

He looks at me hesitantly, as if he wants to say something, but he seems to decide against it. After a beat he says, 'Where do you want to go now?'

'Home,' I say flatly.

As I climb up into the seat, I cast a weary glance at the blankets I brought to wrap around Hannah Smythe. I don't even have enough to pay her small fine.

The cart trundles along the cobbles towards the church.

As we approach the handsome western tower of St Editha's, I spot two figures walking in the churchyard.

'Stop here, Sam.'

I climb down and run to the back of the cart. I open the catch on the trunk, take out a book and thrust it into my satchel.

'I'll be back in a minute,' I say.

The paths in the churchyard have been cleared of snow but they are lined with piles of dirty slush. Above, bare branches stir in the wind. How different it looks from last spring, when the pink cherry blossom drifted over the path so beautifully that I took a longer route around the tree to avoid spoiling it.

I stop at the end of a path, behind a yew tree. Halfway along it, Bishop Divine is strolling with the dean of St Editha's. He is dressed in black with only a purple sash indicating his status. He has a broad, pleasing face. He was walking with Henry in the spring when I came upon them. I heard the bishop's sonorous voice saying, 'According to Townsend, your wife has one of the broadest collections around.' And when Henry saw me, he said, 'That's my wife now,' and the bishop had greeted me warmly, saying, 'Mrs Wolfreston, tell me about all these James Shirley books you have.'

I wait till the men come nearer then step into their way.

'My lord,' I say, smiling.

The bishop stops. 'Mrs Wolfreston!' He turns to the dean. 'Dean Wishaw, this is the rector of Statfold's good wife.'

The dean gives a curt greeting, clearly irritated by the interruption.

'I've just been to the bookshop,' I say. 'Then I saw you and I wondered if I might have a word.'

The bishop returns my smile, although his eyes are serious. Glancing at the dean, he gives the slightest of nods, and the dean duly murmurs, 'I'll wait by the north door.'

The bishop indicates the path he has just walked down with the dean. We walk in silence until we come to a bench beside a yew tree. Bishop Divine sits at one end of the bench and I take the other.

I reach into my bag. 'Oh, I have a work by James Shirley here,' I say. 'I remember you telling me you were fond of his work.'

He smiles and reaches for the volume.

'*The Constant Maid*,' he says, looking slightly disappointed. 'Now, what can I do for you Mrs Wolfreston? I have only a few minutes.'

'I wanted to explain to you the unfortunate mix-up that caused the recent issue at Statfold. I hope to set your mind at ease.'

He looks amused. 'Mix-up?'

I smile pleasantly. 'It was not Mr Wolfreston's fault, you see. The error—or should I say the omission in the parish records—was my mistake.'

'Go on,' he says. His grey eyes are sharp now.

'Well, I keep the parish records for my husband. Under his supervision, of course, but I write them. In the case of the recusants, Mr Wolfreston assigned the recording of them to me.'

'And this woman who wrote to see me?'

'Mrs Edwards . . . She gave me a list of names, and it was my job to check them and write them up.'

The bishop frowns. 'There seems little scope for a *mix-up*.'

I clear my throat. 'Well, there was one parishioner who lives on the boundary between the parishes, and I had trouble finding her name. I would normally discuss this with Henry, but I was called away by a pressing family matter before I could.'

His eyebrows and his eyes narrow at the same time, giving him a peculiar look—like the Broughton hounds just before they are let loose on a trail.

'It was my mistake. Henry knew nothing of it.'

His fingers tap his knee, the gold ring with the bishop's mark catching the light.

'Mrs Wolfreston, nothing you have said affects what must happen. There will be a full inspection of all parish finances and records. Penalties will be issued and reparations demanded accordingly.'

He stares at me as if challenging me to say more.

I have made a mistake coming here. This is not the pleasant man who commented on my books in the churchyard last year or who came to Statfold for the Easter meal. There is no sympathy in his gaze.

A sluggish wasp buzzes around us and he bats it away, all the while scrutinising me, judging me.

'We have a significant financial problem. Some of your parish benefactors no longer support the rector.' His voice is cool, calculated. 'So, how do you propose we rectify that? The rector was at a loss when we last spoke.'

I stare at him, surprised, and trying to grapple with the financial implications. Why has Henry not told me this?

His eyes rest for a moment on the ring he wears. 'I may be forced to merge Statfold into Rivermead parish.'

I bow my head and stare at my clasped hands. My legs tremble beneath my skirts and I put my hands on them, forcing them to be still. It is always about money. How could I have misjudged this so?

He stands and looks down at me. 'Good day, Mrs Wolfreston. Give my regards to your mother. I hear she is . . . confined.' The trace of scorn in his voice is unmistakable.

I watch as he walks past the bare cherry trees towards the north door of the church, his black robe billowing in the wind.

38

As the cart turns into the stable yard, George and Middy come running to meet us.

'Where have you been, Mamma?' George calls.

'Tamworth,' I say kissing his head.

'Did you buy anything?'

I hadn't bought or sold anything. I'd achieved nothing.

'No.'

They look disappointed but soon rally, each taking one of my hands and steering me towards the kitchen.

'There's potato and cheese pie,' George says.

My stomach growls.

I call over my shoulder, 'Will you take the trunk back to the library, please, Sam?'

The boys watch while I eat the pie, which is light and delicious. When only a crust remains, George says, 'Can we go play with Sam?'

'Yes,' I say, 'but stay near the house. It looks like rain.'

A blast of cold air enters as they open the back door. Peg tuts, closing the door after them.

I take my bowl to the basin on the bench to rinse it. Peg takes it from me and dries it.

'Where is Mr Wolfreston, Peg?'

'He's gone to see Mr Dawson. Left about an hour ago.'

While I wait for Henry's return, I take out the accounts. I review the incomings and outgoings for the last ten years, looking back beyond the time the country was at war. I am familiar with the accounts, of course, but I've never considered our household income as separate from that of the parish. We have some income from the flax and the wool. We have a small amount of rent from a tenant farmer. We grow much of our own food, but we also rely on the tithes and benefactors' donations to the parish. If the bishop were to merge Statfold with Rivermead, the parishioners and their tithes would go to Rivermead church. Statfold would become little more than a family chapel.

I rest my hands on my belly and breathe out, feeling a rasp in my throat. Perhaps I'm getting a cold. I should take some honey. Outside, there's a sudden flash of lightning. I listen carefully for a distant rumble, but when it comes it is so quiet I am unsure if it is thunder. A flurry of fluttering kicks nudges my hands and I turn away from the window.

Perhaps I am being too pessimistic. It's possible that I've made a mistake. While the thunder rumbles closer, I check the figures again.

The baby turns inside me. Outside the heavy clouds that have threatened all day finally burst. Rain pummels the glass. The branches of the copper beech, now slick and black, sway in the storm.

Checking the figures for a third time, I cannot deny the truth of the arithmetic any longer. Without the tithes from the parish and the donations from the benefactors, we cannot cover the basic running costs of Statfold House.

The wind whistles in the chimney and the flames of the fire leap up in response. As the fire slowly settles, I wonder what on earth can be done.

Later, while Peg sets up the bathtub in the kitchen, Henry and I walk in the lane, weaving around the puddles left by the earlier rain. In the fields around us, cows wander between sodden haycocks. Beyond them, on the lower slope of Craggy Hill, the distant haycocks are small as pinpricks.

Beside me, Henry looks miserable. 'Take a good look,' he says. 'It's all disappearing.'

'What is?'

'The common grazing land. The Dawsons are building a fence along all the boundaries of their land. So, there'll be a fence right across there,' he says, pointing, 'halving the common land. Others will follow till there's none left.'

'What can we do?'

He shrugs. 'They are acting within the law. There's no protection for common grazing. The Kavanaghs are furious. Mrs Kavanagh was ranting at me in the village today, in front of several other villagers. She said the church had let everyone down. I tried to tell her that enclosure has nothing to do with the church, but she wouldn't be appeased.'

Mrs Edwards has been the main force behind the protection of the common grazing lands, but Henry would have no leverage with her now.

'Maybe Sir James could do something?' I ask.

'Like what?'

'He has acted to protect tenant farmers before.'

Henry pauses at the turning into the village. 'I'll mention it in my sermon again on Sunday.'

I watch his troubled eyes as he looks towards Statfold.

'We can turn back here, Henry.'

We walk for minute or so in silence, then his hand grazes the back of my own, his little finger curving around mine.

'What's troubling you, Frances? You seemed keen to get away from the house.'

I smile awkwardly. 'I drove into Tamworth this morning.'

'Why?'

'I tried to sell my books to Townsend.'

Henry stops walking, 'What? Why would you do that?'

'I wanted to raise a few pounds to pay towards my mother's fine and to pay Hannah Smythe's.'

He sighs. 'I can't believe you did that.'

A wild rose hangs over the lane. There's a branch full of large orange rosehips.

'It was a stupid idea,' I say. 'He said he wouldn't buy them because I've written my name in most of them.' I nip a rosehip from the bush and hold it to my nose. 'Anyway, afterwards I saw the bishop in the churchyard of St Editha's. So, I had a word with him.' Henry's eyes widen but I continue quickly before he can react further. 'And he told me about the merging of the parishes.'

Henry looks over the fields, his left eye twitching.

'Why didn't you tell me?' I say softly.

His breath puffs out, but he says nothing.

'I checked the accounts. We can't manage without the income from the parish, even if we rent out all the land.'

'I know that, Frances,' he says loudly. 'I'm not a fool.' He's breathing quickly now and shaking his head. 'And I didn't tell you because I knew you would blame yourself.'

My fingers flutter as I think about touching his arm, a conciliatory gesture. But something in his tone stops me; there's resentment in it. I turn away from him. The wind rouses the trees, cows bellow in the distance, and we walk back to the house together without exchanging another word.

Peg has run a rope from the coat hooks by the back door to a hook on the kitchen wall. She has draped two old linens across the rope, cutting the kitchen in half. Behind the linens, near the fire, the boys are splashing in the wooden bathtub.

Henry glares at me as he deposits his muddy coat on a hook.

'I'll be at my desk,' he says.

I bathe the boys together in the tub, soaping their hair while the water is still clean, then scrubbing their ears, their toes and fingernails. They are shining when they climb out and into the drying linens. The water is filthy.

'It's running in the woods with Sam does that,' Peg grumps as she dips the bucket into the water. 'I'll have to tip the whole lot out. You can't get into that.'

While Peg empties the tub, I towel the boys' hair dry and slick it back with the wooden comb. They pull on clean nightshirts then I wrap them in shawls and take them to sit by the fire in the library so their hair can dry off.

Henry's staring into the fire. He barely seems to notice the boys as they sit on the rush mat near the fire.

'Do you want to bathe next?' I ask.

He doesn't answer.

'Henry?'

He looks up, seeming a little dazed.

'Do you want a bath now?' I repeat.

'No. I'll go in after you.'

I look at him for a moment, wondering if he's still angry with me or if he's feeling unwell. Probably both.

'All right,' I say. 'Watch the boys don't go too close to the fire.'

I return to the kitchen and, behind the linens, undress and climb into the refreshed tub. As I lower myself into the warm water, bending my knees so I can lie back against the side, I'm struck with the changes in my body. There are delicate blue lines crossing my bosom and the tops of my legs. I'm thinner than usual, except in my stomach. It's as if all the food I'm eating has gone to the babe. Immediately I hear my mother's voice in my head: *You must eat more, angel. Keep your strength up.*

My head starts to ache and tears smart my eyes. I can't help her, and we have no means to help her, even if I could persuade Henry.

My belly shifts, small soft movements, like a mouse under a blanket. I rest my hand on it and feel the baby ripple under my skin. A salty tear runs into my mouth.

I dip my head in the water and my dark hair weaves around me.

Muffled voices echo in the water. I lift my head and wipe the water from my face.

Peg says something in the hall. A moment later Henry responds. I wash myself quickly, the rough soap scraping my skin.

Peg's face appears around the curtain. She is carrying a drying linen and holds it up while I step out of the tub.

'Thanks, Peg.'

'There's a letter come,' she says.

'Who is it from?'

She shrugs.

Peg helps me wrap a linen around my hair. I put on a clean shift and pull my shawl over my shoulders.

I hover by the library door, watching Henry's expression of discomfort as he reads the letter and lays it down on the desk. He rubs his chin.

'Who is it from?'

He holds up the bishop's seal for me to see.

'Oh,' I say. 'What does he say?'

'He's coming to Statfold on Friday.'

The linen wrap around my hair is loose and water drips down my back, making me shiver.

'That's only three days.'

He rubs his chin again and gazes into the fire. 'Looks like your little talk with the bishop may have sped things up.'

'I'm sorry, Henry. I didn't know.'

Henry continues to stare into the fire, his shoulders hunched. 'He will address the congregation this Sunday. It can't be good news.'

The wrap slips off my head. My wet hair falls over my shoulders, 'Well, at least we'll be clean,' I say, trying to lighten the mood.

Henry doesn't respond.

I go to him and say firmly, 'You are not facing the bishop alone, Henry. Others care for the future of this parish too. Talk to Charles.'

He takes my hand. 'You're right,' he says quietly. 'We're not alone.'

Part 4

'From women's eyes this doctrine I derive.
They sparkle still the right Promethean fire;
They are the books, the arts, the academes,
That show, contain, and nourish, all the world,
Else none at all in aught proves excellent.'

WILLIAM SHAKESPEARE, *LOVE'S LABOUR'S LOST*, ACT 4, SCENE 3

39

The wan evening sky is layered with frayed strands of listless yellow that makes me think of whey spilling into water. I smooth down my old mulberry-coloured dress, made from a length of linen bought from a shop in Tamworth. But it is not a colour that complements my skin tone, and I look as pallid as the sky in it. My head feels dull as I watch Charles, who leans on the mantel, his crisp white shirt fresh against his red doublet. He is speaking rapidly, a breathy whistle coming from the gap in his teeth as he asks Henry questions.

Henry sits by the table with his chin on his hands, staring at Charles intently.

'Have you talked yet with the Edwardses and the Dawsons, Henry?'

Henry shakes his head morosely. 'I just got the letter this afternoon.'

'But you've known since you saw the bishop.'

Henry looks away.

Charles looks at me as if he cannot believe what he has heard. Our eyes meet. I swallow and touch my throat.

Henry hates to ask people for money—he is more comfortable giving it. He may thunder decisively from the pulpit, but it is Tom Dyer who leans on parishioners when they are behind in paying their tithe. With the benefactors, like Mrs Edwards, Henry works his way around the subject, sometimes granting oblique favours, until the benefactor asks what they can do to help the parish and then they reach an understanding. I once tried to rail against the folly of this approach, but my mother-in-law warned me not to underestimate the power of such a strategy.

When Henry turns back to Charles, he looks like a hare in the field just before it bolts.

Charles says through gritted teeth, 'Henry, it's imperative we have a plan before he gets here.'

It is all too late, I think. I can't help Henry any more than I could help my mother or Hannah Smythe.

Charles is still talking. 'My father will have something to say about this. He invested in Oliver Edwards' wool business for more than twenty years.'

'We need to make her see sense,' Henry says, his voice as brittle as linen flax left too long in the field.

'We should visit her first thing in the morning, put some heat under the old witch,' Charles says, slamming his fist on the mantel.

A surge of heat courses through me. I smooth down my dress and walk over to the table. With a trembling hand, I pour myself some ale. A sharp pain radiates from my throat as I swallow it, aware of both Henry and Charles watching me.

When I was angry and would shout out at home when I was young, I was always sorry afterwards, regretting every outburst. But my mother would remind me how Katherine, the shrew, felt. *My tongue will tell the anger of my heart, or else my heart concealing it will break.* The thought steadies me.

I put the cup back on the table.

'Mrs Edwards is not a witch, Charles,' I say softly.

The dawn sky is a torrid red, making the rocks on Craggy Hill glow like hot coals. Below, the mist sits over the low fields like a shroud. There is no birdsong. A cold silence has descended on the land, broken only by the rhythm of my boots on the lane as I make my way to see Mrs Edwards.

The Edwards' stone house is in shadow, its shutters closed. A hard frost grips the garden plants in an overtight vice. When the sun releases them later, they will wither and die.

I make my way around the back and rap softly on the kitchen door. There's no answer, but through the window I can see the orange glow of a fire. I knock again.

Soon, I hear steps approach and I brace myself for a telling-off.

Mrs Edwards opens the door, clutching a shawl about her billowing nightgown. She looks me up and down. Then, without a word, she stands aside to let me in.

'I thought you might still be asleep,' I say as I unwind my scarf. 'That's why I came around to the back door.' My voice is shaking with cold.

She motions me to sit by the kitchen fire. 'Sleep isn't kind to me,' she says.

We sit regarding each other, incapable of smiling or uttering pleasantries.

'You may as well tell me what's on your mind,' she says.

'The bishop is coming to Statfold on Friday. There's to be a dinner; you are invited.'

Her eyes widen a little in surprise, but she says nothing. I smell a sourness on her breath, a sick smell. I wonder if that's why she's having trouble sleeping.

'Henry and Charles Broughton are coming to see you about it today,' I say.

'Why would they do that, if you have already invited me?'

'They don't know I've come.'

She swallows hard.

'They will likely plead with you to reverse your decision not to support the parish. They may talk of the rewards in heaven of giving more of your estate to the church, and they may remind you of your late husband's past borrowings.'

'My husband paid well for everything in life,' she says, a hard edge to her voice.

She reaches for the comfort of her stick, but she has left it hanging on a chair by the table. 'Why are you telling me this?'

'I wanted to let you know.'

'Hmph,' she mutters. 'You're very considerate all of a sudden, Mrs Wolfreston.'

'I wanted to let you know, woman to woman. It's your money; I think you should be able to do with it what you choose.'

'I certainly should, but you would not believe how many think me too old or too silly to make decisions for myself. Everyone watches me for any sign of weakness or any bias that they can pounce upon.'

She pokes at the fire erratically. Sparks fly and two logs roll out from the collapsed fire. She gives an exasperated moan.

I rise to help her.

'I can do it myself,' she snaps.

She crouches awkwardly and works slowly and methodically to rebuild the fire. She's not so unlike me, I think. We're all just pawns in a game.

'You've done a lot for this parish,' I say. 'You've always fought to preserve the common land for grazing. You've contributed to the parish coffers so that families who become destitute don't starve.'

'I do what's right, Mrs Wolfreston.'

She sits back down, her face still flushed from her exertion.

'There are some who do good work only if it benefits them in some way,' I say. 'You do it for the benefit of others.'

'Are you trying to sweeten me up?'

'No,' I say, shaking my head.

She looks at me curiously, as if trying to decide whether she can trust me.

'It is the women of this parish who do most of the caring for people,' I continue. 'We make sure the old and sick are cared for, that families don't starve after their rents and tithes are paid. We do it quietly, our efforts unseen and unheralded.'

'That's true,' she says, her face lined and weary.

'We are like the spaces between the words of a book. The words are what people see, what they argue over, fight wars over, swoon over, collect. Yet without the spaces between, there is nothing at all. We are the spaces, Mrs Edwards.'

'Yet you want to teach all these common children to read those very words.'

'If you can read the words, you can begin to see the spaces.'

Her head cocked to one side, she considers this.

'Spaces,' she mutters. 'Men do enough warring with words, that's for certain. The newsbooks are full of war. The King is removed and still people fight for him, fool though he is. Show me the men who can see these spaces. They do the same thing over and over again, and there's not a damn thing we can do to stop them.'

I am taken aback by the vigour of her speech. She hates war as much as I do, it seems.

'So, what would you have me do, Mrs Wolfreston?' she asks.

I smile grimly. 'Whatever you think is right.'

She stares into the fire, as if the answer might lie there.

A scraping noise comes from the hallway, and I glance up.

'That cat will be the death of me,' says Mrs Edwards, standing. 'I'll show you out, Mrs Wolfreston; you'll be wanting to get home.'

When I reach the gate, I look back at the house and notice someone watching me from a downstairs window. Thinking it is Mrs Edwards, I flutter my fingers. A small hand waves back—it's little Grace Harding.

40

When I reach Statfold House, George is walking across the yard with Sam. Sam has a length of wood over his shoulder and George has a piece of old linen. Behind them, Middy appears, trailing an old bit of rope the pup is pulling on.

'Where are you off to, boys?'

Middy screws up his eyes. George shrugs. 'We're fixing something.'

Sam laughs. 'Well, I'm fixing a hole in the henhouse. The rain's getting into the corner. They're going to help me seal it.'

Sam is handsome when he smiles. I tousle Middy's hair and find myself smiling back at him.

I want to ask him about his intentions regarding Jane, but it is hardly appropriate with the boys nearby.

'Have you seen Mr Wolfreston, Sam?' I ask instead.

He nods towards the lane. 'He rode off on Merlin about half an hour ago.'

'He said he was going up to the manor, Mamma,' George says.

'All right,' I say, relieved to have missed Henry. 'Don't get too dirty, boys!'

I continue on to the house. In the kitchen, Peg is red-faced and simmering. She's staring at the baskets of vegetables in the pantry.

'What's wrong?' I ask, hanging up my cloak.

'Mr Wolfreston said the bishop's coming Friday and I've no idea what to cook. I expect you'll want a pig butchered. And there's milk to be churned, that pile of linens to be washed, not to mention them two cabbages to be pickled.'

I lift the pan lid to look at the porridge.

'Well, I'll churn the milk as soon as I've had some breakfast,' I say, cringing at the thought of hours plunging the stick in the dash churn to make a round of butter. 'And the laundry can wait.'

'But what about them Kavanagh boys? They'll be here shortly.'

'We'll have to send them home. We're too busy for the rest of this week's lessons.'

'And what'll I cook for the bishop? We've no fish or fine meats.'

I want to say, *I don't care what you make for that man*, but of course I don't.

'Roast pork will do very well,' I say. 'And pies—pork and mutton pies.' I spoon porridge into a bowl.

Peg stares at me, wisps of damp hair plastered to her head.

I sit down, salt the porridge and add a spoonful of milk.

'What's wrong?' I ask.

Peg gives an exaggerated shrug. 'Pies?'

'Everyone for miles around talks of your pies. Make your tasty pies, Peg.'

'If you say so, Mrs Wolfreston,' Peg says sceptically.

She reaches for the mixing bowl and measures in the flour for the daily bread.

'That George has been taking all my old rags. I'll have nothing left for cleaning.'

'He's helping Sam.'

'Hmm,' she says, banging a spoon onto the table.

'The porridge is good, Peg.'

She gives the briefest of nods in acknowledgement, then dips her hands into her bowl.

Henry still hasn't returned by midday, and I'm growing worried. I tell Peg to keep the noon meal warm and send George and Middy outside to see what Sam's doing. There's a wisp of smoke drifting up the hill from the orchard, so he has likely lit a bonfire. I stand by the window watching for Henry, trying not to think of all the things that have gone wrong over the last few weeks.

While I stood in the cold buttery for a good hour, churning the buttermilk, I convinced myself that it was a mistake to visit Mrs Edwards this morning, that she will have told Henry and Charles of my visit and will have used it against me in some way. I was glad to lay aside the cursed paddle, strain the butter and shape it into small rounds. What a lot of work for so little butter!

Peg brings more logs for the fire.

'If you don't mind me saying, Mrs Wolfreston, you're not doing that baby any good with all that pacing.'

While she pokes the fire and lays on the new logs, I sit down, breathing so loudly that Peg turns to stare at me. She brings some ale over and sets it next to me. 'Drink that up, Mrs Wolfreston,' she orders gruffly. 'You've had nothin' since that porridge.'

Smiling at the stern tone she employs to hide the softness of her heart, I pick up the book Henry's left on the side table. *The Redemption of Time. Or, A Sermon Containing Very Good Remedies for Them that Have Mis-spent Their Time, Shewing How They Should Redeeme it Comfortably.* Lord, Henry, what dull books you choose.

Sighing, I open it and begin to read.

Outside, horses are approaching. I close the book and hasten to the window.

A carriage is coming from the direction of the Tamworth Road. As it clears the trees and turns off the lane towards Statfold, I try to make sense of what I've seen. Henry mentioned that Sir James might come back this week, but why is his carriage coming to Statfold House now?

By the time I reach the front door Peg is already by my shoulder, rubbing the flour from her hands with her apron.

'Is that him already?' she says, meaning the bishop.

My heart beats rapidly. 'I'm not sure.'

As the driver pulls the horses to a stop, I walk towards them.

A woman's voice calls from the carriage: 'Frances!'

My heart lifts and I run straight across the damp grass, not bothering with the path.

'Frances!' Candace says again. She kisses my cheek, whispering in my ear, 'I'm sorry I left so suddenly. I hope you'll forgive me.'

I put my arms around her, hoping that the tightness of the embrace is sufficient to convey my feelings.

After some seconds, I release her and, wiping my eyes, take her in. She has a glow about her. The amber flecks in her eyes sparkle and her golden hair glistens beneath a dark green bonnet with a long feather.

She squeezes my hand. 'Come, my dear Frances.' She pulls me towards the carriage, and I see her father standing beside it.

'Sir James, I am surprised and happy to see you.' I gesture towards the house. 'Please come into our humble home.'

His eyes crease in a queer sort of smile. He exchanges a glance with Candace. 'We have brought someone to see you,' he says as he turns and offers his hand towards the open door of the carriage.

My heart sinks at the prospect of another guest when we are so unprepared.

The corner of a travelling hood appears. A woman takes his hand. She lowers her travelling hood and turns to look at me. She has lost weight and the dimple in her chin is more pronounced. Her hair is not completely grey as I thought when I last saw her; it is still streaked with blonde.

'Mamma!' I cry.

In a moment, she is in my arms, her soft cheek pressing against mine.

I hold her small frame tight.

'Oh, Mamma. You're here.'

'Frannie,' she says huskily, suppressing a cough.

Her pale eyes are red-rimmed and, despite her heavy clothes, she's shaking with cold.

Candace and her father watch us, smiling.

'How on earth . . .?' Tears fill my throat and I can't say any more.

Sir James takes a handkerchief from his pocket and blows his nose. 'We were passing, so it was convenient to visit your father,' he says.

I look at Candace.

She says softly, 'I suggested your mother come here to . . . recuperate.'

I wipe my eyes. 'We owe you a great debt,' I say, glancing at Mamma, hardly able to believe that she's here.

Candace squeezes my mother's arm gently. 'I'll come and see you tomorrow,' she promises.

'If you have time,' I say. 'But I expect you will be busy.' I pause as I notice her look at me with raised brows. 'Preparing for the bishop's arrival on Friday,' I add.

Candace and her father exchange a worried look.

Sir James says, 'Where is the rector?'

'He is with Charles—preparing.'

Sir James exhales heavily. He nods to the driver, who has already unloaded my mother's trunk and carried it to the house, then he tips his hat and says, 'We'll leave you now to get settled, Mrs Middlemore.'

We watch as the Broughtons return to the carriage and drive off, the horses' hooves kicking up dust.

Mamma says, 'They're good people.'

She grips my arm and leans on me heavily as we walk to the house. I worry that she is too frail, but I say brightly, 'We'll soon get you strong again, Mamma.'

She smiles weakly. 'I'm all right now I'm here,' she says.

41

The bedroom window is open a crack to let in the fresh air. Outside, the wind blows the distant sounds of shouting and hounds barking across the woods and fields. Mamma sleeps—and I sit watching, too scared to take my eyes from her in case this should prove a dream. She is so tranquil that I want to touch her face to check that she is still breathing as I used to do with the children when they were babes.

During the night, I took a blanket and sat on a chair next to her bed just as she did for me when I was sick all those years ago. How tired she must have been, keeping that vigil by my bedside. She did not once complain.

She woke last night, her eyes blinking in the dim light from the candle that I'd placed over on the mantel in case she thrashed in the night and knocked it from the bedside table.

'Frannie,' she said, staring up at the ceiling, her voice distant and unsure. 'Am I here?'

I took her hand. 'You're here, Mamma.'

She breathed out, a light rattle to her breath that made me think of Mr Townsend's kind face, then closed her eyes again. I sat holding her hand, watching her breathe, until Henry came looking for me.

We hadn't talked much that day. He had been at the Broughtons' when Candace and her father returned to the manor. Sir James wouldn't give him any details of my mother's release; he simply told Henry to go home and see his mother-in-law.

'Can't you sleep?' I asked as he stood in the doorway watching us.

He gave a slight sideways movement of his head, his eyes hooded and weary in the candlelight.

'I suppose it didn't go well with Mrs Edwards?'

'No,' he said. 'She refused to talk to us. She said she would see the bishop alone.' Then his eyes turned to my mother. 'I'll sit with her awhile. You go to bed, Frances.'

I stood and stretched out my back. As I passed him the blanket, his hand touched mine. Our eyes met and we looked at each other for a few moments. Then, with softness in his eyes, he rested his hand on my belly. I laid mine over his.

Mamma stirs. Her eyes are open. She tries to sit up and I help her, placing another pillow under her head.

'Help me wash my face and hands,' she says, running a hand through her hair. 'Nance helped me as best she could, but I'm thick with dirt.'

As I wipe her face gently, she says, 'I need a bath, Frannie.'

'We'll get you in the tub later.'

Her hands are flaky and dry, the scarred skin red and sore. She winces as the damp cloth touches them. She lets me smooth the paste I use for Henry's chapped skin over them. But she watches me keenly, her lips pursed as if she doesn't trust me not to hurt her. As soon as I'm finished, she tucks her hands under the covers.

I want to ask her about the gaol, and how she came to be freed, but she keeps her eyes averted.

'I'll go get some potage,' I say.

'Thank you,' she says. 'I feel better for being in a warm bed.' She lifts a finger towards the window. 'Why are those dogs barking?'

'I don't know. It may be the sheriff's hounds. Do you want me to close the window?'

'No,' she says, 'leave it open.'

When she has eaten and rested, I help Mamma downstairs to the bath Peg has prepared in the kitchen. Mamma shoos me away, telling me to see to the boys, that Peg can help her into the bath. I protest and offer to help her myself, but she refuses, just as she had refused my help to undress yesterday, insisting that Peg do it.

Peg winks at me and says, 'I'll look after her, Mrs Wolfreston, don't you worry.'

My mother doesn't want me to see how reduced she has become by the meagre rations in the gaol, I realise.

'All right, Mamma.'

Afterwards, Mamma sits by the fire in the library, where she can look out onto the garden and the copper beech tree. The boys hover nearby, watching as I wrap a blanket around my mother and fold it under her feet. They run and bring a footstool and I lift Mamma's feet onto it.

'Would you like George to read to you, Mamma?'

Mamma's eyes light up. 'I would enjoy that very much.'

'What book should I read?' George asks.

My mother answers, 'Your favourite one, dearest.'

George looks at the empty shelves where his books usually sit then down at the open trunk.

'Why are the books in there, Mamma?'

My face reddens and I notice my mother looking at me.

'I was just rearranging the shelves.' I rummage in the trunk then hand him the book I know he was seeking. 'Go on, George, start at the beginning.'

While George reads *The Famous Historie of Montelyon* in his clear, high voice, Middy watches his grandmother with his finger in the cleft of his chin.

'You have my chin,' Mamma says to him softly, doing the same with her own dimple.

A surge of joy fills me as I watch them.

Candace arrives at eleven o'clock. She asks after my mother's health, commenting on how much better she looks. She urges George to keep reading, and Mamma says, 'Go talk with your friend, Frannie. These young men can look after me.'

I kiss her forehead and say, 'All right, Mamma.'

As we leave the room, I hear her ask, 'But how do you know he's brave, George?'

Candace and I make our way to the drawing room. The fire is not lit yet, but the sun is warming the window seat, making it a pleasant place to sit.

'I can't stay long,' she says, spreading two newsbooks on the seat between us. She points at one I haven't seen before called *The Profectus*. 'This is a new one and the writing is more progressive. There is one article I would like you to read.' She turns the pages and points. 'It's about education. Let me know what you think of it.'

I smile and push it gently aside. 'I will, but first tell me how you managed to free my mother. I thought you had gone to Bridgewater to see your cousin.'

She smiles, her teeth smooth as pearls. 'Forgive me that deceit, Frances. I didn't want to raise your hopes. I went to London to find my father and tell him of your mother's condition.'

Candace tells me that, on the way back from London, her father went into the sheriff's office in King's Norton while she waited in the carriage. Her father insisted on knowing the details of the fine and any other penalties owing. The clerk agreed that, if the fine was paid in full, my mother could be released into Sir James's care.

'So Papa paid the fine, and we took the carriage around to the rear of the magistrate's office and a guard brought your mother out. She looked dazzled by the light and so frail that I was shocked. I realised that she didn't know us, and I did not know what to say or do, but Papa explained that we were friends of you and Henry and that we had secured her release.

'We took her directly to Hazelmere, and there my father came to some arrangement whereby your father would pay the money back in instalments, so that your father would not have to sell his land. In return, my father insisted that your mother be allowed to recuperate at Statfold. Your father wasn't happy about this, but he was hardly in a position to argue.'

'So, my mother didn't need to sign anything?'

'No, there was no requirement for any oath. I asked my father about it, as you had already told me she would not sign such a thing. But it seems to be something only your father needed.'

I stare through the window at the stone chapel sitting among the trees, my lips trembling.

My father had lied to me.

Had Joseph known of the oath? I wonder. My father said he had discussed my mother with him. Then, as clear as the turning of a new page, it comes to me; I am like the fool in the *Shrew* who is not a nobleman but a poor man dressed up as one. I do not know the game that is before me. Joseph is a lawyer. He would have refused to ask my mother to sign something that was not legal. He would have no part in my father's game.

It was always so. My father *always* chose me.

My shoulders begin to shake. Candace's arms encircle me. She holds me while I lean against her. We sit like this for a few minutes. The seat becomes cold as the sun retreats behind a cloud. I take a breath, sniffing, trying to stifle the tears.

Candace remains beside me, watching, without judgement.

'Thank you,' I say, when I am able to speak. 'How can we ever repay you?'

She shakes her head as if the idea of repayment is a silly one. 'It's lovely to see your mother here with you. Now,' she says, gathering her gloves and standing up. 'I must go. I have dinner for a bishop to organise. You've heard we're hosting it at Broughton Manor now?'

I wipe my face and give a half-smile. 'That's another thing I won't be able to repay you for.'

She kisses my cheek.

'But what of Mr Brydges?' I say. 'You are fond of him, I know, and—'

She interrupts. 'I've written to him.'

As I open the side door, she says with a shy smile, 'And he has written back.'

There is no time for me to respond for, as I follow Candace outside, the cold wind gusts fiercely. We struggle to the stable yard, pressing our hands against our skirts.

'I'm glad I came in the carriage,' Candace says through strands of hair that have blown across her face.

The barking is louder, more frenetic in this strong easterly.

'The sheriff's men must be over there in Rivermead,' Candace says, pointing. While Sam holds the door open against the wind, Candace steps into the carriage and calls, 'Now, Frances, don't forget about that news article.'

I watch as the carriage trundles past the house towards the lane. I wave until it has disappeared behind the trees.

Shivering, I turn to see that Sam is still standing there. His eyes are soft but devoid of their usual sparkle. He looks as tired as Henry. These last few weeks have been hard on all of us.

'I've cleaned up that old flask of your brother's,' he says. 'The leather's come up well. I thought you'd like to have it back.'

Sam is good with his hands. The flask probably looks better than it did when Joseph used to drag it around. Joseph loved it because it was my father's flask, but I have no desire to see it again.

'You keep it, Sam. You'll have more use of it than me.'

He smiles, his mouth twisting up slightly on one side. He rubs his face, looks towards the stable then back at me, his dark hair blowing, his face scrunched against the wind. His expression is concerned, and I am reminded of how he looked at me in the barn at Hazelmere— as if there were something I should know but he was reluctant to reveal it.

'What is it, Sam?'

'I just wanted to tell you . . .' he begins. He hesitates.

Peg calls my name and I glance at the house. I can't help shivering as I look back at Sam.

'It doesn't matter. You should go in. Thank you, Mrs Wolfreston,' Sam says. He turns quickly and heads back to the barn, carrying the old flask.

I watch him for a few moments, wondering what's on his mind. Then, shivering, I make my way back to the house.

Mamma sits alone in the library, her head resting on the high back of the chair, sleeping. *The Famous Historie of Montelyon* lies closed on her lap.

The chimney gives a howl and the fire sparks and spits in response.

'Is that you, angel?' my mother murmurs, stirring.

'Yes, Mamma.'

'I think I fell asleep,' she says, nudging the book.

'Do you want me to read to you?'

She shakes her head. 'Come and sit with me,' she says, patting the seat near her. 'You should rest a moment, Frannie—let that baby get fat.'

I sit beside her, my hands cradling my belly, watching the branches of the copper beech bend and stretch in the wind.

'Tell me what happened to that woman,' she says. 'The one who wouldn't go to church.'

A lump grows in my throat, and I swallow.

'She's in gaol, Mamma.'

I see my mother wince.

'I wish I could go back in time, Mamma. There are so many things I would do and say differently.'

Mamma is quiet a moment, her eyes watching me steadily. 'Every life is full of mistakes and regrets, Frannie.'

42

When I wake in the grey half-light, Henry is already dressed and staring out at the chapel sitting among the bare rowans. It's the first Friday of the month and the poor wait for their relief whether the bishop is coming or not.

'Are there many, Henry?'

'More than last time,' he says, heaving out his breath as if carrying the weight of it inside is too much.

He sits on the edge of the bed to tie his boots. His thick curls have been flattened into waves by sleep.

'Do you want me to come?'

'No,' he says, laying his head gently on my belly.

Sensing him, the baby squirms and moves. Henry's lips slowly twitch into a smile, but there is a tear in the corner of his eye.

'We'll be all right, Henry,' I say, stroking his hair gently.

He sits up and wipes his face, turning away so I can't see his tears. 'I'll be back in a couple of hours,' he says.

I pull my shawl around me and watch from the window as he walks by the side of the house. He pauses by a tree, his head down, holding his hat by his side. My heart lurches as I observe him. A bird stirs above him, its breast fat as it trills its morning song. I long for him to look up, so I know he has heard it.

Henry puts on his hat and walks slowly towards the chapel.

I move quickly, washing my face and dressing, trying to keep my mind off Henry. But I find myself sitting on the end of the bed, thinking about how I could have behaved differently, how I could have been more helpful to him these last weeks. He did, after all, take me to King's Norton to see my mother.

A thud from outside jolts me from my thoughts. I finish dressing and tidy the bed.

Another thud.

I look out of the window. One of the stable doors is blowing loose in the wind.

My hair still flowing about me, I run downstairs and slip out of the side door.

I open the stable door wide and fix it to the post.

'Sam?'

Light floods into the stable. Merlin and Lady stand in their stall watching me with their great wet eyes. The horses snort and lift their noses, inhaling the scent of wood smoke that drifts in over the odour of their dung. The first thing Sam does in the morning is take the horses out to the field and muck out the stable.

In the next stall is Hannah Smythe's cow and her pretty calf. Beyond them is the area of flattened straw where Sam sleeps. There's no sign of his coat or his bag. He must be with Jane Harding. I picture him with her, smiling at her as he did in the chapel, tucking a strand of her straw-coloured hair behind her ear.

Strands of hay swirl up and drift past me. I notice that Sam's blanket, usually rolled up during the day, is also gone. In fact, I realise, there doesn't seem to be anything here that belongs to Sam.

The baby squirms inside me. I put my hands on my hips and stretch out my back. Then I lean on the doorpost, breathing hard. If he was with Jane, he would have left her before daybreak; he couldn't risk being seen leaving her house.

And he would not have left the stable door open all night.

I make my way back to the house trying to recall what Sam had said the day before. Had he given any indication that he was leaving?

The smell of fresh bread greets me as I enter the kitchen. Peg lifts a tray bearing two loaves from the oven and sets it down to cool.

'I gave the first two loaves to Mr Wolfreston for them paupers,' she says, glancing at my hair, which is blown about me.

'Have you seen Sam this morning?' I ask.

'No, ma'am.' Peg's face reddens as I continue to look at her.

I loosen my shawl and smooth my hair. Several wisps of hay fall to the floor.

'When did you last see him?'

'Yesterday afternoon. He was heading to the orchard with the boys. I asked George what they were doing, and he said they were fixing something.'

'Are they still repairing the henhouse?'

Pegs tilts her head. 'What?'

'Sam told me a few days ago that there was a leak in the roof of the henhouse.'

The broth on the spigot hisses. Peg stirs the broth and repositions the lid. She turns back to me, tutting and shaking her head.

'There's no hole in the henhouse. I'd be the first to know about it if there was.'

I breathe out through my nose. 'Then why would he tell me that?'

'I'm sure I don't know, Mrs Wolfreston,' Peg says, turning back to the pot. A moment later she says, 'I hope he's not gone off again. He's supposed to help me scald that pig ready for butchering.'

I exhale and look around the kitchen. The lavender hangs above the fireplace as usual, the cat is curled up near the hearth, the pup's blanket lies in the corner. The pup is not there.

'Where are the boys, Peg?'

'They're not up yet. I'll go wake them.'

I hear Peg's footsteps as she clatters up the stairs calling, 'George! Middy!'

I look out of the window at the drying green, the trees in the distance, then the stable wall and its door—still bolted, as I left it a few minutes ago. My chest tightens. Why would Sam lie to me?

Peg returns from the boys' room, looking tense. 'They're not here,' she says. 'Maybe they've taken the pup out. Or could they have gone to the chapel with Mr Wolfreston?'

She knows as well as I do that Henry doesn't let them near on relief day.

My insides feel light, untethered, as if I might be sick.

Peg's hand is on me like a compress. 'You look faint. Sit down.'

'They always get dressed then come and have breakfast, Peg.'

There's a noise on the stairs. We both look up.

'There now,' says Peg.

But it's Mamma who comes into the kitchen. She's wearing her shift, a shawl hanging loose on her thin shoulders.

'What's going on?' she says.

My throat catches. There's a tight pain in my chest.

Peg answers, 'It's George and Middy—we haven't seen them this morning.'

'Well, go look for them,' Mamma says.

Peg takes her shawl. 'I'll check the chapel and the sheds.'

Mamma gives me a shake. 'Think, Frannie. Where do they usually go? You and Joseph used to go to that tree. Where do your boys go?'

I'm trembling as I look at her. Where would they go?

43

When I reach the rise at the top of the orchard, Peg is already running back from the chapel, heading towards the henhouse.

I scan the field and the orchard. My throat feels tight as I hurry down between the bare plum trees, careful not to slip on the frosty ground. At the bottom of the hill, at the edge of the grey circle of ash where the bonfire was lit, there is a pile of leaves and shards of bark. Black spots are scattered on the bark. I push it aside with my foot then cover my nose to block the acrid smell. There's a blackened pit about a foot and a half deep. Black lumpy spots of sticky pitch lead away from the pit.

There's a large footprint in the ash and I can see parts of small footprints here and there—Middy's.

'George! Middy!' I yell.

In the distance, I can hear Peg, too, calling for the boys.

I stare at the pit. Why make pitch here and carry it all the way up the hill? But the splashes of pitch are not trailing towards the house or the henhouse, but away from it, down the hill to the overgrown path that leads to the woods—the same woods Hannah Smythe said she came through.

I call the boys' names again. Where could they be? Holding my belly, I run along the path to the edge of the woods and gaze into the gloom. Ancient ash trees and thick oaks line the steep slope that leads down to the stream. There are no pleasant glades among these trees and the stream's banks are thick with ferns and brambles. Surely they haven't gone in there.

Something catches my eye in the grass near my feet, and I bend to pick it up.

It's a long piece of string, still clean, as if it hasn't been there long. I run my hands through the grass near it, pushing apart the long strands. I spot a carved wooden whistle. I turn it over; on the back is carved the letter M.

I feel sick.

'George! Middy!' I shout.

Then I add, 'Here, boy.'

Silence; not a bird nor a dog answers my call.

I take my kerchief from my pocket and quickly tie it to an overhead branch. Clutching the whistle, I step into the woods.

The path is rough and damp underfoot and my boots are quickly caked with mud. I tie my shawl in a rough knot to stop it catching on the nettles. Here and there brambles have recently been pushed back. The boys have come this way, I'm sure of it. Below me to the right, I can hear the rushing stream. I can't see it, but I can see the trees rising up the slope of its far bank.

After a while, the path drops steeply among the trees. I step from tree to tree steadying myself on branches and leaning against trunks until it levels out. The path runs on parallel to the stream, closer but still several feet above it.

It is some minutes before I see the river glinting through the trees. I stumble on, the stream below me to my right, the river head getting closer. Hannah Smythe had told me the path came up from the river and ran along beside it for some time.

Abruptly, the path stops.

I look around in a panic, wondering what to do. Thick brambles lie ahead, dense ferns cover the rise to my left, and a mess of fallen branches interspersed with nettles runs all the way down to the stream. It's completely impassable. I can't see any birds, but I can hear them calling to each other while the upper branches of the trees creak in the wind.

'Middy! George!' My voice silences the birds as it echoes through the trees.

There's a sick feeling in my throat as I wait; listening, hoping.

There is no response.

I call again, screaming their names this time.

I'm so far from the house I can no longer hear Peg calling. Perhaps she's already found the boys, and I'm the one who is lost. I stare up at the pale blue sky through the treetops. I'll have to turn back. But I can't—I'm certain they have come this way.

Then I remember Middy's whistle in my pocket. I blow it and the sound rises shrill and high. If the boys are anywhere in these woods, they will surely hear it.

Nothing.

I am breathing unsteadily, tears pricking my eyes. I have no choice but to go back and get help. I blow the whistle again.

And then I hear it: a faint whistle in reply. I blow again on my whistle, and this time the response is louder, closer.

'Middy, George, over here,' I shout.

A few minutes later George comes weaving through the trees. He's higher than me, further up the hill. I push up through the thick ferns towards him.

'Mamma,' he says, hugging me.

I squeeze him so hard he says, 'Mamma, you're hurting me.'

I kiss his head. 'Where's Middy?'

He looks behind him. 'Back there.'

'Isn't Sam with you?'

'No,' he says. He glances back along the path again.

'What are you doing in the woods so far from the house?'

He shrugs, his bottom lip sticking out in that stubborn way of his.

'George Wolfreston, you tell me now or so help me I will . . .'

He fumbles with the whistle that hangs from his neck. 'The pup's hurt, Mamma.'

'Take me to Middy,' I say.

I follow George along the high path. After several minutes it drops towards the river. Some tree roots have formed makeshift steps down the worst of the muddy slope, then the path weaves along the bank between the reeds and bushes. It must have taken poor Hannah Smythe—or Jen, as she was then—hours to reach our orchard in her broken and beaten state.

Middy is stumbling along the riverbank carrying the large pup. When we reach him, Middy shoves the pup straight into my arms.

I set the pup down on the ground and pull Middy towards me. He's sniffing, trying not to cry. I pull George into our embrace and hold them both until they sigh against me.

'Promise me you'll never go off like this again.'

'I promise, Mamma,' George says.

The pup whimpers. He can't put any weight on his rear leg, so George helps me gather him inside my shawl. With the shawl tied tightly around my waist, I can carry him for a while. The boys walk ahead on the way back: George sullen and quiet, Middy turning every minute or so to look at the pup.

'It'll be all right, Middy,' I say.

George scowls. He knows what happens to lame dogs.

When we are in finally in sight of the orchard, I send George running for help.

Peg meets us when Middy and I emerge from the woods. I want to cry with relief at the sight of her, but I manage to control myself.

'Lord, help us,' Peg says, taking the trembling pup from me. 'We were worried about you, Mrs Wolfreston. I was on the verge of fetching Mr Wolfreston when George came. Can you make it up the hill?'

'Yes, I'm all right,' I assure her, though I am tired and short of breath. 'You go on ahead.'

'Your mamma's at the top of the hill,' Peg says as she ushers the boys ahead of her.

Every part of me shakes, as if I'm separating into pieces. I tell myself the worst is over, but my body is not listening. I trudge slowly up the hill. Mamma waits on the rise, her face tense with worry. As she wraps her arms around me, I weep into her shoulder, great gulping sobs.

44

'Sometimes it's better to get things off your chest, George.'

George sits at Henry's desk, idly fingering the page of the catechism that I've told him to read until he's ready to talk. He already knows the first chapter of faith well but has been looking at its initial page for the last ten minutes.

'Don't just stare at the page, George—recite.'

George huffs and begins to read. '*What is Man? Man is a reasonable creature which God hath made marvellously consisting of a body and soul . . .*'

He recites dully, as if his mind were elsewhere. Despite this, I find it hard to stay angry with him. He had been very good in the woods, guiding me on the steep slopes, taking a turn with the pup and saying, 'It's not too far, Mamma,' when he could see I was struggling. When we finally got back to the warm kitchen, he'd pulled off my muddy boots, his cheeks almost bursting with the effort. I asked him about Sam and what they'd been fixing but he refused to say.

George turns a page then pauses. He watches Middy, who has come into the room but is standing near the door looking reticent.

Middy hasn't left the pup's side since we got home. He'd watched intently as Peg held the pup while I inspected its leg and foot. He'd drawn in his breath as I found a thorn between its toes and tweezed it out with my fingernails.

'Is the pup asleep, Middy?' I ask.

Middy nods. He holds up his whistle that is fastened onto a new piece of cord, grinning. He walks over to George and swings it under his nose. George bats it away.

'George, you can go play with Middy as soon as you tell me what happened this morning.'

George starts reading aloud again in a monotone.

'Sam,' Middy says, pointing out of the window.

Outside, the solitary copper beech stands like a sentinel. I look around; there's no one in sight.

'Middy, did you see Sam?'

His eyes widen. 'Sam gone.'

George shoves him.

'Stop that, George.'

'Middy, where is Sam?'

Middy looks at George and then at me.

George says, 'He doesn't know, Mamma.'

I narrow my eyes at George, warning him to be quiet.

'Middy, love, where is Sam?'

Middy makes a fist with the whistle inside his fingers. He looks towards the window and says, 'Boat.'

George stares at him, his eyes wild.

'What boat?'

Middy stares at me. He has no more words.

I turn to George. 'What boat?' I ask, my tone stern.

George dips his head so his brown hair hides his eyes.

'George, I'm serious. Sam may be in a lot of trouble. You must tell me. What boat?'

After a moment George mutters, 'Mrs Smythe's boat.'

My heart thuds in my ears as I lean on the back of Henry's chair.

'How did you know about that?'

George swallows. 'I heard her telling you, Mamma. I told Sam about it, and we went looking for it. We found it and Sam's been fixing it.' He looks up, disappointed. 'He said he was going to take us fishing.'

'He was going to take you fishing this morning?'

George shakes his head. 'No, but I saw him from the window. He was running, carrying his bag, and I knew he was going to the boat. So, I followed him. And Middy followed me.'

I breathe out through my nose, trying to stay calm.

'Go on.'

'When we got to the river, Sam was pulling the boat out through the reeds. I shouted to him, Mamma.' Tears well in his eyes.

'What were you shouting, George?'

Tears roll down George's face.

'I asked him to take us with him,' he mumbles. 'He said he would take us in the boat, Mamma.'

I turn away quickly, a small groan escaping from me. I want to say, *Thank God you're both safe*, but I can't seem to get any words out. I wipe my eyes on my sleeve.

I hear my mother's voice then, quick and bright. 'Come, boys, let your mamma rest.' She ushers them from the room, saying, 'Let's have some of that apple pie Peg's just made.'

I glance at the chest of books, which I still haven't returned to the shelves. The book of poetry by Du Bartas is lying on top. It had been given to him by an officer at Naseby, he'd said. I chastise myself for ever having allowed Sam near the boys. My initial instinct that he is a Royalist was right. Why didn't I tell Henry straight away?

Henry's sermon for Sunday sits half-written on the desk. It stops mid-sentence, the quill lying beside it as if dropped hurriedly. I wipe the quill and straighten the pages. My hands are still shaking. I pour a little wine from the jug and sit by the fire sipping it.

There's a soft tap. George stands by the door, his brow furrowed.

I smile at him. 'Come in, George.'

He crosses the room to stand beside me.

'Peg said the sheriff might be looking for Sam.'

I am tempted to deny it, then decide it is best to tell him the truth. 'Probably.'

His lip wobbles. 'I should have told you about the boat and the fishing.'

'Why didn't you?'

'Sam said we should wait till the boat was fixed, and it would be a surprise.'

I fight to keep my voice calm. 'It was wrong of him to say that.'

I wrap my arms around him, breathing in the comforting scent of his hair.

'Has he done something bad?' he says into my shoulder.

'Hush,' I say. 'I'm very angry with Sam, but the truth is, George, we don't know what he's done or even if he's the man the sheriff is looking for.'

He shudders against me, crying now. 'I thought he was good.'

I did too, I want to say. I hold him tighter and tell him, 'We all did.'

We stay like that for a while, then George pulls free of my embrace. 'Are you going to tell Mrs Smythe about the boat?' he asks.

'Eventually,' I say, looking out of the study window towards the orchard. I wonder if Hannah Smythe had known her boat was still there.

'Mamma, is Mrs Smythe a witch?'

'Who called her that?' I say sharply.

He looks down. 'No one. She talks to herself sometimes, that's all.'

'She just misses her husband, George.'

'Oh.' He tilts his head, as if it had never occurred to him that she might have had a husband. 'What does a witch look like, Mamma?'

The late witch-finder general, Matthew Hopkins, arrested nineteen women for witchcraft in one town in 1645. Five died in gaol and fifteen were executed. He was paid handsomely for ridding the town of them. They were guilty of bearing warts or moles, looking old or having a cat.

'I don't know, George. Sometimes old women are mistaken for witches because they look a bit different. But I can tell you that Mrs Smythe is not a witch.'

George looks uncertain.

'There are some people who think there are witches, but some clergy folk like us tend not to believe that. We believe that everybody is made in God's likeness.'

'Like it says in the catechism?'

I touch his cheek. 'Yes, just as it says in the catechism.'

'Even Sam?'

After a beat, I nod.

He looks out of the window as he considers this. My eyes follow his, beyond the trusty copper beech, towards the woods. I wonder where the river will take Sam.

'Now tell me,' I say, tousling his curls, 'did you save me some apple pie?'

One corner of his mouth turns up. 'Yes, Mamma.'

45

My mother is sitting by the library fire with her eyes closed. The pup is curled on the rush mat at her feet. Even though the sun has not yet set, the boys are asleep in bed. Henry is at Broughton Manor welcoming Bishop Divine.

When Henry returned from chapel this morning, I told him that Sam and all his things were gone. He sighed wearily but merely asked if the horses had been fed. I'd forgotten about the horses. He laid his hand gently on my belly and said, 'Go and get some rest.' I decided not to tell him about the boys and Hannah Smythe's boat. Instead, I placed my hand over his.

Mamma opens her eyes. 'I've been thinking, Frannie. Instead of returning to Hazelmere, I will go and stay with Joseph and then with your sister. They both invited me several months ago, but I put it off because your father refused to come with me.' She purses her lips. 'But I think I would prefer to go on my own anyway.'

I give a reticent smile. 'I hope you are not going too soon, Mamma.'

She waves her hand. 'Oh no, I will wait until you tire of me, angel.'

I take her hands and say, 'I will never tire of you.'

'Silly,' she says with a snort.

I study her hands: those scarred, raw hands she always keeps hidden.

She tries to pull them away, but I maintain my hold, rubbing my thumbs gently over them.

'You tried to save your books,' I say. I look at her, waiting till she meets my gaze.

'I was foolish,' she says.

'No, you weren't. I would try to save mine.'

She looks over the bookshelves, still devoid of my books, then down at the chest. 'You've collected so many books, Frannie. I couldn't be prouder of you.'

The air seems to stick so that swallowing is impossible.

'Don't say that. You know I don't deserve it.'

She looks puzzled. In this light, her eyes are somewhere between blue and grey.

'I'm so sorry I hurt you, Mamma.'

'Hush,' she says. 'It wasn't your fault, Frannie.'

I release her hands as the words surge out of me. 'Papa asked Joseph what your favourite books were, and Joseph said he didn't know. And I, thinking how much cleverer than Joseph I was . . . I told him. Joseph knew them as well as I did, but he knew better than to say.' Tears press at my eyes and my voice wobbles. 'Papa told me we would pretend to throw them on the fire. He told me it would help you get better.'

Mamma grips my hands fiercely, sending a warm pulse through me.

'You were a child,' she says, emphasising each word. Her eyes are soft as she says, 'You have no reason to be ashamed, angel.'

'I shouldn't have listened to him. I should have helped *you*.' I duck my head. 'I cannot forgive myself,' I mumble.

She takes my face in her hands. 'Look at me, Frannie.'

Reluctantly, I lift my eyes.

She says slowly, 'You burned the books, but I burned myself. I should have walked away.'

Tears roll down my face. The more she forgives, the more it hurts.

'You must stop punishing yourself,' she insists.

'I should have been loyal to *you*, not him.'

Mamma stands up. 'Let's get a breath of air.'

She opens the garden door, and we walk out past the bare copper beech towards the rise above the orchard.

'Frannie,' Mamma says, taking my arm, 'do you remember how I used to say sometimes that you were like Cordelia? You always wanted to please your father. From the moment you could walk you followed him around. And you're so like him.'

'You think I am like him?' I was horrified.

'You're very like him. You have his thick dark hair, his strong features, his ability to persuade people to do things. You have some of his best qualities.'

I consider this fact unhappily.

She smooths her hair behind her ear and pulls her shawl around her.

'The reason I used to say you were like Cordelia was because she was the dutiful daughter that King Lear desired her to be.'

I look out over the fields towards the brooding shadows on Craggy Hill. Above them the sky is streaked with pink.

My mother says softly, 'She loved him so much that she was blindly obedient to him. She always put his judgement above her own even when she knew inside herself that he was wrong.'

I swallow, my throat aching.

My mother touches my arm. 'I made this same mistake with your father . . . believing that what he was asking me to do was in my best interests.'

'Did you know this fault before you married him?'

'My mother warned me, but I found your father so very handsome. And a part of me thought I could change him, if I tried hard. But one day he told me to do something that he knew I couldn't ever do.'

'What was that?'

'He told me I must never pray again in the old way, even to myself inside my head. Even inside my own head.' Her voice catches. 'I was so angry that I left him. I rode off further than King's Norton, heading towards my parents' house, even though I knew they would simply send me back to him.' She heaves a sigh. 'Anyway, he followed me. Dragged me home, warned me not to humiliate him.'

'I don't remember you leaving, Mamma.'

'He told you I fell off a horse.'

My hands fly to my mouth.

She was hurt that day; bruised and unconscious. I remember him carrying her upstairs. I stare at her, unable to say anything.

She looks away, her face closing as if she has said too much.

'And why did you stop going to church?'

She stares towards Craggy Hill. 'There is a woman who attends the church. She is a . . . a *close companion* of your father. And I couldn't bear to sit under God's roof and pretend that everything was all right.'

'Oh, Mamma,' I say gently.

The pink light is soft on her face. She looks both young and old, as if time were playing a trick. I squeeze her arm.

'Now, Frannie,' she says briskly, 'let's put this all behind us. It makes no difference to me now that my books were burned.' She taps her head. 'I have them all in here.'

46

Mamma sits beside me in church on Sunday morning. Under her warm shawl, she is wearing a dark blue skirt and bodice with a white lace collar. Her grey-blonde hair is pinned back under a crisp white cap. She looks so serene that I can't help gazing at her. In the pocket of her skirt is the little book of sonnets that Nance sent in the basket. I gave it back to her this morning while she was getting dressed for church. 'You'll need this,' I said, and she gave a quiet laugh before kissing me.

'Mamma,' George whispers, turning to stare at the back of the chapel.

'Eyes to the front,' I chide him.

'Did you see the people?'

'George. Please be quiet.'

I glance across the aisle. Mrs Edwards stares ahead steely-eyed and uncompromising as usual. In front of her, the Broughtons are seated in the front row in their usual order: Sir James, holding the *Book of Common Prayer* open in his hand, then Charles, who is gazing at the stained-glass window, and finally Candace, wearing black silk, her head bowed in prayer.

George tugs my hand and points to the back of the church. 'Mamma, look how many people there are,' he whispers.

I turn. The pews behind us are full. Beyond the pews, people I don't recognise are lining the back wall and crowding at the door to get in. They must have come from Rivermead. I wonder if rumours about the parishes being merged has spread already. Tom Dyer opens the doors wide. Outside are still more people.

I catch Mrs Kavanagh looking at me, a curious half-smile on her face. Jane Harding is also staring my way. I turn back to the front. Mamma pats my hand and gives me a reassuring smile, and I realise the two women were staring not at me but at Mamma. There's a sick taste at the back of my throat. I want the service to be over. I fix my gaze on the fancy high-backed wooden chair where the bishop will sit.

I slept badly last night. When Henry returned from dinner at Broughton Manor, he was so discouraged he could barely look at me. He explained that Mrs Edwards had not come, so the bishop's plans to merge the parishes would proceed.

Middy pushes a small piece of carved wood along the wooden pew. George slumps against the pew, watching him.

A bell rings and everyone stands.

I turn around. Everyone is watching the bishop, who wears a golden mitre and a robe that reaches the floor and trails behind him. I glimpse the blinding white of the finest linen peeking from beneath his cassock. I cannot take my eyes from him as he walks behind Henry down the central aisle. He nods to the parishioners on each side as he passes, a strange, pious smile on his face.

As if he has read my thoughts, his crow-like eyes meet mine, sending a shiver of dread through me. I turn swiftly to the front, gripping my prayer book to stop my hands from trembling.

I cannot look up at him when they reach the front. My head remains bowed when Henry starts to speak, welcoming the bishop to Statfold parish. He calls the bishop's visit rare, a special occasion, a deep honour for all of us.

Middy puts his hand over mine. His hand is dirty and there is a rim of dust around the cuff of his jacket, which makes me want to cry. But the warmth of his touch steadies me.

After Henry has read the gospel, he steps down from the pulpit. There's a shuffling of feet and a few coughs from the pews as the bishop climbs the three steps to the pulpit and gazes out at the congregation.

I glance to the side. Candace, Charles and Sir James Broughton stare tensely at the bishop. Behind them, Mrs Edwards looks as prim and rigid as her old-fashioned ruff.

The bishop talks about the importance of belief in the goodness of God, and in the word of God. He talks of the poor harvest, the hard work and sacrifices that people have made, and the rewards that will come in heaven. He talks about the war that people have struggled through these last years and prays that the Royalists will give up their vain struggle to reinstate the King and expresses his hope that peace will be maintained. His voice is strong, forceful, yet somehow soothing. I imagine the words flowing over the heads of those assembled, through the doors of the church and wrapping like a blanket around the poor people who have walked over the fields from Rivermead to catch a glimpse of the bishop.

Bishop Divine clears his throat. 'And now I want to talk about some changes to be made in the parish.'

I look up abruptly, my heart beating rapidly. Henry's hands are tightly clasped as he watches the bishop. I steal a glance at Mrs Edwards. Her eyes flicker towards me and she raises her chin just enough to let me know that she is aware of my gaze. This is it then—the beginning of the end for Statfold.

The bishop rests his hands on the pulpit and looks around, still with that strange, pious smile on his face.

My stomach lurches. I can't bear to listen. Mamma shuffles closer so that her arm is touching mine.

'Starting from next Sunday'—the bishop pauses and swallows, as if what he has to say is unpleasant—'there will be a lesson held after service for the children of Statfold parish. These lessons will be held every Sunday thereafter and will be led by Miss Broughton.'

I squeeze Middy's fingers tightly, unable to believe what he is saying.

'These Sunday lessons will teach the children of the parish to read the *Book of Common Prayer*. Mrs Edwards, principal benefactor of Statfold parish, has agreed to fund the endeavour. I would ask you to ensure your children, both boys *and girls* over the age of five years, attend these lessons every week.'

He looks directly at me, then adds, 'Let us pray for the Broughton family and the Edwards family for their unfailing support of this parish.'

A resounding 'Amen' comes from the congregation.

My mouth falls open as I watch the bishop step down from the pulpit and Henry stand up. My eyes dart to Henry's. He glances at me, and I can tell that he, too, is surprised by what has transpired. Then he continues with the service as if it were a regular Sunday.

The only clue that something unusual has occurred is the slight tremor of relief in his voice as he says, 'Let us pray.'

The boys look up at their father as usual. Either they have not understood what the bishop has said or were not paying attention. I glance at Mamma. She's watching Henry, smiling.

When the service is over, we file out into the churchyard.

Peg comes over and offers Mamma her arm. Mamma accepts it gratefully, with a tired sigh. Together they walk towards the house, while I look for Henry.

I find him standing beside the bishop, talking with Sir James Broughton, Charles, Candace and Mrs Edwards.

I keep my distance and watch the crowd disperse. Most make their way down the lane towards the village. Jane Harding is at the rear, walking slowly, her hair tucked neatly under a cap. She turns and looks at me, her expression miserable. Beside her, Grace is chatting away happily.

I should talk to Jane, although I know she will say nothing about Sam.

Someone touches my arm and I turn.

'How is your mother?' Mrs Edwards asks, shielding her eyes from the sudden burst of sunlight breaking through the clouds.

'She is weak but improving, thank you.'

'I'm glad to hear it,' she says curtly.

'How are you, Mrs Edwards?'

Mrs Edwards considers me as she leans on her stick. 'I want to thank you,' she says, without answering my question, 'for not asking me for money for the parish, even though you knew that the financial situation was dire.'

'If I were a better rector's wife, I probably would have,' I admit.

She gives a wry laugh. 'Well, I know your mother-in-law, Mary Wolfreston, very well, and I can tell you that she would be proud of you.' She taps her stick on the ground. 'Well, good day to you.'

I am so surprised that I can only watch as she turns to walk away. Abruptly, I reach out and touch her sleeve.

She turns back, her eyebrows arched in surprise.

'Thank you, Mrs Edwards,' I say.

She smiles and gives me the briefest of nods. 'Give your mother my best.' She walks between the rowan trees into the lane. She is some way behind her nephew and his wife, but they do not pause to wait for her.

'What's wrong?' Candace asks, appearing at my side. 'You look upset.'

'No, not at all. I'm just . . . confused.'

'Are you pleased about the Sunday school?'

'Very pleased,' I say, tucking my arm into Candace's.

She says in a rush, 'Apparently Mrs Edwards insisted upon it in exchange for supporting the parish. I don't know what you did to persuade her, Frances . . .'

'I did nothing, I assure you.'

She smiles at me. 'I don't believe that for a moment.'

47

Henry is asleep by the fire in the drawing room with the latest *Mercurius* resting on his lap. Mamma is asleep opposite him with the pup curled at her feet, while I am at the table writing in the almanac.

I note that my mother has arrived for a visit and that a Sunday school will start in the village. I also note that the pup had a thorn in his foot and that Tom Dyer is looking after the horses for a few days. I blot the ink and look at the pages. I have made no mention of the fact that my mother was in gaol for recusancy, although that is a matter of public record. I have made no note of Sam's disappearance or of Hannah Smythe's arrest. It is surprising how much I record in the pages of the almanac each week and how little I say about our lives. I dip the quill in the ink again. I write that Candace has brought me a number of penny godlies and loaned me several newssheets to read.

I leave the almanac open to let the ink dry and pick up *The Profectus*. The front page reports a foiled attempt to free the King when in Newmarket, and the move of the King from Newmarket to Hampton Court. Sighing, I turn the pages looking for the article Candace mentioned on education. I am about to start reading when my eyes are drawn to the opposite page.

REWARD
Royalist Captain Christopher Grey,
Evaded capture at Newmarket,
Last seen in Tamworth, district of Lichfield.
Armed and Dangerous.

Below is a sketch, from a fine woodcut, of a man's face, his eyes clear and dark. I stare at the hard eyes transfixed. It can't be. It looks like the same man I saw in Tamworth with Sam—the new smithy who's been staying in Jane Harding's barn.

I stand up, feeling anxious again, as if I'm still in the woods looking for the boys.

Outside the window, the boys are playing at sword fighting with sticks. I slip out the side door and beckon to George. He leaves Middy and comes over, trailing his long stick, clearly fearing that he's in trouble again.

'George, was there another man in the boat with Sam?'

He nods, a quick bob of his head—he's impatient to get back to his game.

'Was it the new blacksmith?'

'Yes, Mamma.'

My breath wavers; what danger the boys were in!

'Why didn't you tell me before?'

He shrugs. 'I thought you'd be angry. Grace said her mamma called him a brigand and we were all to stay away from him.'

My mind is reeling. I look over at the barn, wondering if this was what Sam had been trying to tell me. 'All right—go back to your game, George.'

He runs over to Middy and the clacking of sticks resumes.

Over in the stable yard, Tom Dyer is talking to Peg, who is cradling a large brown hen as if it were a babe. Peg points over at the stable and then looks back at Tom. I can't see the expression on her face, but I imagine it is fierce. Neither of them thought we should have hired Sam.

Tom calls, 'Mrs Wolfreston?'

I walk towards him. 'Yes, Tom?'

'There's something here you should see.'

I follow him into the barn.

He leads me over to the corner where the saddles are stored, bends and lifts something from the hay. 'I was cleaning the saddles and I found this.'

It's Joseph's old leather flask. Sam has done a wonderful job cleaning it. No one would guess how old it is.

'It looks too good to be Sam's,' Tom says, a rasp of accusation in his voice.

I take the flask and gaze at it. The dark brown leather has been oiled and polished to a rich sheen. 'It's my brother's old field flask. Sam was cleaning it and I told him he could keep it.'

'The stitches are loose on the bottom, and look . . .' Tom points to a gap in the leather. 'There's something inside it.'

I push my finger into the gap. There's a hard object, an edge. 'Oh,' I say.

There's a quivering in my stomach. Still holding the flask, I stride back to the house. I enter the library and close the door behind me. For the last few days, I've been so angry with Sam, so cross with myself for allowing him near us. And yet . . .

I unravel a few more leather stitches and walk over to the light of the window. I peer into the gap, unable to believe what my eyes are telling me.

It's the singed edge of my mother's old book.

I hug the flask against me.

The long clock in the hall strikes four as I return to the drawing room. George and Middy have come inside and are playing Noddy with Henry. It's so long since we've played cards, I'd forgotten how much Henry enjoys it. A warmth flows through me as I watch them.

Mamma stirs and looks at Henry and the boys. After a few moments, she turns to me and says quietly, 'Frannie, let's take a walk. I love this time of day.'

We walk slowly arm in arm to the rise at the top of the orchard. There's a warm glow in the sky and the air is still. Cows are mooing in the distance.

'I was so pleased to hear of the Sunday school,' Mamma says with a happy sigh. 'Times are changing, Frannie—thanks to a determined woman.'

'Yes, Candace is very determined,' I agree.

My mother's blue eyes sparkle in the sunlight. 'I meant you, Frannie.'

'Me?'

My mother chuckles. 'Yes, you. You make things happen. You and your books.'

I snort, thinking of the chain of events around Hannah Smythe and Sam. 'Not always good things,' I say.

She stops walking and stares at me. 'You make a difference to people's lives every day. You help run this parish. You teach children to read despite opposition. This would never have happened if it wasn't for you. I wouldn't be here, if it wasn't for you.'

A lump grows in my throat.

'I'm just stubborn, Mamma.' I say, touching my belly. 'Like you. And anyway, it would never have happened if you hadn't taught me to love books.'

She smiles, her eyes sparkling more brightly now.

'I've been thinking,' she says. 'I brought a few shillings with me, and I thought you and I might go into Tamworth and spend them.'

'Of course,' I say. 'Maybe some material for a new dress for you. And I can show you where I buy my books.'

She gives a curious half-smile. 'Well, I thought we might use it to pay Mrs Smythe's fine.'

I grip Mamma's arm. 'Are you sure?'

'I'm sure, angel.'

'She might just end up back in there, Mamma, for she won't go to church.'

'Well, I've been thinking about that. I'll talk to her, Frannie. See if I can't change her mind.'

'Oh, thank you, Mamma. Let's take the cart and be there when the sheriff's office opens in the morning.'

The late afternoon light casts hues of green and fawn on the slopes of Craggy Hill. In an hour or so, the sun will set behind it. We watch it in silence, our arms entwined.

'I wonder what the land looks like from the top of that hill,' Mamma says softly.

'Well, there's a good path to the top. We can walk up it whenever you are ready.'

As she smiles, her face glows with wonder.

And I am filled with love.

Epilogue

February 1648

Soft afternoon light is shining through the window as I drift between drowsiness and sleep. Beside me, my baby daughter is nestled in a blanket. Her eyes are open. Their shape is familiar; she looks like George as a babe, though her features are smaller. Her tiny fist is pressed against her face. She makes a sound in her throat, softer than the purr of a kitten, like the hum of a low tune.

'My lovely,' I say, caressing her curled-up hand.

She gurgles and gives a windy smile.

This is how my mother must have felt when I was born. In these humbling moments after the birthing is done, I feel at one with the women who have laboured before me. We are all a part of a wondrous cycle of birthing and being.

Mamma sits near me, gazing at her granddaughter as if she's never seen a baby so beautiful.

She's holding a book—the first edition of the *Venus and Adonis* quarto. The old cover was badly damaged, and some pages were blackened around the edges, but Mr Townsend had said it was salvage-able. He cleaned and bound it for me, together with my old copy of *Licia* that Mamma returned, in a new dark blue cover with gold lettering.

When I gave it to Mamma, her face shone as if she were seeing something magical.

'Is it truly my old book? How did you save it? I thought it was burned.'

'You saved it, Mamma. Joseph found it on the hearth. He hid it in that old flask he used to carry around.'

Her eyes creased in a smile but then she began to weep. As she cried, I stared out at the copper beech, wondering if it was a mistake to have returned the book to her.

After a few minutes she wiped her eyes. 'After all these years,' she said. Then she smiled as she used to—a smile so warm I knew that I would remember the moment forever.

'Thank you, angel,' she said. 'But I want you to keep these books.'

Mamma insisted that I write my name on the title page of *Venus and Adonis*. Her eyes glowed with pride as she stared at the inscription:

Frances Wolfreston Hor Bouk

My baby girl suddenly unfurls her fist and grips my finger. I give a surprised cry.

'She is strong, Frannie. Like her mother.'

'Like you,' I say with a soft smile.

Mamma looks down at the book in her hand, but her face colours as if she is pleased.

'Will you read to her, Mamma?'

So, Mamma reads her old book, and the words lift and fall around us like notes of the sweetest music of all.

Author's Note

In the Margins is a historical novel inspired by the life and books of Frances Wolfreston (1607–1677). Frances was a remarkable seventeenth-century book collector who managed to collect and preserve hundreds of rare literary works, including the sole surviving copy of Shakespeare's first published work, *Venus and Adonis* (1593). Frances Wolfreston's collection is one of the most significant surviving book collections of the period. It is also one of the scant records to exist that shows what women may have read at a time when female literacy was only around ten per cent.

This novel is a work of fiction; however, I have drawn on factual events, people, settings, and books to create my fictional representation of Frances Wolfreston and the world around her. The story and her views in this narrative are speculative and extend beyond what may be gleaned from her historical records. Any historical inconsistences or errors are unintentional and are mine alone.

Characters

To create the fictional character of Frances, I have used the few biographical details known about her, her detailed will and the brief memorial made by her children. These, together with the many annotations made in her books, give a few glimpses into her character and agency.

I have based the character's reading and collecting preferences on Frances's book collection. Roughly half of her extensive collection was literature, many of which were playbooks and verse. She had eleven of Shakespeare's books, so he seems to have been one of her favourite authors. As well as signing her books, Frances also made brief comments in the margins of some of them. These annotations show some of the books she enjoyed and indicate that she may have had an interest in books that concerned attitudes towards women.

One of the key aspects about Frances that I wanted to capture in developing her fictional persona was her commitment and determination surrounding her books. She was a woman who meticulously inscribed her books with her name as an ownership mark at a time when women had few property rights. It is this signing of her name that has helped enable historians and academics to rediscover and collate her collection over the last forty years.

In addition to establishing and preserving her collection, Frances was a hard-working clergyman's wife who ran a busy household and had many children, including a child with a disability whom she cared for until she died in 1677. For creative effect and to simplify the narrative, I have reduced the number of Wolfreston children and consequently changed their names. I have created fictional personas for her husband and parents. To avoid confusion for the reader, I deliberately changed the name of her husband from Francis to Henry, her oldest son from Francis to George (and made him younger), and her mother from Frances to Alice. I have also used 'Frannie' as the young Frances, as her childhood and her relationships with her parents are imagined. The real Frances was the oldest of twenty-two children.

While the characters in the novel are fictional, one key fact about Frances's mother in this novel is real: her mother was arrested and fined for recusancy (which was sometimes associated with being Catholic) in October 1647. As Frances was married to a protestant clergyman, the arrest of her mother was likely a significant source of tension for the family. Note that I have doubled the size of her mother's fine for dramatic effect.

Setting

I have set the story where Frances lived and in places that she may have frequented: Staffordshire, Warwickshire and London. I have used seventeenth-century maps and descriptions of the towns of Tamworth, Lichfield, King's Norton and parts of London to inform the re-creations of England. Statfold House is the house where the real Frances Wolfreston lived; for its fictional recreation, I used a photo of Statfold House, as well as descriptions of what the original house may have looked like when it was built, as it has been extended substantially in the centuries since. Similarly, I used an old map of Statfold village, which no longer exists as a village, and with imagination recreated a working parish populated with fictional characters. Rivermead village, the river, woods and Craggy Hill are all fictional creations.

To write authentically about the period, I found academic papers about recusancy laws, local court records of recusancy fines and land sequestration helpful. I also researched the English Civil Wars, relevant politics, the locations of King Charles I during the period of the novel, and the types of newsbooks published at that time. To simplify the narrative, I have stated that Oliver Cromwell led the New Modelled Army (also later called the New Model Army), but it is worth noting that the commander-in-chief was Thomas Fairfax, with Cromwell one of his significant commanders. Lastly, while I have made reference to the Pendle witch trials, all the details have been fictionalised. Other witch trial references are also fictional, although informed by the Colchester witch trials in 1645.

Her books

I have referred to several Frances Wolfreston books within this novel. Where I have used quotes from these, I have not always used the old-English language spelling of the original text. To avoid confusion for the reader, I have used one spelling of her signature inscription, 'Frances Wolfreston Hor Bouk'. Also, I have slightly altered her annotation in the Du Bartas to fit the narrative.

Many of Frances's books were thin quartos and octavos, sometimes unbound. In keeping with her collection, I have referred to them all as her books even though *Hic Mulier* may be called a pamphlet in some academic papers. It is also worth noting that the books used within the novel are all printed before 1647 apart from *The Good Woman's Champion* (circa 1650), which I have creatively borrowed and made available in 1647 to assist with the narrative. Note also that *Haec-Vir, The Womanish-Man* and *Shakespeare's Sonnets* are not part of Frances Wolfreston's collection.

Frances wrote in almanacs later in her life, examples can be found her Poor Robin's Almanacks. I have assumed in this novel that Frances developed this type of practice earlier in her life. Note that the Grey's Almanac is fictional. The survival of more than two hundred of Frances's books for over 400 years is amazing. Below is the short list of the Frances Wolfreston books that I have mentioned in this novel. Full bibliographic details including locations can be found on Sarah Lindenbaum's crowd-sourcing website 'Frances Wolfreston Hor Bouks', available at: franceswolfrestonhorbouks.com.

Located books referred to

Chaucer, Geoffrey. *The works of Geffray Chaucer* (1550). ESTC S122266.

Du Bartas, Guillaume de Salluste. *Bartas His Deuine Weekes and Workes* (1605). ESTC S116457.

Fletcher, Giles. *Licia or Poems of Love* (1593). ESTC S105618.

Ford, Emanuel. *The Famous Historie of Montelyon* (1640). ESTC S120140.

Harpur, John. *The Iewell of Arithmetic* (1617). ESTC S103870.

I.A. *The Good Womans Champion* or a *Defence for the Weaker Vessell* (circa 1650). ESTC R11216.

Shakespeare, William. *A Wittie and Pleasant Comedie Called The Taming of the Shrew* (1631). ESTC S111180.

Shakespeare, William. *Venus and Adonis* (1593). ESTC S102412.

Shakespeare, William. *Venus and Adonis* (1636). ESTC S104547.

Shakespeare, William. *The Rape of Lucrece* (1616). ESTC S106350.

Stubbes, Phillip. *A Chrystall Glasse for Christian Women* (1646). ESTC S100019.

Swetnam, Joseph. *The Arraignment of Lewde, Idle, Froward and Unconstant Women* (1645). ESTC R219682.

Vaux, Laurence. *A catechisme or Christian doctrine* (1620). ESTC S95659

Not yet located books

Unknown. *Hic Mulier: or, The Man-Woman* (1620). ESTC S92970.

Hill, Thomas. *The Profitable Arte of Gardening* (1593). ESTC S104120.

Shirley, James. *The Constant Maid* (1640). ESTC S104120.

Lloyd, Lodowick. *The Practice of Policy* (1604). ESTC S1335.

Raleigh, Sir Walter. *The Prerogative of Parliaments in England* (1628). ESTC S1667.

Acknowledgements

This book grew out of a seed planted in a lesson about the history of early books in the Rare Books Room at Melbourne University. During the lesson, I asked whether there were any female book collectors in the seventeenth century. The answer led me to Frances Wolfreston, and I chose to write an essay on her book collection. While researching this essay, I was so moved by her personal will that I decided to focus my Advanced Creative Writing Project on her. *In the Margins* has grown out of this creative work.

I would therefore like to acknowledge the following Melbourne University staff: David McInnis, who introduced me to Frances Wolfreston and her books; Odette Kelada, Rachel Hennessey and Grant Caulfield, who supported and encouraged me during my Advanced Creative Writing Project; and Suzanne Hermanoczki, whose recommendation to extend the project into a novel stayed strongly with me until the day in 2021 when I decided to tackle the book.

It's important to acknowledge the many historians who have researched Frances Wolfreston and her books over the years, including but certainly not limited to Paul Morgan, Sarah Lindebaum, Johan Gerristen, Arnold Hunt, Lori Newcombe and Alison Wiggins. While this is a work of fiction, it would not have been possible without their research and the re-discovery of Frances Wolfreston's books.

I would like to thank Robert Watkins, Ultimo Press Publishing Director; Sophie Mayfield, Project Editor; Andrea Johnson, Marketing and Community Manager; Zoë Victoria, Media Officer; and the rest of the wonderful team at Ultimo Press; you have all been a pleasure to work with. Special thanks go to my fantastic publisher, Alex Craig, for her vision and inspiration, to copyeditor Ali Lavau for her insightful input, to proofreader Libby Turner for her forensic detail, and to Hazel Lam for her beautiful cover design. I'm also grateful to my agent Margaret Connolly for her superb support and for believing in *In the Margins*.

My most important thanks are for my family and friends, who have believed in me and have been generous in listening and supporting me throughout this journey. My special thanks go to my first reader, Morgan Holmes. Thank you also to Lauren, Darcey, Ben, Chris and Andy Holmes for putting up with me when I was lost in the seventeenth century. This book is for you.

Gail Holmes grew up in Scotland, the youngest of seven children and the only girl. She graduated from the University of Strathclyde with a BSc (Hons) in Civil Engineering and a Master of Business Administration. She moved to London to join an energy company and had an international career there for 23 years as a project manager and commercial manager. During this time Gail also married and had five children. She moved to Australia in 2013.

Her creative writing journey began when she was a working mum with very young children in Shanghai, China. Unable to get back to sleep one night, Gail started writing short stories about living in Shanghai. As this writing habit continued to grow, she attended short courses at the City College of Literature in London and then later studied the Melbourne University's Master of Creative Writing, Editing and Publishing programme, graduating in 2021. *In the Margins* is her first novel.